Cast

Judith Onslow. She's the ˅ [illegible] Hospital. She also has a "re———— Like most of the staff, she lives at the hospital.

Dr. Bob Medford. He's the acting head of this country hospital. He and Judith have a "history."

Miss Angie Ewell. A small, white birdlike woman, she's the former head nurse—and still runs the place.

Dr. William Smith, Sr. He owns the hospital but arthritis has crippled him.

Vera Smith. His slim daughter. She stands to inherit half the hospital when her father dies.

Dr. "Willie" Smith, Jr. He gets the other half. He drinks. He might be a good doctor, if anyone ever gave him a chance.

Les. An amiable, wolfish man with a eye and a line for the ladies.

Shirley West. The new day switchboard operator who shows up with too much rouge and lipstick and then mysteriously tries to transform herself.

Elizabeth Barstow. Dr. Medford's sister, who has reason to hate Judith.

Charlie. An ex-doctor, he isn't quite right in the head. He prowls the halls at night in his pajamas wielding a knife.

Jacob Knotty. The chief of police. He's out of his depth.

Betty Robinson. The night switchboard operator. The chief's niece.

Jake. A former orderly, he tried too hard to act like a surgeon.

The nurses: Mary Gore, who believes that faith can do more than medicine to heal the sick; **Eva Babcock** and **Peggy Forbes,** who complain quite a bit; and **Kathy,** who just does her job.

The patients: Mrs. Scubble and **Mr. Lister.** They demand a lot of attention.

The other doctors: George Usall, who lives in town and is thought to be nice. Young **Dr. Burrell**, who arrives near the end.

Other staff. Nora, the maid, and **Lucius**, an orderly.

Books by Constance & Gwenyth Little

The Grey Mist Murders (1938)*
Black-Headed Pins (1938)*
The Black Gloves (1939)*
Black Corridors (1940)*
The Black Paw (1941)*
The Black Shrouds (1941)*
The Black Thumb (1942)*
The Black Rustle (1943)*
The Black Honeymoon (1944)*
Great Black Kanba (1944)*
The Black Eye (1945)*
The Black Stocking (1946)*
The Black Goatee (1947)*
The Black Coat (1948)*
The Black Piano (1948)*
The Black House (1950)*
The Black Smith (1950)*
The Blackout (1951)
The Black Dream (1952)
The Black Iris (1953)
The Black Curl (1953)

*reprinted by the Rue Morgue Press
as of February 2005

The Black Smith

by Constance & Gwenyth Little

Rue Morgue Press
Boulder / Lyons

ISBN: 0-915230-76-3

Any resemblance to persons living or dead
would be downright ridiculous.

Printed at Johnson Printing
Boulder, Colorado

The Rue Morgue Press
P.O. Box 4119
Boulder, CO 80306

PRINTED IN THE UNITED STATES OF AMERICA

About the Littles

Although all but one of their books had "black" in the title, the 21 mysteries of Constance (1899-1980) and Gwenyth (1903-1985) Little were far from somber affairs. The two Australian-born sisters from East Orange, New Jersey, were far more interested in coaxing chuckles than in inducing chills from their readers.

Indeed, after their first book, *The Grey Mist Murders*, appeared in 1938, Constance rebuked an interviewer for suggesting that their murders weren't realistic by saying, "Our murderers strangle. We have no sliced-up corpses in our books." However, as the books mounted, the Littles did go in for all sorts of gruesome murder methods—"horrible," was the way their own mother described them—which included the occasional sliced-up corpse.

But the murders were always off stage and tempered by comic scenes in which bodies and other objects, including swimming pools, were constantly disappearing and reappearing. The action took place in large old mansions, boarding houses, hospitals, hotels, or on trains or ocean liners, anywhere the Littles could gather together a large cast of eccentric characters, many of whom seemed to have escaped from a Kaufman play or a Capra movie. The typical Little heroine—each book was a stand-alone—often fell under suspicion herself and turned detective to keep the police from slapping the cuffs on. Whether she was a working woman or a spoiled little rich brat, she always spoke her mind, kept her rather sarcastic sense of humor, and got her man, both murderer and husband. But if marriage was in the offing, it was always on her terms and the vows were taken with more than a touch of cynicism. Love was grand, but it was even grander if the husband could either pitch in with the cooking and cleaning or was wealthy enough to hire household help.

The Littles wrote all their books in bed—"Chairs give one back-aches," Gwenyth complained—with Constance providing detailed plot outlines while Gwenyth did the final drafts. Over the years that pattern changed somewhat, but Constance always insisted that Gwen "not mess up my clues." Those clues were everywhere, and the Littles made sure there were no loose ends. Seemingly irrelevant events were revealed to be of major significance in the final summation. The plots were often preposterous, a fact often recognized by both the Littles and their characters, all of whom seem to be winking at the reader, almost as if sharing a private joke. You just have to accept the fact that there are different natural laws in the wacky universe created by these sisters. There are no other mystery writers quite like them. At times, their books seem to be an odd collaboration between P.G. Wodehouse and Cornell Woolrich.

The Littles published their two final novels, *The Black Curl* and *The Black Iris*, in 1953, and if they missed writing after that, they were at least able to devote more time to their real passion—traveling. The two made at least three trips around the world at a time when that would have been a major undertaking. For more information on the Littles and their books, see the introductions by Tom & Enid Schantz to The Rue Morgue Press editions of *The Black Gloves* and *The Black Honeymoon.*

The Black Smith

Chapter 1

Judith Onslow looked anxiously around the little country railroad station in search of a taxi. She had two heavy bags, and it seemed useless to expect that anyone would meet her, nor had she any idea where the hospital was located. She moved to the edge of the wooden platform and peered hopefully at a sagging old car that was rattling idly down the dirt road, and at the same time she became conscious of the fact that a woman was standing at her elbow, also peering.

The car circled and drew up beside the platform, where it panted with its fenders drooping. The driver said, "Taxi?" without breaking the rhythm on his chewing gum, and Judith stretched a hand toward the rear door. There was an immediate collision between herself and the other woman, who observed cheerfully, "Pardon me, but I'm just trying to get into this taxi."

"So am I."

"Too bad," said the woman, still cheerful. She climbed into the back seat and kicked off her high-heeled shoes, which appeared to be too small for her bulging feet. Judith hesitated for a moment, and then set her teeth together and climbed in too.

The woman, wriggling her stockinged toes, shrugged and directed the green feather of her red hat toward the driver. "You drop me first, brother."

"Where you going, lady?"

"Smith Hospital."

"Oh." Judith settled back onto the seat. "That's where I'm going."

The woman said, "Swell. Now we don't have to fight it out," and let forth a hearty laugh.

The driver yawned and clashed gears, and the woman yelled, "Hey! Wait a minute! Our suitcases aren't in yet."

The driver turned and surveyed them. "Well, hadn't you ladies better load them on?"

"What's your name?" the woman demanded.

"Luke Andrews. What's yours?"

"Mrs. Shirley West. Come on, Luke. Get the damn bags in and let's get going."

"I got hernia trouble," Luke said simply, "and Doc told me not to lift anything. You ladies got to get them bags in yourself."

Judith sighed and crawled out of the back seat. She handed the bags in to Mrs. Shirley West, and then discovered that there was no room for herself, so that she had to sit in the front beside Luke.

"O.K.," Shirley said, "I guess you can take off. Say, what's hernia trouble, anyway?"

Judith told her, absentmindedly, and in rather technical language.

Luke shuddered. "I ain't that bad off," he muttered, and started the car with a jerk and a roar.

"You a nurse?" Shirley asked from the back seat. "Or maybe even a doctor, huh?"

Judith's mouth twisted wryly, and she rested her head against the seat. She had desperately wanted to be a doctor but there had been no money. Nursing was not the same. But she was a good nurse. She'd done well. She was still young, and newly appointed director of nurses at Smith Hospital. Of course that sounded better than it was, since Smith Hospital was merely a small private institution in the country. Still, rich people had their ills cured there, so that there would always be enough clean sheets. Little things of that sort that took up so much of a nurse's time. Only, maybe they were stingy. Some places were.

"Just what was it you said you were, at this joint?" Shirley asked.

"I didn't say, but if you're interested I'll tell you. I'm a fool."

She was a fool, too, to come out to one of these places with no particular standing. If she'd stayed where she was, she'd have been head eventually. Well, in another twenty years, perhaps.

Shirley laughed. "Oh, sure. We're all fools. I'm the new switchboard operator and receptionist. You know, the poor dope in the hall who answers bells and questions."

Judith experimented with a laugh which she hoped was as natural and hearty as Shirley's. She had a reserve which she longed to be rid of, but it seemed almost impossible to cast it off. After the laugh had died away, she said flatly, "I'm the new director of nurses."

"No kidding?" But Shirley didn't seem too interested. She added, "Here we are. This is the dump, I guess. Jeez, I hope the eats are good."

Luke said amiably, "You're nuts. This place has the best food in town." He drew up under an old-fashioned porte-cochere, and stretched prodigiously.

Judith paid the fare, but Shirley carefully counted out her half and handed it over, and they walked together into the large old house. It announced its institutionalization now by iron fire escapes attached at each end, and the square hall, as they entered, had a dark, blank, polished look that confirmed it. Shirley clutched at her pocketbook, and gave a feeble imitation of her usual hearty laugh. "Gives me the willies," she said apologetically.

A young girl seated behind a switchboard at one side raised her eyebrows and said in a cultured voice, "Yes?"

Shirley took in a breath, but before she could speak, Judith said hastily, "Could you locate Miss Ewell for us, please?"

The girl looked them over. Her eyes dealt rapidly with Judith, but lingered, with a growing chill, on Shirley. She noted the green feather on the red hat, and the spring suit of a green far different from the feather. The shoes and purse were of navy blue, and Shirley's hair, dark and too frizzy, hung to her shoulders. Her face was well painted in a carefree manner that ignored the rest of her color scheme.

Judith said coldly, "Kindly get Miss Ewell."

The girl returned to her switchboard. "Who shall I say?"

"Miss Onslow."

"I'm Mrs. Shirley West, the new switchboard operator. You leaving?"

"Miss Ewell is not in her office," the girl said, giving her attention entirely to Judith, "but Dr. Medford is there, and he'll see you, if you'll go in." She gestured down a narrow corridor running toward the back and seemed glad to abandon them.

Shirley made a rude remark under her breath, and Judith stifled a little gurgle of laughter as they went in the half-opened door which bore the name of "Miss Ewell." Dr. Bob Medford was seated at the desk, reading a newspaper, and he did not look up immediately, which gave Judith a chance to swallow the little gasp that rose in her throat. What could she do now? she thought wildly. How could she stay here? It would be impossible to work with him. Of all the places that she might have come to, why on earth had she picked this one?

Dr. Medford dropped the newspaper and looked up.

"Hi, Doc," Shirley said, straightening her hat. "I'm the new switchboard."

He gave her a brief glance, and then his eyes swung around to Judith and stayed on her face. He rose to his feet and said quietly, "Well, it really is a small world, isn't it? You are the new head, of course. You must be. And yet how is it possible, with your reputation?"

Chapter 2

Unexpectedly, it was Shirley who answered, in a flare of anger. She said furiously, "Well, of all the nerve! My reputation's as good as yours, and then some! Who are you, anyway?"

Judith turned to her quickly. "It's all right, Mrs. West. Dr. Medford was speaking to me, and he was only joking. We—we're old friends."

He considered her for a moment of silence, and then said, "Yes, of course. We're friends, and I was joking. I believe Miss Ewell will be here shortly."

He left the room, and Judith looked blindly down at the carpet. Why had she come here? How could she leave now? And why had he been so easily silenced? Oddly, it made her hate him all the more.

Shirley sank into a chair and eyed her shoes, but decided to keep them on. "Well, who does he think he is, with all that stuffing in his shirt? Nobody likes the men better than I do, but you can have that one, even on Sundays and holidays."

"Probably has something on his mind," Judith said, trying to sound careless. "You know the type, always thinking of his patients."

Miss Ewell tripped in, looking like a small white bird. Her white hair had been done with the correct amount of blueing, and she wore spectacles which she kept adjusting with her little finger stuck well out. Her laugh was a high tinkle, and she used it often. She informed Shirley that the switchboard girl usually lived out, but since they had not been able to get anyone from the village, they'd put her up in the hospital. Shirley nodded, and Miss Ewell asked Judith to excuse her while she showed Mrs. West to her room.

She came tripping back in a few minutes and politely wished Judith luck in her new position. She herself was the retiring director, but was staying on because she was a close friend of the family and had no relatives of her own. She was getting on in years and had earned her rest, and now she intended to take it easy. She would, of course, help Judith all she could. The recital took a long time, and Judith yearned restlessly for her own room.

First, however, she was escorted farther back on the main floor to a suite of rooms which included a large sun porch badly cluttered with potted palms. A white-haired, elderly man sat there in a wheelchair, looking sour and cross; Judith could see that he was crippled with arthritis.

Miss Ewell cleared her throat. "Dr. Smith, this is our new director, Miss Onslow."

Dr. Smith turned his white head and glared at Judith. "She's too young."

"She is not too young," Miss Ewell chirped firmly. "She is perfectly suited for the position. I have investigated thoroughly."

Dr. Smith grunted, and Judith said, "How do you do?" which he ignored completely.

Miss Ewell cleared her throat again, and said, "Well, now, where's Vera?"

Dr. Smith ignored that too, and Miss Ewell murmured, "Come on," and led Judith from the porch, through the living room behind it, and to a door, where she knocked. "I want you to meet his daughter, Miss Vera Smith," she explained, half turning to Judith. "She'll get a half interest in this place, when Doctor goes."

Judith nodded, standing first on one foot and then on the other. She was considerably relieved when there was no answer to the knock, and Miss Ewell decided to take her to her room and save Vera for another time.

They climbed to the third floor. Although these were attic rooms, they seemed large and airy enough. Judith wondered what they would be like in summer, but was too tired to brood on it. She was given a fairly large bedroom which was separated from the hall by a sort of anteroom. The smaller room was furnished with two easy chairs and a day bed, and was part of what Miss Ewell called her "suite."

"You'll find it's very nice," Miss Ewell assured her. "I used to be here, and I always liked it, but I had to move downstairs some time ago because the climb got to be too much for me. I've only a small room downstairs, but of course it's much better than climbing—my heart, you know. I have to be so careful now."

"I hope it isn't serious," Judith said, wishing that she'd go.

"Oh no, not at all. It's just that I have to be careful, you see. I'll leave you now, and I do hope you'll be happy here. Dinner will be ready soon. You're to eat with us. Come down to Dr. Smith's quarters when you've unpacked and refreshed yourself."

She fluttered away, and Judith sank into a chair and pulled out a cigarette. I can't go away now, she thought. Too late. Why hadn't she run away when the switchboard girl had said "Dr. Medford"? Only it hadn't registered, for some reason. And that Dr. Smith—surly and unpleasant. Well, arthritis—pain most of the time. You couldn't expect him to be a ray of sunshine. So here she was, director of nurses, buried out in the country. What could she do on her day off? But that didn't matter. She'd find something. It was Dr. Medford, damn him!

She relaxed into the chair and reflected that it was funny, when you first fell in love, how you thought that it was the only thing that mattered. You found out, in time, that a lot of other things mattered. The man's wife, for instance.

Judith crushed out her cigarette, and rested her head against the back of the chair. She closed her eyes and could see the courtroom again, and this Medford giving quiet testimony. He had seen them here and there, and in Bill's rooms. And then, in the end, Bill and his wife had become reconciled. Embarrassing. Frightfully embarrassing for her. She'd been the goat. Bill had been just a straying husband who loved his wife, really.

Judith grinned suddenly, and shook her head. Bill loved himself—dearly. She knew that now; she could remember things. There were two children, but Bill never stopped to consider them, or his wife, or Judith, either. And so, after it was all over, Judith was the villain. She'd been called a home wrecker, and worse.

She laughed again. She'd never dreamed that a wife would want a husband who was interested elsewhere. She had thought that the wife would simply go off and get a divorce. In fact, she had thought a lot of stupid things, but she had learned a lot too. This Dr. Medford could go to the devil. Of course he might get her fired. There was not such a shortage of nurses now as when the scandal had broken and she was named corespondent. At that time the hospital had been too shorthanded to let a good nurse go. They had begged her to apologize and promise to be a good girl, and perhaps it was all a mistake, anyway.

What was Medford's position here? A visiting doctor, perhaps. She hoped so, because then she need not see so much of him. Possibly she was making too much of the whole thing, only Medford had been the wronged wife's brother, and he could be expected to take the worst view of the affair.

Judith sighed and raised herself out of the chair. No use tying her brain in knots. She'd better get unpacked and washed up for dinner. She moved swiftly around the room and had just finished and was eying herself in the mirror, when there was a knock on the door. She tapped lightly at the lipstick on her mouth with a little finger and called absently, "Come in."

The door opened, and Dr. Medford stepped into the room.

Judith whirled from the mirror and asked sharply, "What is it?"

"Well"—his eyes took her in from head to foot—"it seems only fair to tell you that I am acting head of this hospital, and you might find it unpleasant to work under me."

"It's more of a probability than a possibility," she replied quietly.

"Then why don't you resign?"

So that was it. He was going to try and push her out. Judith raised her chin. "Please don't be absurd. Just because I had an unfortunate love affair, do you expect me to go around with my ears hanging down for the rest of my life? I have no intention of leaving this position unless my work is unsatisfactory or I get a better offer somewhere else."

Dr. Medford said, "I see," and after a moment of silence turned on his heel and left the room.

Judith stared at the closed door for some time. What was the matter with him? Couldn't he let the past die? After all, it was harder for her than it was for him. It was all so unfair. The chances were that he was married and more than probably fooling around with some nurse in the place, which was why he was so anxious to get rid of her.

Shirley walked in without knocking. She said cheerfully, "Holy Mike! You sure got a better room than I did! I'm afraid to turn around in mine for fear of bumping my fanny."

"Oh well," Judith said vaguely, "I suppose it's better than putting up in the village, anyway. There'll be more going on around here. Besides, I'm the director of nurses, remember? I rate a larger room."

"Sure." Shirley yawned. "I just saw that guy leave here. Was he tellin' you not to spit on the floor in this refined joint? He's good-lookin', but he's an awful sour apple. Let's go on down and see if they got anything to eat."

They went downstairs together, and Shirley followed Judith into the Smith suite. There were several people sitting in the living room having cocktails, but Judith scarcely noticed them. She had looked first at Dr. Smith, and his face frightened her. It was gray and pinched, and his mouth worked soundlessly, as though he were trying to speak. Judith took two steps toward him, and saw his eyes roll up to the ceiling.

He spoke, slowly and painfully.

"Your word against mine."

Chapter 3

Dr. Smith's voice had sounded clearly in a momentary lull in the general conversation, and his daughter went quickly to his side. She asked, "What is it, Papa? What do you mean?"

Dr. Smith looked down at his gnarled hands and said crossly, "Nothing."

Miss Ewell fussed over to them and took the daughter's arm. "Vera, this is the new director of nurses, Miss Onslow, and—er—the new switchboard operator, Mrs. West." She turned around and added, "Dr. Smith's daughter, Miss Smith."

Miss Smith looked pleasant, Judith thought, but a bit insipid. She had dark hair brushed smoothly to a neat bun on her neck, and obviously used little else but soap and water on her face. Her clothes made her appear thin, instead of slim.

Across the room Dr. Medford was talking to another man who was introduced as Dr. Smith, Jr. They bowed to the newcomers, and immediately resumed their conversation until Shirley, who had been getting restless, went over and broke it up. She raised her drink on high and said, "Ah, forget it for a while, boys. Always tryin' to do the undertakers out of turnin' an honest penny. Come on, let's drown."

Dr. Medford gave her a blank look, and Dr. Smith, Jr., after a moment of astonishment, broke into a weak smile. Dr. Smith, Sr., immediately turned on Miss Ewell and demanded furiously, "Angie! What's the switchboard operator doing in here?"

Miss Ewell fluttered her hands. "What can I do with her? You know I can't get a local girl, so we have to put her up here. She'll *have* to eat with us."

"Why can't she eat with the nurses?"

"Because they have their own dining room, and they've a right to it."

"So have I a right to mine. I won't have her here."

Miss Smith brought Judith a cocktail, and a deprecating little smile, and Judith asked, "Where is the nurses' dining room?"

"You mustn't mind my father. He isn't well, you know, and he's always fussing about something."

But Judith felt that her meals would be decidedly more pleasant away from this group, and she presently moved over to Miss Ewell and put it to her directly.

"I think it would be better for Mrs. West and myself to eat with the nurses."

Unexpectedly Miss Ewell's face went pink with anger. She made a few tart remarks, and ended up by saying, "Remember, young lady, you are only head nurse, here. *I* am in charge of all housekeeping arrangements."

Judith shrugged and devoted herself to her cocktail, and Shirley presently joined her, muttering darkly, "Did you ever see such a bunch of dead ones, outside the morgue? They look nude, walkin' around without their coffins."

Judith glanced up and saw that the two younger doctors were talking together again, and that Miss Smith was speaking to her father in a low voice while Miss Ewell looked on. She grinned at Shirley, and murmured, "You're going to have to make your own fun here."

The whole dull atmosphere was suddenly changed, simply because another man walked into the room. He was young and good-looking, but it was not that. Judith realized that you could sense his gay personality before he had so much as said a word. He went straight to Miss Smith, bowed low, and kissed her hand, while she smiled down at him. He surveyed the room then, and grinned over at the two younger doctors. "Leave me out of that discussion, fellas. I'd rather die decently of alcoholism than have to wait at the pearly gates for my appendix to catch up with me." He turned to Miss Ewell, who was smiling at him, and kissed her on the cheek. "Hello, Angie. You get prettier every day. Only don't forget your manners. Introduce me to the two charming young ladies."

Shirley's entire drooping surface revived and vibrated, but Judith continued to feel tired and depressed. The man was introduced as Les something, and she nodded indifferently. He said, "Darling, what a bright and cheerful smile," and she murmured impatiently, "Oh, go and get yourself a drink."

"Hmm, yes. And stop bothering you, you mean?" He departed in the direction of the cocktail shaker, and may or may not have been surprised to find that Shirley was clinging to his arm.

Miss Smith sat down beside Judith and said seriously, "I want to welcome you to our hospital. I know you have done very fine work, and I am sure we shall all be happy together."

Judith assumed a conventional smile, and said, "I shall do my best, of course." No use telling the woman about Dr. Medford, or of her consequent feeling of disappointment and depression.

Miss Smith made some further remark, but a burst of laughter from Shirley, Les, and the two doctors drowned it out. Judith noticed that the elder Dr. Smith, silent in his wheelchair, watched the gay group from under his heavy eyebrows.

Miss Ewell announced that dinner was ready and efficiently extracted them from their cocktails. She led the way to the dining room, which was out of the suite, but close by. It was a large, gloomy place, with heavy furniture, and depressingly, if elegantly, lighted by candles. They were served by a woman called Nora, who was as dour and forbidding as the elder Dr. Smith, and even Les quieted under the overall gloom. Judith felt that if she were required to take all her meals here, she would lose weight rapidly.

She had been seated, by Miss Ewell, between the two younger doctors, it being Miss Ewell's expressed opinion that they would have many things to discuss. Not a single word passed between Judith and Dr. Medford during the course of the meal, but the younger Dr. Smith was courteous and seemed serious about his work. He described the patients, in detail, and Judith found herself feeling lower than ever. There was nothing really interesting: wealthy people with not too much wrong. It seemed that the elder Dr. Smith had had a wealthy practice, and had established the hospital before he became ill. "We carry on for him now, and the patients call me Dr. Willie. I wish they wouldn't. But once a name like that gets attached to you, it's hard to shake loose. You see, Dad's name is William too."

Shirley, talking to Les across the table, yelled, "Well, ain't that the nuts!" and Dr. Willie raised his eyebrows a little. He said with a faint distaste, "Where does your friend come from?"

"She's not my friend, really," Judith explained. "I never saw her before today. She and I happened to come here in the same taxi."

Dr. Willie nodded, and his eyebrows relaxed. Judith idly watched the woman Nora plod into the room with a bowl of fruit jelly and some plates, which she banged down in front of Miss Smith. "I ain't got no time to dish this out in separate plates and serve it, Miss Vera," she announced firmly.

Miss Smith looked distressed, but said nothing, and proceeded to spoon the stuff onto the plates and send it around the table. Miss Ewell murmured, "Now, Vera, you know she hasn't time for things like that. We all like gracious living, but until we get more help in the kitchen, we'll have to be patient."

Coffee was served in the living room. Evidently Miss Smith had held out for that particular phase of gracious living, and they all trooped back to receive tiny cups of coffee poured from a silver coffeepot. Shirley said, "I hope I don't swaller this thing along with the corfee. You got plenty more in that pot? I like two cupsa corfee with my meal. And I mean cups, not little spit buckets like this."

Judith was very tired by this time, and she drank her coffee quickly and left, after a general good night. The last thing she heard was Dr. Smith saying sourly, "I still think she's too young."

Her bed proved to be comfortable, and she stretched out with a little sigh of pleasure and relaxation. She closed her eyes and was becoming drowsy, when there was a sharp knock on the door. She raised her head from the pillow, feeling startled and confused, and at the same moment the door opened and a figure walked into the room. She fumbled for the unfamiliar light switch, and could not find it–and a man's voice spoke into the darkness.

"I got this knife, see," it quavered, in the accents of old age, "and I think I'm going to let him have it. That was an awful thing Willie did."

Chapter 4

Judith slid out of bed on the side away from the door and pulled her robe around her shoulders. She fumbled for the switch again, but before she could get the light on, the old man had shuffled out of the room. She heard him make his way through the smaller room and out into the hall, and she waited only long enough to belt her robe and put her feet into slippers before she hurried after him.

He was going down the stairs and seemed to be wearing hospital pajamas. A patient, then. Judith drew a breath of relief and followed him to the second floor, where he made his way down a long corridor.

A nurse came out of one of the rooms, and, paying scant attention to the old man, hurried up to Judith with a touch of deference. "You're Miss Onslow, aren't you? Is anything wrong?"

Judith explained about the old man, and the nurse glanced at him and laughed. "Oh, he's all right. He's a bit batty, that's all."

"But he says he has a knife."

"Well, gosh, I can't go around searching him all the time. I have enough to do without playing nursemaid to a nut. He shouldn't be here, anyway. They ought to shove him in the asylum where he belongs."

"Who is he?" Judith asked.

"Just an old employee. He's a doctor, as a matter of fact. He used to work here, but I guess he never amounted to much."

"This place has been established for some time, then?"

"Oh, sure. Ages."

Judith glanced at the old man, who was standing a short distance away, looking at them. He did not appear to have a knife, and she said, "Well, you'd better search him."

The nurse nodded and walked briskly away on trim white feet. She led the old man to one of the rooms, and marched him in, closing the door firmly behind her.

Judith stood for a moment, looking down the corridor. This must be a wing, built off from the side of the old house, she thought. It was decidedly more modern. She made her way back, and as she came to the stairs she realized that she was now once more in the original old building. It had been a beautiful place, in its day. The stairs were wide and graceful and the hall spacious.

She had turned to go up when she heard voices and a slight scuffle from below, and saw that Dr. Medford was supporting Dr. Willie and urging him up the stairs. Dr. Medford wore a look of dark fury, and Dr. Willie, obviously very drunk, was giggling. Judith stood watching them, and as Dr. Willie was eventually propelled onto the landing, he bowed low before her and murmured, "Beautiful! Is she not beautiful, Bob?"

It was too much for Judith, who started to laugh, which seemed to make Dr. Medford more furious than ever.

"Why do you stand there doing nothing?" he demanded between his teeth. "Can't you give me a hand with him?"

Dr. Willie nodded and lurched against Judith. "Yes, you help me. Like that much better. Don't give him a hand, give me a hand. Give me both hands—"

Dr. Medford grasped him again and ran him up to the floor above, and Judith followed, smiling faintly. She saw them go into the room next to her own, and waited until Dr. Medford banged out again, dusting his hands.

She stood directly in front of him and said, "Look, I'm going to need a lock for my door. What with him being directly beside me, and another old doctor wandering around with a knife—"

Dr. Medford brushed by her, and flung over his shoulder bitterly, "You don't need anything. You can take care of yourself."

Les appeared suddenly, running up the stairs, and called, "Hey, Bob! Before you bed down there, may I use your couch and stay overnight?"

Dr. Medford had approached the door next to Dr. Willie's, and Judith cried out involuntarily, "Oh, God! You don't live here too?"

Dr. Medford said, "All right, Les, although I don't know why you can't get home. It isn't likely to snow in June." He turned to Judith and added coldly, "Yes, I do live here, all the year around."

Les smiled at her. "Have you a lock on your door, honey? With this gorilla so close— But I'll look after you tonight."

"Come on, Les," Dr. Medford snarled. "If you're going to sleep with me tonight, I'm going to bed now."

"Good boy," Les murmured, still eying Judith. "I mean, you always were, weren't you? If I shed my shoes, may I come in later?"

Dr. Medford gave him a sour look and slammed into his room without further words.

Les grinned at Judith. "He's really a good guy. I don't know what's eating him tonight."

She made a little face. "You know, I *would* like a lock on my door.

An old man came into my room a little while ago, and I think I'm entitled to some privacy."

"An old man?" Les asked.

She nodded. "Used to be a doctor here. I guess he's a patient now."

Les laughed. "Oh, him! Used to be an old beau of Angie's—Miss Ewell. You mean he just wandered in?" Les laughed again, more heartily. "Angie has been downstairs for some time now, but his mind is going, and he still thinks she lives here." He considered it for a moment, grinning, and added, "Shame on Angie."

Judith smiled at him. "Aren't you jumping to conclusions?"

"That isn't much of a jump. Look, will you have a drink? I have—"

"No." Judith shook her head. "I'm tired tonight, and I'll have to work tomorrow. I'm going to bed."

Les nodded. "Yes, of course. I'll see you in the morning."

Judith pushed a small bureau in front of her door this time, but she was unable to get to sleep at once. There were various noises that she could not identify, including a peculiar whirring that came twice and was not very loud. But for some reason it disturbed her.

When she did at last go off, she slept well, and was awakened at six-thirty by Miss Ewell pounding on the door and calling querulously, "What's the obstruction here, dear? I can't get in."

"Nothing. It's all right," Judith muttered, and rolled out of bed with her eyes still closed.

"But there's something against the door. I can't open it."

"Wait a minute. I'll be right out."

There was no privacy here, Judith thought crossly, and pulled on her robe. She pushed the bureau away from the door, and Miss Ewell entered immediately. "What is it? What was holding the door?"

"An old man wandered into my room last night. I'll have to have a lock on this door."

"Oh now, my dear, nonsense! We never lock doors around here. It isn't necessary. Nobody is going to hurt you."

Judith, still half asleep, muttered, "Good! I wouldn't want to get hurt."

"Breakfast is at seven sharp, dear. You haven't much time. Better get dressed in a hurry."

She tripped off, and Judith yawned, picked up her sponge bag and stumbled off to the bathroom. It was rotten, having to share a bathroom with the two doctors, and Shirley too. Shirley's room was up here somewhere.

It developed that Shirley was already in the bathroom, singing at the top of her voice. Judith leaned against the wall and closed her eyes again, since she dared not abandon her position as next in line.

Shirley presently emerged, followed by an aura of steam, trilled, "Hi there," and disappeared into her room. Judith bathed in haste, but when she came out, Dr. Willie was propped against the wall outside, and gave her a feeble "Good morning."

She hurried over her dressing, and managed to make the dining room by seven. She was surprised and a little resentful to find that Dr. Smith was the only one there. But at least he was in a decidedly more amiable mood than he had been the night before. He asked Judith about her previous experiences, and told her a few of his own. She found him quite interesting, and was a little startled when he suddenly stopped in mid sentence and stared at the door behind her. Judith twisted in her chair and beheld Shirley, makeup going full blast on her face, and with her hair incongruously twisted into the same neat knot on the back of the neck that seemed so appropriate to Miss Vera Smith.

Chapter 5

Judith repressed the hilarity that bubbled up within her, and composed her face. She wondered what on earth had possessed Shirley to change from the shoulder bob, hanging in unset permanent waves to her shoulders, which looked bad enough, to this prim and utterly incongruous little bun.

Dr. Smith said, "Young lady, what is your name? I seem to have forgotten it."

Shirley seated herself at the table and replied pertly, "I'm Mrs. Shirley West, the new switchboard."

Dr. Smith bowed. "The new switchboard. Yes, of course. Well and freshly painted, as new switchboards should be. You said 'Mrs.'? Where is your husband?"

Shirley narrowed her eyes and said, "He was killed in the war, see? He was a hero."

"Ah, yes. And so now you are out looking for a new one."

Shirley's face burned with sudden color, and she banged her coffee cup into its saucer. "Go ahead, get it off your chest if you feel mean. I can take anything *you* can dish out."

Dr. Smith laughed in genuine amusement, and Miss Ewell walked into the room and gave him a keen look.

"Well, well. We all seem very bright and happy this fine morning."

"Sit down and eat your breakfast, Angie," Dr. Smith said in a bored voice. "The morning is as lousy as usual, if not more so."

Miss Ewell proceeded to eat a huge breakfast. Shirley watched her with round eyes and at last asked in honest wonderment, "How can you wrap yourself around all that and still stay so thin?"

Miss Ewell almost simpered. She explained kindly, "Some people simply do not put on weight, and others do. Now you, my dear, have arrived at the point where you should eat your breakfast toast without butter, and drink your coffee without cream or sugar."

Shirley looked uneasy, but she said with bravado, "Nuts! I hate black corfee and dry toast."

Dr. Smith leaned back in his chair and smiled almost amiably. He said to Miss Ewell, "You're wasting your breath. These fatties can never reduce, and you know it."

"They can and they should," Miss Ewell snapped, "and *you* know it."

"Don't mind me," Shirley muttered, "I'm just sittin' here." She turned to Judith and asked uneasily, "Honest, now. Am I really bulging as bad as that?"

"No." Judith considered her. "But you could take some off, because if you don't make the attempt, you'll start to put more on, and I really don't think you should."

"I guess not." Shirley frowned and then sighed. "But toast without butter, and corfee without anything—what's the usea living?"

Miss Ewell, having finished her substantial breakfast, leaned back in her chair and noticed that Judith was smoking. She frowned and said, "Oh. I didn't know you smoked."

Judith gave her a level look. "Yes, on all possible occasions. It's my favorite vice."

"Oh, well—" Miss Ewell shelved it, and stood up, rubbing her hands briskly together. "Come now, and I'll show you around. You, too, Mrs. West. Time's getting on."

Shirley stuffed the rest of her toast into her mouth, and they went out to the switchboard. A girl with stringy blond hair and a languid manner stood up as they approached, and after acknowledging introductions, took herself off, yawning.

Shirley sat down in her place, and Miss Ewell explained, "You are the desk clerk and receptionist. You are right at the front door, and no one is to pass you unless he has legitimate business here."

"Yeah?" Shirley eyed the switchboard. "Who decides whether their business is legitimate or not?"

"You must ask them and find out what they want. And if you are in doubt, phone me."

"Oh, sure." Shirley gave her a bleak look. "With you flittin' all over the place, I guess I gotta make up my own mind, mostly."

"You must not be difficult." Miss Ewell turned away. "Come, Miss Onslow."

Judith was introduced to the patients and to the nurses on duty, and the general inspection took up most of the morning. Shortly before noon she met a Dr. George Usall, who seemed pleasant and greeted her with impersonal courtesy. After he had gone, Miss Ewell informed her that he lived in town and had a nice practice. He also had a nice wife and two nice children. Further, he lived in a nice house. Miss Ewell ended up by observing that he was a nice person.

They ran into Dr. Medford once or twice, and Judith was relieved when he greeted her in a quietly polite manner. He gave her a note which he said, indifferently, was from Les, and she stuffed it hastily into her pocket. Miss Ewell was obviously of the no-mixing-business-with-pleasure type, and Judith had no wish to offend her at this stage. She longed for a cigarette, but knew that she could not smoke on the floor, at least out in the open. She had been a nurse long enough to know how to get a quiet cigarette at regular intervals, but it could not be done as long as Miss Ewell stayed at her side. She became conscious again of an old resentment that the doctors could smoke openly, wherever they pleased, while the nurses had to sneak under cover.

"Now, dear, don't look so upset," Miss Ewell said, misinterpreting her frown. "We shall be getting the new ones in shortly."

Judith brought her mind back and realized that she was staring at a row of chipped bedpans. She laughed, and Miss Ewell gave her a curious glance. Such an odd girl, quiet and refined, seemingly, yet flirting with that Les already.

Vera's voice, calling for Angie, sounded from downstairs, and Miss Ewell hurried off. Judith watched her go, and then turned and made straight for the lavatory for women. She took out a cigarette, and Les's note as well, which stated that he would like to make a date with her on her day off. She stuffed it back into her pocket, feeling pleased. A day off was always more fun if you had a date to pass the time.

When she had finished her cigarette, she went out onto the floor again and did a quiet investigation of her own. She discovered that there were no semiprivate rooms. They were all single and fairly well appointed. She came upon the old man who had disturbed her the night before, but he was sleeping peacefully and looked quite harmless. She saw that his name was listed as Dr. Charles Woods.

She went out and made a determined effort to be friendly with the two nurses on the floor, Eva Babcock and Peggy Forbes. Peggy was young and pretty, but Eva was older and wore what appeared to be a permanent worried frown. She was a complainer, and started in at once.

Judith had had experience with that sort of thing and had a talent for dealing with it, and she was able to soothe Eva in short order. She attempted to get a smile out of her, but this was going a bit too far for Eva, who said fretfully, "There goes Peggy into Mrs. Scubble's room, and she knows that I'm the only one who can look after Mrs. Scubble."

She started off, but Judith stopped her with a hand on her arm. "I don't want either one of you to take exclusive care of any of the patients. I'll go in and see how Peggy is making out."

Peggy was smiling cheerfully, but Mrs. Scubble was not responsive. She was saying querulously, "It's the expense. Simply frightful. And I don't see why we don't have better sheets. I wouldn't put sheets like these on my servants' beds. Very poor quality. I've always been used to the best, you see. Were my husband still living, he would have something to say. And it's lucky for Smith Hospital that his lips are sealed."

Judith was used to this too, and she dealt competently and briefly with Mrs. Scubble. She was able to follow Peggy out within a few minutes, and asked in the impersonal atmosphere of the corridor, "What's supposed to be the matter with her?"

"Nothing," Peggy said simply.

"Nothing?"

"Not one thing. She was lonely in that big old house of hers, and couldn't keep any servants, even though she did give 'em better sheets than we have. So she came here."

"Whose patient is she?"

Peggy grinned. "Dr. Medford's."

Judith murmured, "Hmm," and added, "What does he say is the matter with her?"

Peggy giggled. "He says her head needs examining, and he's going to do it." She glanced into a door close by, and changed the subject abruptly. "Oh, darn! Old Charlie's gone again."

"Dr. Woods." Judith wrinkled her brows. "Where would he have gone?"

"Well, we think he used to have a secret crush on Miss Ewell, because he always goes right up to her room. Even now, when she's moved downstairs."

"That's my room." Judith nodded. "I'll go up and see."

As she left the floor, Eva called after her self-defensively, "I didn't see him leave, and I'm always watching for him."

Judith hurried a little. She supposed that it must be almost lunchtime, and she had an uneasy feeling that if she missed lunch in Dr.

Smith's dining room, she'd have to go without.

It was dark in the hall upstairs, and she saw no sign of old Charlie. She made a hasty search of her own rooms, but he was not there, and she went out into the hall again. There were so many doors, she thought confusedly, and all of them closed. Some of them must lead to closets, and one to a back stairs. There must be a back stairs in a huge old place like this. She went into the bathroom and pulled out a cigarette almost automatically.

As she puffed she heard the whirring sound that had disturbed her last night, and wondered again what it could be. It presently stopped, and there was a deep silence, but people could be walking around, she thought uncomfortably. With so much heavy, over-all carpeting, you could not hear footsteps.

A voice, low and angry and vicious, spoke outside the door. "I'm going to get rid of her, despite what you say."

Judith realized, with a shock, that it was Dr. Smith. But how could he possibly be up on the third floor, when he was chained to that wheel-chair?

Dr. Medford's voice said clearly, "Do as you like, of course. It should be easy. Just fire her. You can't do it any other way."

Dr. Smith laughed nastily. "Can't do it any other way? You just said we couldn't give her a black eye because of vague suspicions. So how can I fire her, and be consistent? But I'll get rid of her. I'll see that she goes, and forever, too. The presumption of her! The utter, damned presumption, coming here! Look, stop wasting my time. Get me your fancy hammer, and let me get on with it."

Judith took a quick, gasping little breath. Were they talking about her? Had Dr. Medford told Dr. Smith about her, so that he was determined to get rid of her? She lit another cigarette and smoked furiously, determined to stay where she was until she could feel sure that they had gone.

She had just perched herself more comfortably on the edge of the bathtub when the door opened and Dr. Medford walked in.

Chapter 6

Judith felt exactly like a small boy caught smoking a cigar, and was infuriated because she wanted, instead, to be cool, poised, superior, and even a little amused.

Dr. Medford looked annoyed. "There's really no necessity for eaves-dropping, not while you're in a bathroom. There is any amount of running water if you want to drown out conversation that is not meant for your ears."

Judith brushed past him. "Of course. But then I wouldn't have been able to hear." She went off to her room with the remnants of her effort to be cool, poised, and superior.

Dr. Medford washed his hands, splashing water viciously. After all, he thought, trying to calm down, it didn't matter to him one way or the other, but the old man seemed to be going a bit batty. Where did he hear about the girl's reputation? In fact, why hadn't they known about it before she came? But in any case, that sort of thing had never bothered the old man before. Must be getting prudish in his old age.

No. There was something wrong somewhere. What had he said? He'd blamed it on Angie. What did Angie think she was doing, bringing a girl like that into the place, a girl with an obviously bad reputation. He'd see that she was kicked out. He'd backed down a bit after that and explained that he'd have to do it, to save her reputation. And yet she was supposed not to have a reputation, at least not a good one. Inconsistent. But that didn't matter. It was the bitterness he didn't like. Why should the old man be so bitter and so determined to fix her? It would be really bad if his brain had gone a bit. And constant pain did queer things to people at times.

He glanced at his watch and sighed. Lunch, now, a happy family party in the dining room, the heads and owners of Smith Hospital. God! He'd have to get out of the place.

Judith was ahead of him on the stairs going down, and he slowed his pace a little. He found that Dr. Smith and Miss Ewell were already at the table, while Vera walked in ahead of him with Judith.

Vera was annoyed. She said directly, "Angie, when I put the drapes and slip covers out to be washed, I do *not* see why they should be pushed to one side to wait for another time."

Angie looked up, and her voice was a little shrill. "I told you not to take them down this week. They can't possibly be done. They'll simply have to wait. In fact, I don't know *when* they can be done, I'm sure."

Vera's face burned with ugly patches of red. "Well, *I* know. They're going to be done today, and I'll see to it myself."

Dr. Smith said, "Shut up! Both of you!"

Shirley bounced in and yelled, "Geez, I'm starved. Have I ever had a time! I was supposed to be relieved, but nobody came. I hadda go and get somebody myself." She pulled up her chair with a sharp lunge, and crockery rattled on the table.

Nora came in and banged food down, but Vera was looking at Shirley. She said finally, "You are doing your hair in a different way."

Shirley nodded. "Yep. I kind of like that hairdo of yours. It's plain, but it's got class, so I copied it. Cute, huh?"

Vera relaxed into a smile and murmured, "Thank you."

The food was bad, and was eaten in almost total silence, and Judith was glad to escape back to her work. She found that there were two floors to the actual hospital, a ground floor and a second floor, and both were in the wing that had been added to the house. There was more accommodation on the second floor, since some of the rooms of the original house were used for the patients. The new wing had a third floor, which was given over to an X-ray room and an operating room. There was also an elevator large enough to accommodate a stretcher, and later on Judith found an elevator in the old part of the house as well. It was much smaller, and the shaft had been put into the space which had originally housed the back stairs. She discovered, too, that it was used exclusively by Dr. Smith; that no one else was allowed to touch it. It went all the way to the third floor, and he was able to operate it himself. Judith realized that this elevator made the whirring noise which had puzzled and disturbed her, and it explained how Dr. Smith had been on the third floor that morning.

She wondered a little about Dr. Smith and his desire to oust her. He had been quiet at lunch, and had ignored everyone. And where was Dr. Willie? She had not seen him all the morning.

She had news of him almost immediately from Peggy, who told her that he had left early in the morning for the city. Dr. Smith had sent him in to perform some errands. Peggy lowered her voice to a whisper and expanded a little on the subject of Dr. Willie. He had been a great disappointment to the old man, and there was no doubt that he wasn't half the doctor that his father had been. He was useful about the place, of course, but he just couldn't take hold. They'd had to get Dr. Medford in to shoulder the responsibility. Dr. Medford had a private practice with an office right here in the building. "And if you ask me," Peggy said, glancing around cautiously, "I think he'd like to get out. But he can't, exactly, not until they get someone else in ,because Dr. Willie can't run the thing."

"Well, he's younger," Judith said, feeling a little uncomfortable.

Peggy shook her head. "But that's just it. He isn't. They're the same age, and Miss Smith too. I mean, Miss Smith and Dr. Willie are twins. Miss Smith is the older by half an hour, and there are plenty who think she should have been the doctor and Willie should have run the housekeeping." Peggy smothered a giggle in her handkerchief, and then put it away and tried to compose her face.

At three o'clock the nurses went off and a new shift came on. It developed, however, that Shirley was on from eight in the morning until eight at night, when the stringy blonde took over. She was relieved by a nurse on the first floor for meals, or when it was necessary for her to leave the switchboard for a few minutes, but that was all. She started yelling at about five o'clock, but no one seemed much concerned. Miss Smith, passing by, disclaimed all responsibility for the switchboard, and it was considerably later when Miss Ewell showed herself. Nor was she disposed to show sympathy. She said coldly, "We have always had these hours for our switchboard, and I see no reason to make any change at this time. In any case, it is not twelve hours, since Mary relieves you for dinner at seven, and the night girl comes on at eight."

Shirley eyed her with open dislike. "Yeah, sure. Only eleven hours. Listen, where the hell is the local union? I'm gonna join."

Miss Ewell said, "Nonsense!" and tripped away on light feet. Shirley kicked over an adjacent wastebasket.

Judith was tired by the end of the day. She longed to have a tray sent to her room, but felt that she did not know them well enough for that yet. She resented the fact that she had to change her uniform for a dress, but Miss Smith liked as formal atmosphere as possible at the dinner table, and felt that uniforms did not match cocktails and candles.

Shirley was being relieved at the switchboard as Judith came down, and she tore up the stairs, yelling, "God's sake! I get off at seven, and I'm supposed to be there at seven! Save me a drink!"

Judith laughed a little, and went on, feeling a lightening of her mood. It was an odd outfit, this Smith Hospital. But, after all, there were few such places that gave you a cocktail before your dinner–even though you had to take it in the company of Dr. Smith and Dr. Medford.

Dr. Smith was extremely polite to her, as it turned out, and talked shop with every appearance of genuine interest. She wondered, warily, whether he were trying to trap her, but she talked to him quietly while she made up her mind to try and find another place. Dr. Willie sidled up once, but his father merely gave him a cold glare and he backed away again.

Miss Ewell approached and said, "You know that Charlie hasn't come back?"

"Come back from where?" Dr. Smith demanded.

"Well, he left his room, and he hasn't returned."

"Oh, shut it off, Angie," Dr. Smith said irritably. "He's a lucky devil to be able to walk at all. Look at me."

"Yes, of course. But you know he's somewhat missing in the head."

"So are you, to be worrying about him. He'll come back when he's hungry."

Les did not appear, and Judith missed his high spirits. Shirley arrived in time for a couple of cocktails, although she had trouble getting the second one. Miss Ewell told her that she thought one was quite enough, but Shirley muttered, "Put it in your hat, sister. A whole bottle wouldn't be enough in this joint," and went straight to Dr. Willie, who obliged her.

Dr. Medford was very quiet, and even Shirley fell silent after confiding to Judith, in a loud whisper, that they oughta have a few stiffs laid out around the room to make the place more natural. Miss Smith did most of the talking. She droned along dully, telling stories of her past experiences with friends who were all of the highest social standing.

The call to dinner was a relief. They ate it in silence, all still except for Miss Smith, who hadn't finished her reminiscing.

When the meal was over at last, Shirley went around the table to Dr. Willie and persuaded him to go with her for a walk in the grounds. He agreed rather helplessly, but Miss Smith made it plain that she did not like the arrangement. "Willie needs his rest," she said, frowning at them.

"O.K., he can come right back and take his hot milk and go to bed," Shirley said cheerfully. "Come on, Doc. I bet you're always tellin' other people to get some exercise."

She walked him off, and Judith escaped to her room. She was surprised and considerably relieved to find that a bolt had been fastened to the door of her bedroom, although there was still no lock for the small outer room. She secured the bolt and went to bed with a book and a comfortable feeling that the roving Charlie could not get to her with his little knife.

But she'd have to leave here and get another place. She'd made up her mind to that. Dr. Medford seemed to have been talking to Dr. Smith, and Dr. Smith was determined to oust her. Still, he was not going to do it brutally, so she'd have time to look around. She didn't want private work; she preferred a hospital job. Supervising head. In fact, this was just what she wanted, and were it not for that damned Medford, she'd be completely satisfied.

She fell asleep against her pillows with the book in her lap and dreamed that she was married and living in a nice house, and that Dr. Medford was her husband. She woke up with the dream still in her mind and a feeling of helpless fury about it. She looked at her watch and discovered that it was twelve o'clock, and that she'd been asleep much longer than she had supposed. The room was stuffy, and she got out of bed, put her book away, and opened the window. She went over to the door and looked again at the bolt, which was still in place, and then she froze, with her eyes wide and round on the blank panels of the door.

Directly on the other side, in her little sitting room, someone was snoring gently.

Chapter 7

Judith stretched her hand toward the bolt, and then drew it back. Charlie. It must be Charlie. He had been unable to get into the bedroom, and so he was sleeping out there. What was the use of going out and making a fuss? Maybe he had his knife with him, anyway. She took out a cigarette, and walked around the room, smoking in nervous puffs. And once she went over to the bolt and shook it a little, but it seemed to be quite secure.

She went back to bed, in the end. Let him sleep there. What difference did it make? She knew that she was afraid to go out, and was a little ashamed of her fear, but she turned the light off and was presently asleep in spite of herself.

The next morning at breakfast Les walked in and gave forth a cheery, blanket greeting. He announced that he was just back from a business trip in his car, and he'd take a bite of breakfast with them, if Nora didn't mind.

"Why, of course," Miss Ewell chirped brightly, "Only, it's such a pity, Vera never gets up for breakfast."

Les coughed and became absorbed in picking a piece of lint from his sleeve, and Shirley grinned over at him. "Never mind, pal, you got plenty of company, anyway. It would help me from goin' nuts if you would come in to breakfast every morning. Do you know what I got to look forward to? Twelve hours at that stinkin' switchboard."

Miss Ewell carefully stuck her little finger out while she took a sip of tea. "Now, Mrs. West, don't be absurd. You know you get relief."

"Yeah, yeah, I know, so I can eat and go to the can."

Les choked severely over some cornflakes, and Miss Ewell thundered, "Mrs. West! Please!"

Dr. Smith came out of a long abstraction and looked up at them. "What's the matter?" he asked abruptly.

Dr. Willie walked into the room, and Dr. Smith's attention was diverted. "Right on time as usual, Willie," he said with bitter sarcasm.

"Nice of you to join us, too, when you know we'd be delighted to send a tray up to your bed."

Willie sat down and helped himself to black coffee, with every appearance of being stone-deaf.

Dr. Medford came in a few minutes later, and Dr. Smith said immediately, "Bob, I'd like to see you for a while, after breakfast. There's something I want to discuss with you."

Judith could feel Dr. Willie tighten up beside her. She supposed he was jealous, and it was understandable enough. His father practically ignored him, and when he did speak to him, it was usually a reproof. She wondered why Dr. Willie put up with it, why he didn't demand a little respect, at least in front of other people.

Les leaned over and murmured to her, "How many times do I have to speak to you before you'll notice me?"

"Oh." Judith smiled at him. "I'm sorry, I really didn't hear you."

"I said it was a lovely morning."

"Is it?" Judith glanced at the window, and Les laughed.

"I knew you wouldn't take my word for it."

"God almighty!" Shirley muttered, "my stomach is flappin' like a wet sail."

She reached for the toast, and Miss Ewell poised her cup halfway to her mouth and shook her head. Shirley flung the piece of toast onto the table, pushed her chair back, and walked to the window. She mourned, more to herself than to anyone else, "What's the usea starvin' just to get a figger that no sailor would look at twice?"

Judith glanced after her, and felt a little conscience-stricken. Shirley was plump, certainly, but a slim figure was really not her type.

Les said, "I have never met such a quiet nurse."

Judith looked at him. He was used to attention. He wanted hers, and he would not be satisfied until he got it. She stood up, and said flatly, "I have work to do."

He followed her out of the dining room and immediately made a date with her. She went on upstairs, smiling a little, and decided that she'd forget her worries. She'd go and buy herself a new outfit. She needed clothes, and there hadn't been much time, lately, for shopping. There wouldn't be much in a town as small as this, but she might be able to pick up something.

On the second floor Eva Babcock waylaid her, and began to give her a detailed description of several of the patients. She swallowed a yawn or two and broke away at last to answer a light that had been burning over a patient's door for some time.

Peggy tripped up to her and announced, "We're having an operation this morning."

It immediately developed that Judith was to be on duty in the operating room, since they had no one else except the retired Miss Ewell, who appeared promptly and escorted Judith upstairs.

The equipment was modern, and of the best, and Judith found her spirits rising. She had realized by now that her title was more or less bait, that Miss Ewell was still in charge, and that what they had really wanted here was just another nurse. They were shorthanded, of course, as most of the places were, but at least she could see to it that she was not put back on the bedpan and bed-making routine. She had always rather liked the operating room. It was more interesting.

The operation went off smoothly, with Dr. Medford officiating, and Judith felt that she had done well. But then she had always been good in the operating room, and she knew it.

She accompanied the stretcher down to the patient's room, guiding one end, while Lucius, the orderly and man of all work, propelled the other. Lucius turned out to be a chatty soul, and informed her almost at once that he was married and the father of seven children. The work here was too much for him, of course. It would be too much for an elephant. But what were you gonna do, with a wife who had no better sense than to produce seven children?

Judith asked him if the missing Charlie had returned to his room, and Lucius shook his head comfortably. "Nope, but you ain't got no need to worry about him. His brains is gone, but he's harmless. He's off on a bat somewheres. Here they try to make out like he don't go off on bats no more since he quit practicing, but we all know he does. And why not? is what I want to know. Me, if it wasn't for the old lady and the seven, I'd go on bats too. But I ain't got the money. The old lady is standin' right outside the door, paydays." He paused to laugh, and added, "Sure is a tough one, that."

Judith gave some instructions to Eva and then went up to her room for a cigarette. She was resting her tired back in an armchair when she heard the whirring noise again and realized that Dr. Smith must be using his elevator. What could he possibly want up here now? But he had to pass the time somehow, poor creature.

She dragged herself from the chair, and went to the mirror to touch up her face. Better not put too much on. Think of Shirley. Judith laughed at her reflection. Shirley was all right. She was better adjusted than most people.

She paused suddenly, with the powder puff upheld in her hand. Someone was in her little sitting room. But then, her bed was still unmade, and she was supposed to get service. It was probably the maid. She went to the door, but as she put her hand on the knob, she heard Dr. Smith's voice.

"Nora, where's Charlie?"

Nora replied indifferently, "How should I know?"

"Of course you know. Stop stalling. Where is he?"

"Honest to God, Dr. Smith, I don't know, not this time. He ain't in any of the usual places. And if I was you, I'd get them to look through all the saloons in the village."

"Don't be silly," Dr. Smith said impatiently. "If he were down there, somebody would have brought him back by now."

"Mebbe they're gettin' scared to bring him back. He's much worse lately, and you know it."

There was a silence, and Judith wondered uneasily whether to go out or to stay where she was. But Nora would surely be coming in at any minute to clean her room. Might as well face it. She squared her shoulders and walked out with as blank a look as she could manage.

Nora glanced at her indifferently, and Dr. Smith moved his chair from the door so that she could pass. He said mildly, "I heard that they were very pleased with you in the operating room."

"Thank you. I've done a lot of that kind of work."

He said no more, and she went on down to the first floor to look things over. She passed Shirley, who was mournfully chewing gum at the switchboard, and went along to the chart desk. A nurse, who had been introduced to her as Mary Gore, sat there studying her middle-aged and unlacquered fingernails. She looked up and said, "Hello, Miss Onslow," without enthusiasm.

"How are things here?"

"Slow," Mary said, swallowing a yawn. "They all think they're pretty sick on this floor, and that keeps them quiet. Kathy's been in and out, putting tubes in and pulling tubes out, and sticking them with needles when they come to a bit—"

"Hush," Judith said hastily. "Suppose one of them heard you talking like that! We'd lose half a dozen patients at once."

"No, we wouldn't." Mary settled her cap. "No matter what we do to them, or what mistakes we make, they come howling back for more. If it was me, I'd stay quietly at home and get well in a hurry, but not these dopes. They want it the hard way. Have an operation, get the tubes and the needles, and go tottering home full of holes."

"I don't see how you've kept your job here for so long, if you're accustomed to airing opinions of that sort," Judith said coolly.

"Well"—Mary took a long breath—"maybe I ought to tell you that

I believe in healing by faith. I always tell the patients that they're not really sick at all, they just need a little faith. So from this floor they go home much sooner. A thing like that gets to be known, and—"

"Ah, shut up, Mary," Kathy said, appearing from behind them. "Miss Onslow, will you come and see Mr. Omsted?"

Judith nodded, and Mary watched them as they walked off together and disappeared into a room. When the door had closed behind them, she got up quietly and went out to the lobby. As she passed the switchboard Shirley yelled at her, but she called back, "You'll have to hold it for a while," and went on to a small room at the back of the hall.

She entered quietly, closed the door behind her, and stood for a moment, looking at the man lying on the bed. He did not move, and she advanced a few steps.

"Now, Charlie," she said softly, "you're not sick at all, really. It's just that your thoughts have fallen into error, and you lack faith."

Chapter 8

Charlie made no move of any sort, and his glazed old eyes stared through half-closed lids at the ceiling. Mary continued to talk softly to him until a sound from the door startled her and she swung around.

Miss Ewell came in and closed the door quietly behind her. She whispered, "How is he?"

"I've been talking to him, telling him that he'll get well. You must leave it to me, and you'll see that everything will be all right."

Miss Ewell's little face puckered doubtfully, and Mary added in a slightly louder voice, "You must believe too. You must have faith, or you'll spoil everything. He can't get well if you surround him with doubt and disbelief."

"No, no," Miss Ewell said agitatedly, "I don't disbelieve. I have faith, I promise you. If you can only—"

Mary nodded her head. "All right. Now, don't worry. Everything's going to be fine." She left the room, crept quietly past Shirley, who was looking the other way, and returned to her seat at the chart desk.

Judith, who had just finished rounds, saw her come from the end of the hall, and said to Kathy, "Miss Gore seems to believe in faith healing of some sort."

Kathy laughed. "She has some dopey ideas, but I don't know exactly what they are. I made fun of her once, so she won't tell me a thing any more."

"But I'm afraid she might interfere—"

"Oh no." Kathy shook her head. "She's a good nurse. She doesn't do much, any more, mostly relief work. All she does is tell the patients that they're fine and that there really isn't anything the matter with them. Some of them don't like it, of course."

Judith smiled, and Kathy went on, "Mary's an old-timer around here. Not as old as Miss Ewell, to be sure, but Miss Ewell will never get rid of her now. She comes in handy, as a matter of fact, because she's here all day, twelve hours, and I guess she likes it. She's a widow with a married son, and she lives with him. Or maybe he lives with her, I don't know. Anyhow, she has all her meals here. She just goes home to sleep."

Judith nodded absently, her interest already waning. Her mind was occupied with a list of new equipment which she felt was badly needed, and she spent some time in making it up and going over it. She took it in to lunch with her, because she was determined to try and send it over Miss Ewell's head. She felt sure that Miss Ewell would regard the list as a ridiculous and unnecessary expense. She was the type to frown on anything new, as she got older, and Judith wanted the list to go straight to Dr. Smith. It didn't really matter to herself, she thought wryly, since it seemed probable that she would be out of the place very shortly, but the comfort of the patients concerned her, and she felt in duty bound to do her best for them.

They were all at the table for lunch, including Les. Judith waited quietly for an opportunity, and at last, during a momentary pause in the conversation, she looked straight at Dr. Smith and said, "I am a little surprised, Doctor, at the old and out-of-date equipment that I have found on the floors."

There was a rather stunned silence, and Judith was amused. Surprise came first, of course, and she had no doubt that fury would follow.

Miss Ewell recovered first, and exclaimed, "Well! Really, Miss Onslow!"

"I don't entirely understand you," Dr. Smith said coldly. "Miss Ewell—"

"I am not criticizing Miss Ewell," Judith said quickly. "It is not the fault of any of the nurses. It gets to be a matter of habit with them to do the best with what they have. But since the equipment in the operating room is of the newest and best, I felt sure that you would want the floor nurses to have what they need too. I am sure Miss Ewell would agree with me."

Dr. Willie and Dr. Medford, seated on each side of her, had suspended their forks and were waiting in interested silence.

"Are you implying that I have indulged my doctors and stinted my nurses?" Dr. Smith inquired acidly.

"I am making no implications of any sort. I am merely submitting a list of things which I feel are necessary for the floors."

"May I see the list?" Miss Ewell asked with chilly dignity.

Dr. Smith snatched the list from Judith and read it with his brows drawn together.

Les said plaintively, "*Must* you people always talk shop at the table?"

Dr. Medford turned to Judith and asked, "May I see the list when you get it back?"

Judith nodded, and Dr. Willie murmured, "Don't forget me."

Shirley yawned. "What are you all yappin' about, anyway? Me, I'd like a new switchboard."

Dr. Smith snapped, "You may get that sooner than you think," and handed the list to Miss Ewell.

Judith returned to her lunch, and was not entirely surprised when the list was not returned to her. She saw Miss Ewell stuff it into her pocket.

Dr. Willie said, "Father, I'd like to have a talk with you after lunch," and Vera nodded her head and murmured, "Yes."

Dr. Smith turned on her and barked, "What do you mean, 'yes'?"

Vera showed a little spirit. "I mean that Willie wants to talk with you, and why shouldn't he? I don't see how you can prevent it."

"I can prevent it by going into my room and locking the door."

Vera drew an exasperated breath. "Now, Father, don't be difficult. You're just mean today." She turned to Judith and added fretfully, "It's your fault, anyway, giving him that list. He hates to think his hospital isn't up to date, and it *is* up to date. We have everything that the most modern—"

"No," Judith said quietly, "I'm afraid you don't."

Les sighed, and apparently addressing the ceiling, observed, "God! What a bunch of bores. What's the matter with me, anyway? It must be a pretty face."

Dr. Smith glanced at him. "You don't find us amusing?"

"No."

Miss Ewell muttered, "I don't approve of these newfangled notions."

"Was it your face you were calling pretty, Les?" Dr. Willie asked. "Because it isn't. Looks more like a mattress than a face." He sat back and laughed heartily.

Dr. Medford leaned toward Judith and spoke in a low tone. "What do you think you are doing, throwing that list in their faces? Can't you be more tactful? Where is the list, anyway?"

Judith looked full at him. "I don't have it. I think Miss Ewell put it into her pocket. And why should I bother being tactful when I know that he intends getting rid of me as soon as he can do it in a nice way?"

Dr. Medford assumed a bothered frown. "I suppose I should have told you. It's not you he wants to fire, it's the West woman. Matter of fact, he can't get rid of her, anyway, because Miss Ewell won't have it."

"Miss *Ewell* won't have it!" Judith repeated. "What has she to do with it?"

"I don't know." He looked down at her. "Miss Ewell was very pleased with you, until now. And Miss Ewell is boss."

Judith shrugged. "I thought I was being pushed out, and it seemed a good idea to get things ready for whoever came after me."

He shook his head. "I doubt whether you'll get anything at all. Miss Ewell gets what she wants, when she wants it. And although I haven't seen the list, I'm pretty sure that she prefers things the way they are."

"Well"—Judith drew a long breath—"no harm trying."

There was complete silence at the table for a moment, and then Dr. Smith spoke.

"The Black Smith," he said distinctly, "had better behave. Or else."

Chapter 9

"Oh, Father!" Vera exclaimed. "You're always talking in riddles. What on earth do you mean?"

Miss Ewell got up. She hated him in that mood, and she left the room without a backward glance. She must have another look at Charlie. Perhaps this time she would find that he had really come out of it.

A distinct odor floated against her nose as she opened her door, and she went in quickly and closed it firmly behind her. She stood there for a moment, looking at the still figure on the bed, with her small face puckered unhappily. She had known yesterday that he was dead, of course. Only she hadn't wanted to admit it to herself. Mary had been so confident, and she had wanted to believe her. But all the time she had really known that he was dead, and that it was no use. How could she keep him here now?

She sat down in her rocker and pulled a handkerchief from her pocket, and Judith's list fluttered to her lap as she shook it out. Fury suffused her face with pink, and she picked the paper up and looked it over. She hadn't read it in the dining room. She'd been too angry, but now she looked at each item carefully, and then said loudly into the quiet room, "Nonsense!"

She looked fearfully over at Charlie, but of course he hadn't moved. How could he? He was dead. She put the list back into her pocket and began to twist the handkerchief nervously through her fingers.

A rap on the door brought her flying to her feet. She stood for a moment with one hand on her agitated chest, and then went and opened the door a crack. Nora stood outside, and Miss Ewell slipped out and closed the door firmly behind her. It was a good thing, she thought wildly, that there was a strict order of long standing that no one was ever to enter her room. She had always hated to have people touching her things, and she had insisted upon doing her own cleaning. Even when she was upstairs, that rule had held. She had allowed them to attend to the outer room, but they knew that they were not to go into her bedroom.

Nora said, "Miss Vera tells me I got to make an apple pie for dessert, and I ain't got the time, outside of the fact that I already made jelly. Anyways, I ain't stayin' here much longer if I have to put up with that one and her old-maid frills. She oughta have a man—"

"Oh, be quiet!" Miss Ewell interrupted impatiently. "Have the jelly, but put some whipped cream on it and a cherry on top."

"Only one?" Nora asked. "Don't think I'm goin' to serve them desserts separate, because I ain't. That jelly is in a bowl, and that's the way it's goin' on the table."

Miss Ewell sighed. "Nora, put the cherries in another dish, and then Miss Vera can put one on each dessert as she serves it out."

"Oh." Nora seemed a little disappointed at this simple solution, and went off with the air of one pondering fresh grievances.

Miss Ewell returned to her room and the rocking chair, and began again to twist her handkerchief through her fingers. She had to face it now, and quickly. Charlie was dead, and something must be done with his body. *He* was not to know that Charlie was dead. Only how could she keep the myth alive? Well, she'd have to, somehow. She couldn't bring anyone in here now and exhibit Charlie. They'd want to know what she'd been doing with him. So she'd have to dispose of him, but where? And what about Mary? Her mouth would have to be kept shut. Think. She must think. Perhaps it wouldn't be so hard to fix Mary, who was a bit weak in the head, anyway. She'd merely tell her that her faith healing had at last been successful with Charlie: he had got up off the bed and walked away. Mary would believe it because she'd want to. All right, that would do. But Charlie had to be removed. He was light, of course, but she was small herself. Could she do it? For a short distance, perhaps. But where was a short distance from here?

The sudden whirring of Dr. Smith's private elevator set her heart to fluttering. That was the answer, and a very simple one. There was a space at the bottom of the shaft, small, but just enough, and that would do it. If by any chance he were found, they would suppose that he had fallen there, and since he had died a natural death, there would be nothing to disprove it. Even Mary would suppose that it was just an unfortunate accident. In any case, the fact of his death, and his knowledge dying with him, would be delayed. Oh, if she could only hurry things up! But that girl, that frightful girl! How could she hurry her? She'd have to stop him from smelling. There were so many angles, so many things to think about.

Miss Ewell found that she had torn her handkerchief right across the middle. She crushed it into a ball in her little hand, and her darting thoughts hovered over Dr. Medford. He wanted to get out. She'd known that for some time. It seemed absurd to suppose that they couldn't get another, but she hadn't been able to move Dr. Smith. And that nurse. She didn't want the knowing kind around. They were too inquisitive. You'd have thought they'd have taken to each other, but of course Vera wanted him, or anybody she could get, for that matter. There was Les. She'd be glad to take him, although she liked Medford better. Vera didn't give up easily, either, but neither did Medford.

She thought of the shock treatments that Dr. Smith had given someone a year or two ago. He wouldn't tell her who the patient was, and she'd never been able to find out. Oh well, never mind. That girl Medford had been engaged to— The engagement was off, but Vera didn't know it. She herself had seen the letter when she went into Medford's room for something. She hadn't told Vera. After all, she might be able to use the information sometime. You never knew. You'd think this new nurse would give him a play, but she hadn't, didn't even bother to look at him. It was annoying, because it would have made it easier to get her out. She was a help, of course. Much better than the usual lazy nurse, or how could she be sitting here now, thinking in peace? Perhaps she'd let her stay, after all. But Medford would have to go. He was getting too nosy. And the audacity of Vera, telling Nora what to have for dessert!

She rocked silently for a while, and then her face tightened with sudden purpose and she got up and left the room. She locked the door after her this time, her mind busy with the thought that no one must find him again.

She went in search of Mary, and found her talking to a patient, an elderly man by the name of Lister. Mary was working against odds, since it was quickly obvious that Mr. Lister preferred talking to listening.

He was saying "—and you can tell that to your damn pompous, butchering doctors too."

"Why bother with the doctors?" Mary asked softly. "They only annoy you. You don't need them. You need just yourself, your *whole* self."

"My *whole* self!" he repeated, in a tone of bitter outrage. "You'd have to go through the blasted garbage cans in the operating room to assemble my whole self again. My ruddy stomach is flopping against my backbone because there's nothing in there to keep them apart any more. How d'ya expect a man to keep going when you've taken out his goddamn engine and thrown it away?"

"Whatever they removed was only physical," Mary said composedly. "Let the doctors have it. You don't need it. But your soul is still within you, and it's *yours*."

"Be damned to my lousy soul!" Mr. Lister howled. "Take it away and put it under one of your infernal microscopes. I want something inside me that'll digest a red steak!"

Miss Ewell said, "Miss Gore, it is time for Mr. Lister's nap."

"Oh, nap, flap, snap," Mr. Lister said peevishly. "What makes you think I can sleep with all these birds building nests inside of me?"

Miss Ewell walked to the chart desk, where Mary presently joined her, after preparing Mr. Lister for his nap to an accompaniment of infuriated shouts. Miss Ewell had been bracing herself, and she turned to Mary with an air of what appeared to be genuine excitement.

"You were right! You were *so* right, and yet I couldn't keep myself from doubting, once or twice. My dear, your faith has actually restored Charlie. He got up off my bed, said he supposed he must have had a nap, and walked out. I told him to go to his room and get to bed, and he promised that he would."

Mary's face reflected several emotions in quick succession. Disbelief was followed by amazement, and then her eyes glowed with a fanatical light. "Do you mean it? Do you really *mean* it?" she whispered.

"Yes, yes, of course. I had to let you know at once, because I knew how you'd feel about it."

Miss Ewell went off in a bit of a hurry and made her way to the kitchen, where Nora was airing her wrongs to her assistant, Linnie. Miss Ewell ignored them both, and pattered over to the cake bin, where she put a piece of frosted cake on a small plate. She poured a glass of milk, to which she added a little cream, and arranged them daintily on a tray.

Nora had suspended her recital in order to watch, and she asked now, "What are *you* up to?"

Miss Ewell said severely, "I doubt if that's any of your business."

"I got me own doubts about it too," Nora admitted, "but I'd like to know."

Miss Ewell elevated her chin and walked out, carrying the tray. She went to the Smith quarters, and entered as quietly as possible. She didn't want to see the doctor. He'd only want to eat the food.

She was lucky, as it happened. She found Vera alone in her bedroom, writing letters.

"Here you are, dear," she said in a voice of cheerful friendliness that caused Vera to look up in surprise. "You've been looking a little tired and thin, and you know you're supposed to eat something in the afternoon."

"Why, thanks," Vera said uncertainly, and put the tray awkwardly on her desk.

Miss Ewell nodded and sat down. She'd have to tell her about the jelly that was coming up for dessert, or there'd be an explosion at the dinner table, but not now. Later on would be time enough. There was something else for now.

"You know, Vera, I never did like Dr. Medford," she said tentatively.

"Why?" Vera's voice went up a shade, and her eyes were unfriendly. "I'm sure I don't know what you mean. I always thought he was very nice."

Miss Ewell shook her head and lowered her eyes to her clasped hands. "I have never been really easy in my mind about him, and now it seems that I was right. Engaged to a nice girl, and yet at night he sneaks into the room of the new nurse."

Chapter 10

Vera put her glass down with a little clatter and said shrilly, "No!"

Miss Ewell noted with satisfaction that she had finished the milk, and the cake as well. She gathered up the tray, and said mildly, "Oh, don't take it too seriously. It's probably just a brief infatuation. And for heaven's sake don't tell anyone."

"But she'll have to go," Vera protested, her voice still high. "We can't have a woman of that sort here."

Miss Ewell rested the tray against her hip. "Now, my dear, don't jump to conclusions. He merely goes there to her little sitting room.

She's a fine type of girl, and I don't want her exposed to that sort of thing. No, we must get another doctor, and it can be quite easily arranged. After all, it's time Willie took over, and we can get him an assistant. Your father never gives him a chance, and it isn't fair. Willie is very capable—I ought to know—and I simply can't understand why your father doesn't trust him."

This worked very well. Vera's eyes flashed, and she elevated her chin. "You're absolutely right. It isn't fair, and it's going to stop. Willie must take his rightful place here. I intend to have a serious talk with Father, and I want you to be there when I do."

Miss Ewell nodded and walked off with an odd little smile on her lips. She'd be there, all right. The smile faded and gave place to a sigh. There was so much that she had to do. And if only the weather would turn cold, poor Charlie would last a bit better.

Judith was busy in her own way too. She worked hard and conscientiously, and in a week she found that things were moving smoothly and well. Dr. Smith and Dr. Medford were both courteous, and even Miss Ewell seemed to have adjusted her temper over the list that had been given to her. She went so far as to say that she might get some of the things.

The warm June weather turned suddenly chilly, and Judith found that she needed a sweater. The hospital wing had its own heating unit, and the few patients' rooms in the main house were supplied with electric heaters, but the furnace had been closed up for the summer and the rest of the house was chilly. Vera complained that the furnace had been cleaned out too soon, it was bad organization, but Miss Ewell merely raised her eyebrows and said that she liked a cool atmosphere.

Judith walked into the village with Shirley one afternoon. She had only the sweater to buy, but Shirley said that she had quite a lot of shopping to do, and Judith asked if she intended to spend all her first week's pay.

"Yeah—yes. All of it."

Judith glanced at her curiously. Shirley, she thought, must have decided to go refined. Her hair, and now her speech. And perhaps this shopping tour meant a change of clothes. She was losing weight too. But at least she was as vividly painted as ever.

Judith suggested a soda at the drugstore, and Shirley made a little face. "Sure, you get a soda. I'll have black corfee."

"What are you trying to do?" Judith asked. "You've lost plenty of weight. How far do you want to go?"

"Old skin and bones," Shirley muttered. "What's the usea livin', anyway?"

She shopped feverishly for clothes that were so different from the things that she had been wearing that Judith feared for her sanity. She bought costumes that were dowdy in their refinement, and most of them were too small for her.

"They'll fit, though," Shirley said, and gave Judith a rather crooked smile. "I just gotta take some more off, that's all."

Judith shook her head a little, but forebore to comment. Whatever Shirley was up to was certainly her own business.

They returned to the hospital, and Shirley made a face at Mary Gore, who was sitting at the switchboard and calling loudly for relief. Judith had started up the stairs when Dr. Medford appeared in the hall and gestured to her. She descended again, and he hustled her into his office. He seated her, established himself at his desk, and then asked with restrained violence, "When did I ever enter your sitting room at night?"

Judith stared at him. "You tell me," she said at last. "When?"

"If you can't name a time, what makes you think I go there?"

"But I don't think you go there," she said indignantly. "What are you talking about?"

"Have you told anyone that I come into your rooms at night?"

Judith's eyes began to spark with anger. "I have never told anyone that you come to my rooms at night, since, as far as I know, it isn't true. If you did, you would not be admitted."

"Has anyone been admitted?"

"Everyone," Judith said furiously. "I'm that kind of a woman. Remember?"

Dr. Medford thrust a cigarette case at her and said, "Here. Have a cigarette."

She took one and then wished that she hadn't. He held a light for both of them, and for a while they puffed energetically until they were sitting in a bit of a fog. It cleared away as they became more relaxed, and Judith said presently, "Somebody has been making fun of you. Why do you take it so seriously?"

He flung the ash off his cigarette and missed the ashtray by at least an inch. "Look, I'm willing to leave this place. I want to, but I won't go under a cloud. And it seems people think I have been playing fast and loose with that fine and lovely girl, our new head nurse."

Judith laughed, heartily and at length. "Annoying, isn't it?" she said, recovering herself, and touching an immaculate handkerchief to her damp eyes. "But I really can't pretend to sympathize. I've been there myself, and with your help."

She got up and left before he could answer, and went her way with a little spring in her step. He had always seemed so utterly above reproach. And now look at him, accused of being a low-down despoiler of her own womanhood! She was too human not to enjoy it, and she laughed all the way upstairs, ignoring Mary Gore's plaintive wail that she ask Shirley to hurry back to her post.

Judith went to her room and tried on the sweater, and was further uplifted. It looked well on her, a particularly good buy. As she turned slowly before the mirror she wondered a little who had been sleeping in her sitting room that night. Could it have been Medford? And someone had seen him come in? But she shook her head at her own reflection. Outside of the fact that he'd have no earthly reason to do such a thing, he could never have fitted on that small couch, anyway. No, it must have been the currently missing Charlie.

She removed the sweater and prepared to take a bath and dress for dinner. She rather liked the change of clothes and the gathering for cocktails by this time. It had become something to look forward to in the evening. In fact, she liked her job, even if the title of "head" had proved to be a bit empty. Miss Ewell was head, and she was a sort of acting assistant, but it didn't really matter. She pulled on her robe and went along to the bathroom.

Vera was bathing, too, and she was a little late and therefore somewhat bothered. But she had so much on her mind. Father, for instance. He just didn't like Willie, and he had said straight out that Willie was no good. But how could the finest doctor prove himself when he wasn't given a chance? He'd never had a chance, poor boy. Even when they were children, Father had always slighted him. Yet Willie had done well in medical school, and as an intern. It was just here that he couldn't show his skill, because he was never allowed to do anything. She'd ask Bob Medford if he could push Willie into things more. Only, how could she? He'd think she was crazy, and she wanted him to think well of her. She wished she could marry him. It would be so suitable. And—well— she liked him too. He was supposed to be engaged to some girl, and then sneaking into that nurse— Of course Les was rushing Judith too. And it was Vera he had always come to see before. The woman was attractive, but probably no better than she should be. And that type of woman always attracted the men. But then, when they wanted a wife, a real woman they could depend on— Vera's thin chest expanded, and she felt a pleasant glow. She herself was a real woman, honest, decent, and dependable. She dallied happily with the thought that perhaps Ju-

dith was the girl to whom Bob was engaged, and she had come here to
see what was going on because she felt that he had another interest
locked within him. Vera's soaring thoughts sobered, and she shook her
head. If he had any interest in herself, he certainly kept it locked within
him.

She put on her robe and went along to her room, and almost immediately there was a knock on the door. Miss Ewell came in with a little
air of apology and declared that she wouldn't stay a minute, but she'd
just had *such* a time in the kitchen. Nora was really getting impossible,
wasn't she?

Vera agreed, and Miss Ewell sighed. "Well, my dear, I won't hold
you up. I see you're dressing. What are you wearing tonight? I wish
you'd put on the green print. You haven't worn it for some time, and it
looks particularly well on you."

Vera said, "Perhaps," and closed the door on Miss Ewell as she
went out. So annoying to be disturbed at this time, especially as she
was late. Angie knew perfectly well that she'd be dressing at this hour.
She had to set the cocktails out, and she hated to be rushed. Still, it was
pleasant to think that they always dined, instead of just eating. Of course
there was Father, but she had to put up with him, and there was no use
in fretting.

Vera glanced down at herself and was surprised to find that she had
put on the green print without having given it a thought. Usually her
choice of a dress was a matter of some deliberation. But in any case,
she had no time to change now.

She hurried to the living room and began to set out cocktail glasses,
and became flushed and slightly peevish when several people came in
before she was ready. Willie amiably gave her a hand, and she was
presently able to take the first sip of her own drink with a sigh of relaxation.

The door opened, a figure entered, and Vera's glass slid from her
hand and broke its fragile stem on the carpet. She thought, wildly, that
she was looking straight at herself, external from herself.

Chapter 11

It had been just a momentary impression, of course. It was that abominable West woman. Vera felt her face flushing violently as she groped
with her foot for the broken cocktail glass. Behind her, Willie drew
breath in a little gasp, and muttered, "What does she think she's
doing?"

Shirley smiled around at them without her usual impudence. "How's this, Vera? Don't I look better? Sort of more refined, I mean, like you."

Vera looked at her helplessly and was still struggling for words when Dr. Smith wheeled himself into the room. He looked at his daughter and at Shirley, and smiled grimly.

"So your style is being copied, Vera. A very sincere type of flattery, I'm told. I'm a little at a loss to understand the young lady's motive, since you're not exactly of the glamorous school—"

Shirley slitted her eyes and said, "You button up your lip, Doc."

He swung his chair around to face her, while Vera and Willie stood frozen and speechless. He let a moment pass, and then said deliberately, "You are impertinent and offensive. I shall accept your resignation as of tonight."

"Oh no." Shirley shook her head. "I got a contract, see, for a year. The only way you can break it is to pay me plenty, and I mean plenty too."

Dr. Smith shifted his body in the wheelchair and asked, "Who signed your contract?"

"I did."

"Who else?"

Shirley sent a quick glance around the room. "Miss Ewell. And she's got the authority, see?"

"I see." His hands gripped the arms of the chair, and in the little pause that followed Miss Ewell came forward with her small hands fluttering impatiently.

"Come, now. All this fuss. I'm sure you look very nice, Shirley, and Vera should be flattered. I wish someone would copy my clothes; it would please me immensely. Dr. Smith, you don't seem to realize how difficult it is to supply workers for this place, or you wouldn't start picking fights with people all the time. Of course Shirley has a contract. How could I expect to get anyone out here, otherwise?"

"What is the enormous sum we'd have to pay her to get rid of her?" Dr. Smith asked.

Miss Ewell settled her lips into a thin line, and then opened them to say, "We're not getting rid of her. We're keeping her, and that's final."

Shirley said, "Yeah, if I decide to stay."

Dr. Smith muttered, "We'll see."

Shirley flung her arms in a wide gesture, and made a very rude comment, which had to do with a horse. She added, "For God's sake, Willie boy, give me a drink. I'm dyin'."

Miss Ewell raised her eyebrows at the vulgar expression, and Vera gasped, but as Judith and Les entered at that moment, she busied herself in getting cocktails for them, and tried to put the whole thing out of her mind.

Dr. Smith wheeled himself into a corner and sat there pulling at his lip until Dr. Medford came in, when he hailed him and began a low-voiced conversation.

"Why," he asked, "in the name of God, *why* did you let her see you? Now she has Vera all hepped up. And Willie—he's floating on pink clouds. You know they all want Willie to take your place here. And you know that he can't handle it."

Dr. Medford settled himself into a chair. "Now, look. Willie will never be able to handle anything if you don't let him try. I think he can manage perfectly well if I come in every day, which is what I expect to do. I'm not staying here forever, you know that, and I might as well go now. But there's one thing I want clear in your mind: I did not go into that girl's room. I barely know her, and I'm not attracted to her at all."

"All right, son," Dr. Smith said pacifically, "you don't have to explain anything to me. You know I don't care. Only, just keep it quiet."

Dr. Medford stood up and walked away. Inside he was seething, but he knew the futility of trying to convince the old man of his innocence. Shirley caught his eye, but he was too abstracted to give her more than a puzzled glance, and he made his way straight to Miss Ewell.

"Look here," he said directly, "I'm leaving, as you wanted. But I'm not leaving with a cloud of scandal over my head in connection with Miss Onslow. The whole thing is a tissue of lies, anyway. And if I hear of any whisperings, I'll be back at once."

"Oh, Bob!" She fluttered her hands at him. "You must not be so silly. You know it will be better for you and Willie both if you go out now. You have your own practice, and you have the facilities of the hospital here. I hate any talk in connection with my nurses. You know that. And so of course I had to protest when I saw you—"

"You did not see me," Dr. Medford said hotly, "and you know it perfectly well. But you've wangled what you wanted, so you'd better be quiet and let it drop."

Judith was watching Shirley and Vera while Les poured a stream of gay talk into her ear. They both wore green print dresses, with sensible black shoes, medium heel, and hair brought back to a bun on the nape of the neck. Shirley was still considerably plumper than Vera, of course. But what was Shirley up to? Trying to annoy Vera? Judith shook her head. It would be far too expensive a joke. She remembered that Shirley had paid twenty-five dollars for the dress, and ten for the shoes—not too extravagant a price in either case, but more than Shirley could afford purely for spite, since her other clothes were of a decidedly cheaper variety.

Les said, "Come on, honey, tell me, won't you?"

"Tell you what?"

"Did you know him before you came here?"

"Who?"

"Bob."

"Who on earth's Bob?"

Les sighed. "Dr. Medford, honey. Why are you trying to fool me?"

Judith felt herself changing color, and slid her fingers up and down the stem of her cocktail glass in silence. She wondered uneasily why he was asking her the question.

"Oh." Les sat back and nodded his head. "So you *have* met him before. I see it all now. Look, honey, why don't you forget all about him? He thinks of nothing but his work, and that's why you didn't hear from him. I'll admit I don't know of any other woman, but his work is just as absorbing to him as another woman would be."

"What in the name of *heaven* are you talking about?"

Judith looked so puzzled that Les wondered if Vera was mistaken. Or perhaps he hadn't heard her properly. She'd whispered to him hurriedly a few minutes ago that Miss Onslow was the girl Bob Medford was engaged to, and that she'd got this job quietly, without his knowing, to find out what was holding up the marriage. He realized that it could easily have been spite. Vera was always trying to get a man by discrediting the other girls, and yet somehow this one gave the impression that she had known Medford somewhere before.

"Well"—Les shrugged—"I heard a rumor, honey, that you are the girl Bob is engaged to, and that you'd come here to check on him."

Judith laughed. "I didn't even know his first name until you told me."

"All right, sugar, but you had met him somewhere before you came here."

"Certainly, but that's not even interesting to me, so I don't see why it should concern you. Can't we talk about something else?"

"We could talk about us," Les said, putting his head close to hers and lowering his voice. "I think I could be more interesting to you than Medford. You'd find that I wouldn't put off our marriage because of business pressure."

Judith started to speak, but he wasn't listening. He drew her up from her chair with an arm around her waist, and took her over to the cocktail table, where he poured her another drink. She disposed of it, too quickly, because she was angry and exasperated. There was no use telling people anything, she thought, because they made up their own stories and stuck to them, no matter what you said.

Shirley, talking to Willie in an undertone, was unusually quiet, and Miss Ewell was uneasy. It was not quite nice, somehow, and she tried twice to part them, but was shrugged off each time. Les and the Onslow woman were paired up, and of course Vera was trying to make Medford again. Idiot, Miss Ewell thought, to make a fool of herself that way. She glanced at Dr. Smith, and decided that he was sulking over in his corner. What was holding Nora up, anyway? Dinner should have been on before this. She was hungry. There was Les, getting more drinks. Of course he never showed it much when he'd had too many, but Willie did. That Onslow woman—why did she dislike her so much? Perhaps because she had taken over her own job, and the rooms that she had had upstairs for so many years. Medford was trying to get away from Vera; he was getting himself another drink. No more for Vera. She never took more than one cocktail.

Medford passed close to Judith, and Miss Ewell felt the shock out to the ends of her fingers and toes when the girl leaned toward him and said, "Darling! How nice to know that you and I are engaged."

He stopped short and stared at her, and then glanced at Miss Ewell, who was frankly listening with her mouth hanging a little open. As his eyes met hers, she closed her mouth and turned aside. This was going wrong; she shouldn't have mentioned it to Vera, after all. Perhaps he wouldn't go now.

Dr. Medford's voice was quite mild as he said to Judith, "I'm glad you told me. It's always better to know these things. But who told you?"

Judith smiled amiably. "It was Les. He told me to throw you over for him too."

Dr. Medford swung around to face the room, and called for silence. Into the ensuing quiet he announced clearly, "You'll all be glad to know that Judith and I are bringing our secret engagement out into the open, and making it official."

There was a blank pause, during which Les dropped his cocktail and Vera turned and left the room. Shirley broke the silence by yelling, "Gee, fellas, that's swell!" and Willie stepped over and offered quiet congratulations.

Dr. Smith was looking at Miss Ewell with an odd smile. She was staring at the broken cocktail glass. The second one—the carpet would be ruined. And besides, the glasses were expensive. But that wasn't it.

There was something else, something that had been nagging at her for the last five minutes, something awful.

The furnace was on.

Chapter 12

They'd find out about Charlie now, lying there underneath the elevator. It had been so cold that he'd lasted pretty well, but with the heat on, they'd surely discover him.

Miss Ewell was suddenly furious. It was Nora, and that was why dinner was late. Nora hated to be cold, and she'd gone down and started the furnace. She'd got permission from Dr. Smith or Vera, of course; she was shrewd enough for that. June, with the heat on. It was absurd. But Miss Ewell felt herself helpless to do anything about it.

Vera came back into the room and said quietly, "Dinner's ready."

She looked over at Les. Perhaps he would give her some attention now, after Bob's announcement. But he had taken Miss Onslow's arm and was talking to her, and Bob didn't seem to care. He was talking to Willie, and seemed absorbed in the conversation.

Vera walked into the dining room alone, and found Shirley there, already seated. "Gee-zus!" Shirley said simply. "Am I ever starved!"

Vera seated herself in silence, and Les took Dr. Medford's usual place beside Judith. He said by way of explanation, "Now that you're engaged, boy, you're not supposed to sit beside the gal any more."

Dr. Medford nodded, and went over to the other side with Dr. Smith and Shirley.

"Oh, nuts!" Shirley said, around an olive that she had just put into her mouth. "All the decent men over on the other side." She laughed heartily, and alone.

Dr. Smith gave her a cool glance. "There is still a difference, you know, between yourself and my daughter. She has an innate refinement, and your manner is crude."

"Yeah." Shirley took another olive. "She's so refined it drips out her ears. I'm more like you—picked our manners outa the gutter."

Dr. Smith frowned, and tackled his food.

Judith was feeling quite happy. She knew that Medford had made his announcement in a burst of emotional fury. Now let him get out of it as best he could! She didn't mind. It was all fun, and it was amusing to see him writhe. She found herself smiling, and allowed the smile to stay on her face.

"Such a quiet little mouse," Les murmured in her ear. "But I have a date with you, and I'm going to hold you to it."

"Of course. I'll keep it, and I'm looking forward to it. I'm sure my fiancé won't mind."

Dr. Medford, looking at her, wondered what she was up to now. He had been a fool, of course, to let temper lead him to make that announcement. But why hadn't she denied it? Because she was enjoying it, and he knew it damned well.

Vera wanted a game of bridge when they returned to the living room, but Les said he had a business appointment and would have to go.

"Blonde business?" Shirley suggested.

Unexpectedly, Les got a bit huffy. He said, "Nothing of the sort," and took himself off, looking offended.

Dr. Smith went to bed, and Miss Ewell went along to help him. Vera got out a table, and she and Shirley, Dr. Medford and Willie sat down to play. Judith took a chair close by.

Shirley didn't last long. She was restless from the beginning, and at last threw her cards onto the table with an exasperated snort. "Honest to God, guys, I can't play this game. I thought you was gonna play poker, with everyone for himself. But this stuff, with all of you holding your cards close to your stuffed chest— Listen, who wants to go to a movie? Nobody? O.K., I'll go and get one of the nurses. You fellas can sit around here and hold services without me."

She flounced off, and Judith was immediately drawn into the game by Vera and Willie, who appeared to take their bridge with deadly seriousness.

She shuffled cards, and turned to Vera with a little smile.

"Miss Smith, how did you guess that Dr. Medford and I are engaged?"

Vera's eyes had gone as cold and chilly as a pair of oysters. She said thinly, "Please! I really don't care to hear any more about it. I've known for some time that you're the girl he's engaged to, and you ought to know that I dislike these secret things. Suppose we get on with the game." She picked up her hand and made a bid in a nasty tone of voice.

Judith drew a breath through her teeth and gave Dr. Medford an artificial smile.

"I think we shall have to talk things over," he said easily. "We must make some plans, and of course there are several things on which we don't see eye to eye."

"Will you make a bid, Bob?" Vera asked with careful patience.

Miss Ewell, having helped Dr. Smith to bed, made an unnecessary adjustment to the pillows behind his back, and patted his shoulder.

He said dryly, "Stop fussing, Angie, and get back to your dirty work.

You've plenty to do, I know."

She huffed away from him, offended that her little ministrations were not appreciated, and said sharply, "Certainly I have, and don't think that I won't get it done."

She went out and closed the door behind her with a firm click. She passed the bridge game with a vague nod of her head, and sighed a little at Dr. Medford's solid back. How could she have been so stupid as to ruin her chance of getting him out? Such a pity. No use thinking about that now, though. She walked to her room, lay down on the bed, and went immediately into an uneasy sleep. She awoke to a restless, compulsive feeling of something to be done, and she presently got up, smoothed her hair, and went straight out to the elevator.

She ran the cage up a little, but it was too dark to see down into the shaft. If she had her flashlight— No. What was she doing? She wasn't supposed to know anything about it. And if someone saw her here— She returned the elevator to its original position in a hurry, and then stood there for a moment, twisting her hands together. There was no odor, none at all, and there should be. Soon—it must be soon, with the heat on—

She forced herself to go quietly to her room. She must stop worrying so about things. Everything was all right. The girl had come through well tonight. Just a little more weight off, and he'd have to come to his knees. She would prove it to anybody. Charlie would be discovered shortly. It couldn't be long now, and she'd have to tell him that Mary Gore knew, and that Charlie had told Mary.

She began to undress, hanging her clothes away neatly. What had Medford meant by saying that he and the nurse were engaged? And the girl had not denied it. Well, why should she? She could hold him to it, and make him marry her. He'd made the announcement in front of several people, after all. It had been fury, of course. She knew his temper. Now, if she'd only had a break like that— But she hadn't. No use thinking about it. And she was afraid of Bob Medford. She had to admit it to herself.

She pulled on a dressing gown and stood for a moment, hesitating. She couldn't sleep yet, it would be impossible. She had to see.

She found her flashlight and slipped out of the door. She ran the elevator up again, hoping frantically that no one would hear it, and cautiously played her flash into the blackness of the shaft.

She stood there for a long time, moving the flash wildly from side to side, but it was no use.

Charlie was gone.

Chapter 13

Miss Ewell ran back to her room with quick, birdlike little steps. She closed the door and stood leaning against it while her heart pounded wildly. Where was he? Who had taken him? And what would she do now? Perhaps he wasn't dead, after all, and he'd crawled out of there. No, that was stupid, impossible. He was dead, all right. She ought to know, she'd seen so many dead people. Charlie was dead, but somebody had stolen him.

She moved restlessly around her room for an hour, her mind busy with anxious, troubled thoughts, and then the walls seemed to close in on her and she struggled into a dressing gown and went outside. She moved forward, but as she neared the front hall she heard someone coming down the stairs, and she slipped back into the shadows and waited.

It was Willie. He came down quietly, paused to say something to the girl at the switchboard, and then went on toward the back somewhere. Probably looking for something to drink. Miss Ewell padded after him silently, but lost him almost at once. After a moment's hesitation, she went into the Smith quarters and headed for Vera's room. She knew that Vera would be reading.

Vera had been reading, but the book was lying on her lap, and she was staring into space. Maybe she could get Les to take her to that dance at the country club. It would be nice to go, and he certainly owed her something. He'd eaten enough meals here.

Miss Ewell tapped and entered, and Vera gave her a look of only partially suppressed annoyance. Miss Ewell saw it, but chose to ignore it, and said brightly, "My dear, wasn't that awful, that creature dressing up exactly like you? Really, I didn't know which way to look. Such impertinence!"

Vera frowned. "It was abominable. I'm not going to have a woman like that mistaken for me. I'm going in tomorrow afternoon and have my hair cut."

"Are you? I mean, really?" Miss Ewell breathed.

"Certainly. If I can get an appointment."

"I don't blame you." Miss Ewell seated herself on the foot of Vera's bed and sighed. She couldn't go back to bed now—she'd never be able to sleep—and after a moment's thought, she brought up the subject of Judith's list. The mere thought of it made her glow with anger, and she said warmly, "It's that kind of head nurse that can put a hospital in the red. These new contraptions sound all right, but they're frightfully expensive, and we've always made out quite well enough with what we have."

Vera yawned. She didn't really care much, one way or the other, about the list. She patted her lips with a handkerchief onto which she had tatted a neat border, and murmured, "Can you imagine her pursuing him all the way out here just to see what he was doing?"

"Oh, well—" Miss Ewell took a long breath. "But I doubt if she's the girl he was engaged to."

"Oh yes, she is. I happen to know it." Vera looked at the handkerchief for a moment, and then crumpled it into her moist palm. "She came down here to find out why he wasn't in a hurry to marry her."

"But I picked her out myself, Vera."

"That doesn't mean anything. She must have known you were looking for someone, so she got people to recommend her. After all, she's a bit young for the kind of job she has here, although I would say that she's well into her thirties."

Miss Ewell said, "She's just thirty," and felt that she was enjoying herself for the first time that evening.

"You mean she *says* she's just thirty," Vera observed acidly.

Miss Ewell's lip curled, and she sent an austere glance at the ceiling. Vera was thirty-two, she knew. And Miss Onslow looked at least five years younger, if not more.

Vera caught the look and interpreted it correctly. She said, coldly, that she wanted to read, and that she would be shortly turning out her light. And if Miss Ewell didn't mind—

Miss Ewell went out slowly, her thoughts circling around Judith. The girl had been recommended by various people, but she began to wonder for the first time if Vera's theory could possibly be right. Certainly, the girl and Medford had behaved in an odd way toward each other, hardly a word passing between them, as though there were an active dislike before they even knew each other. She'd seen Medford go into the girl's room shortly after her arrival, and she had inferred that it was at night when she passed the information on. But it was only an inference; she never really told lies. Well, not when they could be avoided. Sometimes, of course, a lie was absolutely necessary. But if this Judith really was Medford's girl, perhaps something could be done.

Judith, in her room on the third floor, was preparing to go to bed. She listened at the door as she usually did before turning out the light, to be sure that no one was sleeping in the outer room, as had once happened. There was no sound, and she backed away. It had been only that one night, and she still wondered who it could have been.

She got into bed, but her eyes were wide open in the darkness, and she knew that she was too stimulated to sleep. The effect of the extra cocktail seemed to have worn off, but she was uneasy. She should have denied Medford's announcement of their engagement at once. It was silly to play around with things of that sort. What must he think of her? She blushed, and hoped violently that he wouldn't think she was trying to pick him up.

She turned restlessly on her pillow and tried to put her mind onto something boring, so that she could go off to sleep. She was becoming drowsy when the whir of Dr. Smith's elevator brought her wide awake again. It was getting late, and yet he was coming up. Why? Perhaps he was like herself, and couldn't sleep. But it seemed odd that he should come up here to the third floor.

Judith strained her ears, but with the small sitting room between her and the hall, she could hear very little. Some time passed, and then she heard sounds in the room next to hers, Dr. Willie's room. Evidently the father had gone in to have a talk with the son, and yet there was no sound of voices. Dr. Willie was not there then, and Dr. Smith was waiting for him. Had Willie sneaked off on a date? He'd certainly catch it when he came back. Judith smiled to herself, and stretched a hand toward the cigarette box on her bedside table. She'd really have to stay awake and listen; it would be an entertaining row.

She smoked her cigarette to the end, and since there still was no sound of Willie returning, she decided that she'd better go to sleep and forget the whole thing. She settled back, and then found that she was holding her head at a peculiar angle in order to keep both ears free of the pillow. Dr. Smith seemed to be moving around in there, and her mind followed him persistently. It was no use. She couldn't sleep. She'd better get up and take a couple of aspirins. She found the bottle in the dark, and then realized that she had no water. She'd have to go to the bathroom and get some, might as well make up her mind to it.

She listened at the door of her sitting room to make sure that her onetime guest was not sleeping there again, but there was no sound, and she slipped out quietly. She switched on the light in the sitting room with nervous fingers, and when the room proved to be empty, she shook her head at herself. What was it that made her so stupidly timid and afraid in this place? Probably it was Charlie's fault for wandering in that first night.

The hall was in darkness, and she could see a line of light showing under Willie's door. She passed it quickly, her eyes turning backward to it, so that she did not notice the light under the bathroom door. She turned the knob and walked in, and was considerably confused to find

Dr. Medford standing at the basin, washing his hands. He swung around, with water dripping onto the floor, and Judith tried to back out, but in her haste and embarrassment she stumbled against the door and it slammed shut.

Dr. Medford said, "You will forgive me for mentioning it, but the bathroom is supposed to accommodate only one person at a time."

Judith, fumbling frantically for the knob, muttered, "That's unreasonable," and pulled the door open with a jerk. She walked out into the hall and found that Medford was right behind her.

"It's all yours," he said politely. "I'll dry my hands by blowing on them. But remember, after we're married, you will discard red as a color entirely. I don't care for it on you."

Judith glanced down at her red robe, and murmured, "I'm sorry. I'll throw it away immediately."

She closed the door on him and locked it, and then stayed in the bathroom long enough for him to get back to his room before getting her glass of water. But when she opened the door again, he was standing directly outside.

She jumped and spilled some of the water, and he glanced down at the wet spot on the carpet before saying deliberately, "I was waiting to ask you if you'd mind dyeing your hair, as well. I'm not too fond of the brunette shades, but I figure you can blond it up a bit."

Judith looked at the glass of water, and raised it a little. "Are you, perhaps, asking for it?"

He had opened his mouth to reply, when a hoarse scream sounded from behind the closed, blank door of Willie's room.

Chapter 14

Willie looked down at his hand in a dazed fashion, and swallowed convulsively. He shouldn't have yelled like that. Someone might have heard him. He ought to stop drinking; he wished that he could stop. It was his own finger there, firmly attached to his own hand. It wasn't that other one, dismembered, dead. He had thought for a minute that it had followed him upstairs, all by itself. If only he could stop drinking— He'd have to; he must. No more of the stuff. He was through from now on. He needed his wits about him.

Someone opened the door behind him, and he whirled around as Dr. Medford stepped in and exclaimed, "My God, Willie! What's the matter?"

"Oh, damn! I suppose I woke you," Willie muttered. "I'm sorry. I— I had a nightmare."

Dr. Medford glanced at the neatly made bed, and then looked at Willie, who was still fully dressed. He said flatly, "Nightmare?"

Willie knew what he was thinking, and his face flushed with anger. Just because a man drank sometimes, people were always ready to accuse him of being drunk. "I was too tired to undress," he explained coldly, "and I dropped down on the bed and went straight off to sleep. I woke up yelling with this nightmare."

Judith appeared at the door, and Willie felt a cold sweat break out on his forehead. He'd awakened her too.

"You'd better undress and go to bed properly," Dr. Medford suggested. "You'll be all right then."

"Of course I'll be all right," Willie exploded. "Haven't you ever had a nightmare, for Chrissake?" He glanced at Judith, still standing in the doorway, and in a lower voice, "Oh—er—sorry."

Judith smiled. "I'm glad it was a nightmare. I'll go back to bed. Good night."

Dr. Medford followed her out, but she went to her own rooms and closed the door firmly, without looking back. She took two aspirins and went to bed, but her mind continued to work busily. Dr. Willie had been alone in his bedroom, so where was Dr. Smith? Unless it had been someone else using his elevator. That was it: Willie himself had used it, and gone into his own room, and had a nightmare. Only, she couldn't make herself believe it, because she felt pretty sure that Willie wouldn't dare to use his father's elevator. Shirley would use it, of course, probably was using it already. But not Willie. And yet Dr. Smith was not up here. You couldn't hide a whole wheelchair. Unless he was in someone else's room. Who had rooms up here? Shirley. Who else?

Judith was asleep before the elevator descended again, with Miss Ewell standing precisely in the center of its small floor. She couldn't use the stairs, because she didn't want that one at the switchboard to watch her comings and goings. Besides, she had every right to use the elevator. She didn't use it in the daytime, because she never knew when he might need it, but it was different at night. That Shirley, now. She wasn't in yet, and the movie must have been over long ago. Miss Ewell shuddered to think what the girl might be doing in the village at this hour. She'd have to give her a stern lecture, as soon as she could catch up with her.

The elevator shuddered to a stop, and Miss Ewell stepped out and went along to her room. She'd rest for a while, but not for too long. Something must be done about Charlie. She had to find him. Anyhow, she had found out something: those two in the bathroom together, no matter whether she was the girl he was engaged to or not. And all that pretense downstairs in front of everybody, simply put on. Bob so angry, too, when she said she'd seen him go into the girl's room. What was that thing, Shakespeare, maybe, about protesting too much? Bob had protested too much. Well, he'd have to learn. They'd all have to learn that this was a place for respectable people, a hospital that was absolutely above reproach. If she could only get all this cleared up! And Willie would have to stop drinking; he couldn't take over while he was drinking like a fish. It was disgraceful. He'd have to stop it. The way he'd yelled out, up there. She'd almost come running out of Shirley's room and revealed herself. Fine thing that would have been.

She stood up abruptly and made for the door. It was all very well to sit around and think, but she had to find Charlie. She'd try the morgue first, that small room in the basement where they put the bodies and did autopsies. She hated to go there, but she couldn't afford to overlook anything. It would be locked up, but she had her keys.

She went toward the back, and through the kitchen to the basement stairs. The kitchen was dimly lighted. She kept a light going there all night in case the nurses needed anything, but the basement was a black hole at her feet, and she switched on her flashlight as she went carefully down the old wooden stairs. She did not want to put the lights on down here. It might attract attention. She made her way slowly across the old cellar, her little hands cold and clammy on the shaft of the flashlight. When she came at last to the door that led to the basement of the new wing, she hesitated, turning the key nervously in her chilly fingers. This door led directly into the morgue, and there was another door on the other side opening into the new basement. Someone might be in there right now, Dr. Usall, perhaps, but it was unlikely. He did most of his work there in the daytime.

She fitted her key into the lock and opened the door on darkness. That was all right, then. No one here. But it was a frightening place to have to go into alone. She knew, too, that there was a body in the freezer. She should be accustomed to such things by now, but it would have been easier if the freezer were empty. Anyway, she'd leave it to the last.

She walked around the room, playing her flashlight over the walls and floor, but it was clean and orderly and empty. In the end, she approached the freezer and was annoyed to see the light from her flash begin to waver. This was absurd, she told herself angrily. She'd been a nurse, and a good one, all these years, and here she was behaving like a green student.

She forced herself to look through the freezer, but there was just the one. No sign of Charlie. Her fear gave way to sudden fury. Where was he? Who was doing this to poor Charlie's helpless body? It was desecration, and she'd see that somebody was punished for it.

She left the morgue, and shut and locked the door behind her. She was less nervous now, and she swung the flash around, frowning at the dust and disorder that the light picked up. The place should have been cleaned out long ago, but they were so short of help. It had never been like this in the old days. Barrels of rubbish, the old washtubs stained and dirty, instead of gleaming white, bits of wood and plaster left lying around after the new wing had been built, pushing its new bricks into the side of the old house, scarring its ancient dignity with new doors.

Miss Ewell sighed and moved across the cement floor to inspect the old morgue, which had long since been abandoned. The wall that had separated it from the main part of the cellar had fallen down, and she looked at the rubble with a disapproving frown. She *must* get this cleared away. The wall could be repaired, and it would make a nice storeroom. The old freezer was tipped to one side, where it had moved when the wall fell, and the whole mess had simply been abandoned where it lay. She'd tried to get the workmen to do something about it, but they'd mentioned Saturday, and time and a half, and a lot of jargon that she didn't understand, because there'd been nothing of the sort in her day. What did emerge clearly was the fact that it would cost a preposterous amount of money to have the workmen stay and clear up the mess they'd made. So she'd sent them off, and the mess had been here ever since.

Miss Ewell's thoughts fled suddenly before the sound of cautious steps descending the stairs. She switched off the flashlight and backed against the wall, her breath light and shallow in her throat. The footsteps reached the bottom and stopped, and then a flashlight shone out, and moved slowly over the floor. The intruder seemed to be searching for something, and Miss Ewell, huddled against the wall, twice opened her mouth to speak out and ask him what he wanted, but fear closed it again in silence each time. She did not understand the terror that held her still, even when the flashlight fell to the floor and rolled close to where she was standing. She felt as though she were outlined in light, and she stopped breathing and pressed against the wall, but the next moment the flashlight had been retrieved, and was moving away again. It was moving faster now, and she realized that the intruder was retreating. He was less cautious, his steps more noisy, and she knew that he was hurrying. She relaxed away from the wall and drew a shaking breath. He was frightened, something had frightened him. But what?

She moved toward the stairs, and suddenly there was a noise: a confused, whirring noise, that seemed all around her. She felt her knees buckling, and the flash dropped from her hand. She stooped and fumbled for it, and then struggled frantically with sweating fingers to switch it on. It went out again immediately, but she had seen her path to the stairs, and she dragged her trembling legs over it and began to climb. Her heart was thudding painfully, and the whirring noise seemed to fill the whole cellar, and to be buzzing inside her head, as well. Even in her fear and confusion she wondered wildly whether her heart would stop. She knew she had a bad heart, even though they had told her it was all right.

She reached the top of the stairs and closed the door with a little crash. She stood for a moment, struggling with her breath, and then went and sat down in one of the kitchen chairs. She was still trembling and breathing hard, but she could not help noticing that Nora had gone to bed leaving the stove in a soiled and spotted condition. She must speak to her, first thing in the morning.

She could still hear the noise in the cellar, but only faintly from here. It dawned on her that there was something familiar about it, something—

Miss Ewell drew a quick, sharp breath. She knew now. She knew where Charlie was, but she was more frightened than ever.

Chapter 15

Shirley crept into the front hall at two o'clock in the morning. The girl at the switchboard was sound asleep, and Shirley made a face at her as she passed. She did not go upstairs, but wavered down the hall to the kitchen where she began to open doors and closets in search of coffee. She had to have coffee, strong and black. How could anyone be expected to hold their liquor when they were on a goddamn diet? Not that she could hold it, anyway. She knew that. And certainly she didn't want to eat anything right now, just the coffee. She wouldn't be able to get up in the morning. But, what the hell, a person had to be sick once in a while. And she was sick now, or she would be in the morning, good and sick. Just now she wanted to sing. She giggled as she thought of a song that a sailor had taught her once. Mustn't sing that here, though. Vera would blush out to the ends of her skinny ears, and that other little snake might take away the offer of riches. God, it would be swell to get hold of some money. What was the old devil up to, getting her to dress up like that hag, Vera? She wouldn't have minded copying some dames, but of all the lousy-looking characters that Vera was it. It hurt her pride to have to walk around looking like that, especially with some decent-looking men around the place. Well, it wouldn't be forever, just for a while. And it would be worth everything if she got some money out of it.

She shook back her hair, which was hanging loose again, and wriggled her shoulders with pleasure. Having to wear that bun on the back of her dome was almost the worst part of it. It must have taken poor old Vera months to think up such a stinking way of fixing her hair.

Where was the goddamn coffee, anyway? Some of the closets were locked, and presumably the coffee was in one of them. Oh well, to hell with it! The stingy hags could keep their lousy coffee. She'd go to bed. Better hurry too. She could hear someone down in the cellar, and he was coming up sorta quietly. Better get out. She didn't want to meet anyone.

She hurried through to the front hall and kept her eyes away from the girl at the switchboard, although she knew that she was stirring and yawning. She went up the stairs, wondering uneasily whether the girl had seen her or not. Twice she lurched against the banister and had to steady herself before she went on up. She had an uncomfortable feeling that she was being followed. As she started up the second flight, she was sure of it, but she was afraid to turn around. She was running by the time she reached her room, and she slammed her door and stood leaning against it, panting. She felt safe enough in her own room, but she had to go to the can. Might as well make up her mind to it. Well, she'd wait until she calmed down. Only she felt so sick. Sick as a dog.

She undressed and got into her pajamas, and then approached her door slowly. What was she worried about, anyway? There was no one outside; it was just her imagination. After all, she was a bit tight, might as well admit it. She opened the door and went out, boldly and casually. She made the bathroom without mishap, and felt safe behind its locked door. But now she had to get back. Well, she had the light from her room to guide her, and she was acting like a nut, anyway.

She went out into the hall, had an odd sense of swaying and confusion, and found herself lying on the floor. She had a vague feeling that she'd been sleeping there, and she wanted to go back to sleep. But she mustn't. It wouldn't do to be found sleeping on the floor in the hall; it wouldn't look right. But she was dizzy and all mixed up, and she couldn't seem to get on her feet. In the end, she crawled, slowly and painfully, and had to crawl up over the edge of her bed like a snake. As her head fell onto the pillow, she saw that she had left the door open. She shouldn't have done that; she must get up and close it. But her head was so queer, and she was sick, and it seemed to be daylight outside— Funny, daylight. Her head was aching frightfully. She had never had such a headache. She was drowsy, and she wanted to sleep, but there was such a noise. That nurse, what was she doing?

Judith was standing just outside the door, staring with horrified eyes at a pool of blood. Shirley's door was open, and the blood was just outside, and Shirley was stretched out on her bed, flat and still. Judith went into the room and saw at once that Shirley had a wound on her head. She examined it briefly and then hurried back to the hall, where she ran into Dr. Willie, still wrapped in a dressing robe. Judith spoke to him briefly and he followed her to Shirley's room, his hand nervously busy with his untidy hair.

He leaned over Shirley, and then asked confusedly, "What happened to her?"

Judith shrugged. "I'd better go and get some bandages."

"This needs stitches." Dr. Willie straightened up. "You stay here and keep her quiet. I'll get the stuff."

He was back shortly, and worked silently over Shirley while Judith helped as she could. Dr. Medford came in once, but Willie gave him a faintly challenging look and he departed again without comment. Vera appeared briefly, and huffed out of the room when Shirley caught sight of her and muttered, "Scram." She called over her shoulder, "Breakfast is ready, Willie. Please be as quick as you can."

They left Shirley at last, apparently in drowsy comfort, and went down to the dining room, with Willie still attired in his dressing robe.

Dr. Smith ran a cold eye over him and then asked for a complete description of the wound.

It took some time. Dr. Willie loved to expound at length in medical terms, and was of the "Let's see, was it Wednesday or Thursday?" school of raconteur. Judith, listening in secret amusement, decided that he knew his medicine, by exposition, at least.

Dr. Smith eventually lost all patience and said testily, "All right, all right. But what happened to the girl?"

"She was hit."

"She was hit," Dr. Smith snarled. "That, of course, explains everything. Now we know exactly what happened to her. Would you care to tell us who hit her, and what weapon he used? Or did she bump into something?"

Willie lowered his eyes to his coffee cup and said sulkily, "I don't know."

Vera had finished her breakfast, but she was still sitting at her place with a worried little frown between her unshaped brows. She said, "Please, Father. The girl was drunk and fell down. I was talking to Betty before she left, the night girl at the switchboard, you know, and Betty said she was drunk. Said she must have come in the back way, because she came from the back, and went upstairs. It seems she was swaying all over the stairs, and bumping into the banister, and her hair was hanging all over the place. You know, Father, we don't want that sort of woman around here."

"You go to church every Sunday, Vera," Dr. Smith said dryly. "Don't they teach you to be charitable? The girl is trying desperately to turn herself into a refined woman like yourself, and you won't allow her even one lapse from grace."

Vera gave him a rather helpless look and fell silent, and Willie said doggedly, "Well, I'll tell you what I think. She'd have to have fallen hard to get the wound she has, and I believe someone hit her."

"So." Dr. Smith swung around on him. "She could not have acquired this wound by falling on anything?"

Willie stared into space for a moment, and then stuck to his guns. "I don't think so. In any case, there was nothing for her to fall on."

Dr. Medford backed him up. "Willie's right. I saw the wound, and it wasn't produced by any fall, not up there in the hall, anyway. Someone hit her. There was blood on the floor where she must have been lying for a while before she made her way back to bed. If she fell on something sharp enough to do that damage, then someone removed the object, and that's absurd. So someone hit her."

Dr. Smith said, "I see," and his voice was quite mild. Willie muttered, "That's the way I see it too."

"Well"—Dr. Smith flexed his gnarled hands—"if you stick to agreeing with men of sense, Willie, you won't go too far astray. Can you tell me, in a few simple words, whether the girl's wound is serious or not?"

Willie revived a little, cleared his throat, and was launched once more. Patience eventually evolved the fact that Shirley's wound just missed being really serious.

Dr. Smith muttered, "All right, Willie, shut it off, for God's sake. So we don't need to do anything about it?"

"Aren't you going to get the police in?" Dr. Medford asked.

Dr. Smith frowned. "Don't be silly, Bob. That wouldn't do the hospital much good, would it? We must find Charlie. I think he's responsible for what's going on. Tell the girl she fell and cracked her head against the wall. If she was drunk, she wouldn't know the difference, anyway."

Vera pursed her lips. "Angie's going to be good and mad about this, if we ever see her again, that is. Did you know that she is missing?"

Chapter 16

Dr. Smith glared at Vera from under his heavy eyebrows, and growled, "What are you trying to be dramatic about? Just because Angie doesn't show up for breakfast, you must have it that she's missing. You know how she is. Chances are, she's dieting again. Probably discovered half a pound of flesh on herself somewhere."

Vera stood up, looking offended. "All right, Father. But Nora woke me early this morning to tell me about that West woman, because she couldn't find Angie." She turned and left the room.

Judith finished her coffee with a chill little shiver creeping along her spine. What sort of place was this, where people disappeared, and no one seemed to care? That old man, Charlie, had been gone for over a week, and all they said about him was that they'd better find him. Sometime, when they got around to it.

She was half inclined to speak to Willie about it during the morning, but in the end she said nothing. Once you got him started, he talked on forever. And besides, he had screamed, there in his room last night, apparently for nothing. She didn't believe that nightmare story. There was a certain sound peculiar to the cry of a nightmare, and somehow Willie's voice had sounded alert and terrified.

She kept an eye out for Miss Ewell and even followed a couple of white skirts that turned out to be other nurses, who were darkly suspicious of her motive. She cornered Dr. Medford at last, and asked him directly, "Has Miss Ewell turned up yet?"

"What do you mean?"

"She's missing. And that old man, Charlie, has been missing for over a week, and nobody seems to want to do anything about it. What's the matter with this place, anyway? It's a madhouse. Shirley is hit on the head, but we must on no account have the police in. You and I are crazy too, with a publicly announced engagement—"

He said in a quiet voice which throbbed with restraint, "Shut up, will you? You ought to know by now that all hospitals are nuthouses, no matter how well they're run. So Charlie and Miss Ewell have disappeared, and it's none of our damn business. The Smith family probably know all about it; they know them better than we do. As for little Shirley, when people are drunk some very odd and inexplicable things happen to them, as you should know. When she comes out of it you'll find

that she won't want the police herself. And touching on our engagement, it suits me very well at the moment to be engaged to someone.
And it suits you too, whether you realize it or not. If you were out in
the open, Les would be bothering you, and Les is not the right man for
you."

"It's kind of you to take such an interest in my affairs," Judith said,
when fury at last allowed her to speak. "Les is—"

"I'm busy," Dr. Medford interrupted rudely. "I'm not trying to decide on the right man for you, I'm merely telling you that Les won't do.
I'll have to go now. Sorry."

He made off, and Judith stared after him, with her upper and lower
teeth doing each other no good. She made an instant resolve to encour-
age Les as much as possible. Her date with him was for this afternoon,
and she started planning her most attractive costume.

As it turned out, she did not go at all. An emergency came in, and as
Miss Ewell was still missing, she was obliged to stay at the hospital
and help. Les came in for lunch, but when he discovered that she would
be unable to leave, he went off again immediately.

Dr. Smith, obliged at last to admit that he was uneasy about Miss
Ewell, called Lucius, the orderly, and started a search. He decided to
begin with the old house, and it took them the rest of the afternoon,
since nurses kept seeking them out and demanding the services of the
orderly. After several such interruptions, Mary Gore turned up, and Dr.
Smith shouted at her in complete exasperation. "For God's sake, what's
the matter with you women? Can't you give a man a urinal without
getting the vapors?"

"Oh yes," Mary said composedly, "but this case is different. Miss
Ewell never liked us to—er—Well, anyway, she said it wasn't quite
nice. You see, he can't use his arms, and of course we'd have to—"

"So what's he objecting to?" Dr. Smith snarled. "Doesn't he know
he's in a hospital?"

"Yes, sir. He's not objecting. In fact, I had to close up my ears,
because I don't think it's anything to joke about. But you ought to
know that he's in a hurry."

Lucius went off, grinning, and Dr. Smith began to swear softly. Mary
moved closer to him, and said in a low voice, "Oh, if you would only
do as I say, you could get up and throw away your crutches."

"Crutches!" Dr. Smith whispered savagely. "Do you think I'd trundle
around in this blasted, infernal gocart if I could get about on crutches?"

"I meant your wheelchair, sir. You could throw it away, see?"

"No, I don't see." He gave her an evil look, and his gnarled hands
clutched at the arms of the chair. "But if you don't make yourself scarce,

I'll get up and hurl the thing at your head, if it's the last act of my life."

Mary departed in a hurry,and was back on her own floor before it occurred to her that she should have held her ground. She should have stayed and preached the word to him, no matter what he threatened. But people were so combative, and one was only human, oneself.

Dr. Smith, left to himself, muttered angrily for some time. What was the matter with Angie, letting a woman like that stay on at the hospital? What harm might she not do, with her crazy notions?

Lucius returned, and Dr. Smith became absorbed once more in their search. Vera wandered up and offered to help, but he merely said irritably, "For God's sake, get out of our way, will you?" and she went off with her lips folded and her back bristling with offended dignity. He looked after her for a moment, and then returned to Lucius with a shrug. She was his daughter, of course, but what could he do about that? You weren't able to pick your children.

Anyway, Angie must be found. She was up to something, as usual, and this time he didn't know what it was. Well, he'd find out. It was odd for her to disappear just now, when she apparently had her campaign well under way.

He had been avoiding her room, but he suddenly got impatient and decided to go there without further delay. She wouldn't be there, but she might have left something that would tell the story. He swung his chair around, and called to Lucius, who was opening closet doors in a diet kitchen.

The orderly reappeared, brushing vigorously at his white coat. "She ain't in there, boss, unless somebody washed her down the drain. She sure is skinny enough. Make six of my old woman. Or maybe it's the other way around."

"This is not a joking matter," Dr. Smith said coldly.

"You think she hadda accident, or what?"

"What," Dr. Smith snapped.

"Well—" Lucius considered it, unperturbed. "Maybe you think she's hidin' out for some reason?"

"Never mind what I think. Leave my head alone and stick to your own thick skull." But it was so close to what he *was* thinking that he was uneasy and annoyed.

He was sorry now that he had sent Vera away. She would have a better idea than anyone else about Angie's clothes, and whether anything was missing or not. He considered sending for her, and then abruptly decided against it. See what he could do himself first.

When they arrived at Angie's closed door, he told Lucius to knock. No sense in getting her riled, if she did happen to be in there. However, there was no response, and after Lucius had opened the door, he rolled his chair over the sill and looked about him. Everything in order, of course. Neat and tidy, prim. He felt a little foolish as he ordered Lucius to look under the bed and in the closet, but he might as well be thorough. Lucius, withdrawing his shoulders from under the bed, grinned up at him. "Nothin' there, Doc. Not even dust nor them things my wife keeps for emergency. When you got seven kids——"

"I never had seven kids, thank God. Go and find Miss Vera, and tell her I want her here at once."

Lucius departed, whistling, and Dr. Smith eased his chair over to the bedside table. A book lay exactly in its center, and an envelope, thrust between the pages, had caught his eye. It was unlike Angie to have an envelope out of place, even as a bookmark. He pulled it out, and saw that it was sealed and addressed to "Dr. William Smith, Sr." He held it for a few moments, tapping it against his thumbnail. A note for him, explanation. He might have known that Angie would never take off without carefully and precisely explaining why. Only the catch in that was that she would never take off, period. Well, might as well read the thing, since it was directed to him.

In neat handwriting it informed him, "I am going off to die where I shall be given a decent funeral."

Chapter 17

Dr. Smith frowned down at the letter and shook his head a little. For once he didn't know what she meant. She was indicating something, and thought he'd understand, but he didn't. Perhaps he'd missed something. His hands were so bad that it was difficult to hold even a lousy piece of paper. Yes, here it was on the other side, a P.S. It said, "Like father, like son."

He crumpled the note savagely and stuffed it into his pocket. He still didn't know what she meant. She was a fool. She'd always been a fool. Like father, like son. The damn woman was ripe for an asylum, with her nonsense. He pushed painfully at the wheels of his chair, and propelled himself out of the room.

It was dark in the hall outside, and he nearly ran into Vera. She let out a little scream, and cried, "Father! You really should be more careful. You very nearly knocked me over."

"Ahh, why don't you wear headlights?" he muttered. "You're so thin I thought you were one of the stripes on the wallpaper."

She said patiently, "What did you want me for?"

"Nothing."

"But, Father, you sent for me. You know how busy I am, especially with Angie gone. And then you do a thing like this to me."

"For God's sake, stop your jabber," he said irritably. "I wanted you to see if any of Angie's clothes were missing, but I found a note from her in the meantime. She's gone off."

"Gone off? But why? Where?"

"How do I know? She didn't tell me. Simply said she was going elsewhere. She may be back, and she may not. Just forget it."

"Forget it!" Vera repeated tragically. "How can I forget, with all that extra work piled on my shoulders? The housekeeping, and the work she does in the hospital—"

"The hospital work has nothing to do with you," Dr. Smith said sternly. "I absolutely forbid you to stick your nose into it in any way whatsoever, do you understand? We have a head nurse who seems very competent, and what you can do now is to find her and tell her that I want to see her immediately."

"Father, please! I'm not an errand girl."

"Shut your silly mouth, and do as I say."

Vera went off, because she was afraid to argue any further, but she was furious. Father had no right to treat her this way; he really was becoming impossible. If she were in her own room, she'd break down and cry. Everything seemed to be going wrong, anyway. Dr. Medford engaged to that woman, and Les running after her too. Vera had hoped that the engagement would release Les to herself, but it hadn't worked that way. And why did she want him, anyhow? Someone else's leavings.

She ran across Dr. Willie and stopped to do a little complaining. He soothed and cheered her, as he usually did. He said he'd take her away on a trip, soon. She'd been working too hard and she needed a change.

She went on, feeling vastly comforted. Willie was the one human being in the world who really cared for her, and she loved him too. After all, they were twins, and had a special affinity for one another. She felt a warm glow seeping through her, and raised her chin. Her brother would take care of her. He would see that she was all right. He loved her better than anyone else.

When she at last found Judith, her manner was quite pleasant. "It's too bad to disturb you, but Father wants to see you right away. Miss Ewell seems to have left us, although I can't imagine why or where she could have gone. But if you could just go and talk to him—"

Judith sought Dr. Smith at once, although she was busy. Miss Ewell had done a great deal more than anyone had realized, and she wished that the old man had saved his interview until later.

She had an immediate impression that Dr. Smith looked well. She had no way of knowing it, but he felt well too. Somehow, things seemed to be better. He'd keep abreast of things and keep a finger in the pie. He could direct this nurse. She seemed honest and out in the open. Angie's underhand methods of doing what she wanted, regardless of all opposition, were over. She'd come back, of course, that was to be expected, but he wouldn't give her her head again. She was out of it, and he intended to see that she stayed out.

He said, "Miss Onslow, Miss Ewell has left, and you are superintendent of nurses. You are to take no orders from anyone but me, and if you are in doubt about anything, you are to come to me at once. I am satisfied of your capability and feel sure that you can run things competently. If there is any necessity for an outlay of money, you must come to me. That list, for instance. You may go ahead on all of them. I want things to be of the best at Smith Hospital."

Judith was surprised, but she composed her face and thanked him quietly. She talked to him for a few minutes, but cut it as short as possible, and returned to her work.

She was called down again, during the afternoon, and realized that he was going to be a nuisance to her. This time he wanted her to dismiss Mary Gore.

Judith talked him out of it. She explained about the switchboard, and the twelve hours' duty that Shirley could not possibly do without Mary's help. He agreed, reluctantly, to keep her on, but instructed Judith to keep an eye out for someone to take her place.

Judith returned to the hospital wing, rubbing a fist across her tired forehead. They'd have to find someone else, anyway. Mary and two others, who were fortunately able to handle it, had been on the switchboard all day, but that left them shorthanded on the floor. She would not have minded releasing Mary so much, but Mary had protested that she could not sit at a switchboard all day. It was not her job, and she really could not do it.

It was a relief when the night operator, Betty Robinson, showed up. Judith had been wondering, fretfully, what they would do if Betty, too, failed them.

She felt that she needed a cocktail tonight. Only she wouldn't drink more than one. Well, maybe two, but no more. Perhaps it was bad to get into the habit of a cocktail or two every night, but somehow you needed it in this place. Dr. Medford had said that all hospitals were crazy. Well, it might be that he had been too long at Smith.

She heard Dr. Smith's elevator descending and waited to help him out, but when the door opened, it was Shirley who emerged.

Judith gasped. "For heaven's sake, what are you doing down here?"

"I need a drink," Shirley said defiantly, "and I knew it wouldn't come up on any tray. I need company too. You ever get the howling horrors all by yourself?"

Judith followed her into the Smith quarters, wondering a little. Shirley did not look like Vera this evening. She was garbed in a vivid red dressing gown, and beneath the dead white of the bandage her hair flowed to her shoulders.

She made a distinct impression as she entered the living room. Vera's reaction was relief, because Shirley no longer looked like anyone but herself. Les, blinking at the bright red of the gown, thought, "Maybe there's something to this babe, at that." Dr. Willie decided that she was cheap, and turned his eyes away. Dr. Medford was looking at Judith, and Dr. Smith rubbed his crippled hands together and smiled.

Shirley went and got herself a drink, and then Judith made her sit down in a low chair. She was not happy about the arrangement, because she liked to stay on her feet and circulate while she was drinking, but Judith was firm. Shirley was a little sulky, but she leaned her head against the back of her chair and admitted to herself that she was feeling better. She saw Dr. Smith easing his chair in her direction, and she slid her eyes around to him suspiciously.

He was still smiling when he drew up beside her. He said quietly, "Did you know that Miss Ewell has departed and left you holding the bag?"

Shirley lowered her eyes to her drink, and took time to compose her voice before she replied, "Nuts. I don't believe it."

"You had better. I have a note from her. She left in a bit of a hurry. I suppose she figured that she'd gone too far and had better get out before she found herself behind bars. I suggest that you follow her as quickly as you can pack."

Shirley continued to gaze into the depths of her cocktail. So the old goat was telling her to beat it. Seemed there was no doubt about that nasty little creep, Ewell, having taken a powder. Nora had brought her the news with her luncheon tray, as a matter of fact. And this old stinker was pleased about it, figured he could get rid of little Shirley now. Well, she wasn't going. There was money to be picked up here in some way. She should have made Ewell tell her more. But she wasn't going to run, because there was certainly something. She shivered a little, and took a quick gulp of her drink. Somebody had landed one on her head, all right. You couldn't fool her on that. She'd been drunk, but not too drunk to know that someone had conked her. She mustn't get stewed again. It was fattening, and, anyway, she ought to keep her wits about her.

She gave Dr. Smith a sunny smile. "I like it here. I think it's real nice. I'm staying."

He shrugged. "We can fight that out later. In the meantime, there is one change that will have to be made. In the future you will take your meals with the nurses."

Shirley's eyes blazed, and she gave him the full malevolence of their glare. "I'll do nothing of the goddamn sort," she said fiercely. "I'm gonna stay right here with you, where I belong."

His face lost color, and he wheeled away from her abruptly. Perhaps the girl knew. It sounded a bit as though she did. But surely Angie would never have told her! She would lose her own power if she told anyone. He thought of her note again, and suddenly his hands went slack on the wheels of his chair. Like father, like son.

He remembered clearly about the father. He used to cut up the dead bodies to see what was inside. Only once he had made a mistake, if it was a mistake, and he had cut up one that was still breathing.

Chapter 18

Dr. Smith looked slowly around the room. No one was paying any attention to him, and it was just as well. Angie should not have gone off and left him. After all, he wasn't dead, not yet. He might even have a chance. This new treatment—he'd be getting it soon. He supposed, though, that he looked almost dead to most of them here. Perhaps he ought to go away. Only he'd have to come back again. No, he wouldn't. Why should he? He'd go away for good, and Medford could take over. That new nurse was good; they could run the place between them. He'd have to take Vera with him when he went, of course. She'd be pleased, all the new people she'd meet. Oh, what was he thinking about? This was his own place. Why should he run away? And what would there be for him to do in some lousy resort? Stare at the sea, and pass the time of day with the creaking old relics that infested such places? No, at least he had something to interest him here. It was his own place, and he'd built it up himself. Well, it was all his own fault, but he'd do something; he'd fix things some way. He smiled. Of course he could. What was he being chicken-hearted about? He'd go and phone right now. He wheeled quietly off to his own room, and no one saw him go.

Willie was getting drunk again. He kept telling himself to stop, and at last he did. His head was whirling a little, and his step was unsure, but he told himself, several times, that he had stopped in time. He had this drinking licked; he could take it or leave it alone. Shirley, who had been drinking with him, had stopped earlier. She hadn't had much. She didn't want to be drunk tonight. In fact, she mustn't get drunk again while she was in this place. She'd have a good binge after she left, and she hoped it would be soon. It was so stinking dull. Willie was the best bet for picking up some fun, but he was such a drip. That Les was quite a guy, but he was all tied up with Judith, and Shirley knew why. He wasn't getting anywhere with her, and he was so conceited that he just couldn't stand it. Well, she'd like to pick him up herself, and she would, too, if it was the last thing she did.

Vera was boring the ears off that stuffed shirt, Medford, and he deserved to have his ears bored off. Shirley laughed loudly at the thought, and Willie laughed with her.

Shirley composed her face and asked, "What are *you* laughing at, mac?"

"Same thing as you," Willie said vaguely.

Nobody noticed that Dr. Smith was missing until they got into the dining room, and then Vera went off to look for him. She met him emerging from his room, with an odd smile on his face.

Dinner was dull, because Les did not stay. He had wanted Judith to come out with him, but she was too tired; she was going to bed. She was sorry. Next time she hoped to keep her date with him. This time, as he knew, it had not been her fault.

"Will you be able to make another date with me?" Les had asked.

"Of course."

"That's some engagement you're tangled up in. If you were engaged to me, I wouldn't let you make dates with other fellows."

"I'm not engaged. It's just a joke."

"I've heard that before, baby. I know you're still trying to keep it secret."

Shirley was silently cursing her luck because of the bandage on her head. Had it not been for that, she could surely have gone off with Les. Of course, her lousy head was aching like the very devil. But she didn't feel like going back to bed. She'd horse around with Willie for a while.

But Willie disappeared, and Judith came up and ordered her back to bed at once. "You'd better get all the rest you can, because I'll need you for a few hours tomorrow."

"But I can't work with a head like this on me," Shirley protested.

"Yes, you can. You came down to dinner, didn't you? I don't expect you to put in full time, but you can ease the situation a bit."

Shirley was led off, still protesting feebly, and Judith helped her

into bed. She gave her a mild sedative, urged her to try and relax, and
then went off to her own rooms.

Dr. Medford was comfortably established in an easy chair in her
sitting room. He glanced up as she paused in the doorway and said
absently, "Sit down and rest your feet."

"Certainly not. I'm tired, and I'm going to bed."

"So am I tired, and I'd like nothing better than to go to bed. But
there are things to be done."

"Why don't you go and do them then, and let me get my sleep?"

"Stop wasting time with your silly huff," he said irritably. "Sit down."

Judith sat down and lit a cigarette, but she almost dropped it when
he asked casually, "Do you know of anyone around here who has lost a
finger?"

She squeezed the cigarette between her thumb and forefinger. "Are
you trying to scare me?"

"Don't be silly. You're a nurse. You shouldn't scare so easily. I found
a finger down in the morgue, lying on the floor. It shouldn't have been
there, and I don't know where it came from."

Judith was silent for a moment, and then she said, half to herself,
"How I wish I had never come here."

Dr. Medford shifted in his chair and idly turned a cigarette lighter in
his fingers. "It's nice country around here, nothing wrong with it. Any
place can have its troubles; most places do. But there is something not
right here. I think they ought to have the police in to look for Charlie,
and they won't hear of it. Now Miss Ewell has disappeared, but Dr.
Smith says he had a note from her, and that she's just gone off for a
time. It sounds a bit odd to me, because I don't think she'd go off as
abruptly as all that."

Judith shook her head. "She wouldn't. And why is Shirley dressing
up to look like Vera? It isn't natural."

"Mrs. West?" He shrugged. "I hadn't noticed that she looked like
Vera."

"Well, I noticed it, and everyone else did too. She's fatter than Vera,
but she's been making a serious attempt to reduce, and I don't suppose
she ever dieted in her life before."

He raised his eyebrows. "Perhaps I'd better talk to her."

"No. I've given her something to make her sleep. Anyway, I don't
see why you want to make all this your business, and mine too."

"You're still in a huff," he said mildly, "and you're not thinking
straight. Shirley was brought in by Miss Ewell and steered into our
dining room over the protests of Vera and Dr. Smith. It *is* my business,
and yours too, because something is going on that might break wide

open at any time. Chances are, it's dirty, and you and I will be connected with it in the minds of people on the outside. It could do us a lot of harm."

"You can take that sort of thing when you have to," Judith said coldly. "I've weathered one storm, and I suppose I can take another."

He said nothing for a while, his eyes staring absently at the wall behind her. Judith wished that she could recall her words, and then decided that he hadn't heard her, anyway.

But he had. He said at last, "That's just the point. You'd be really done for this time. You'd have a reputation of bringing scandal with you wherever you go. That's why I'm here, talking to you. My honest advice to you is that you should leave immediately, before it breaks. And I'm not trying to get rid of you, either. You probably have no idea how much more satisfactory it is to work with you than it ever was with Miss Ewell. You could manufacture a sick relative, and then wait a day or two until they are able to replace you."

Judith shook her head. "I have no relatives, none that count, and nowhere to go that would not cost money. And I've very little money."

"Then tell them the country air stirs up your hay fever, and make arrangements to get another job."

Judith realized, with an odd little sense of surprise, that she did not want to go; she wanted to stay. What he said was right. She knew that. But she couldn't go, not yet. She'd take her chance, for a while at least. She found that she was twisting her hands nervously together, and she dropped them into her lap.

"I'm going to take a walk. Perhaps I can get the cobwebs out of my head."

Dr. Medford dropped his cigarette lighter into his pocket and stood up. "Good enough. I think I'll come too."

They went out into the hall, but as she started toward the stairs he put a hand on her arm. "If that West frill can use the elevator, I suppose we can too."

Judith followed him into the back hall, and they stepped into the little cage. Dr. Medford pressed the button, and they moved slowly downward and vibrated to a stop at the bottom. As they walked out, an odor floated up against their faces.

"Oh, God!" Judith moaned, her eyes going wildly around the small, blank hallway. "Someone has been sealed up in the wall!"

Chapter 19

Dr. Medford glanced around the walls of the small hallway and shook his head. Not in the walls. In fact, there was only one place it could be. He ran the elevator up a little and peered into the pit, but it was too dark to see anything. He went into the dining room and got one of Vera's candles, and he and Judith leaned over the pit together, while the light flickered between them.

The pit was shallow, and they could see at once that Charlie was there. He wore only the brief bed gown that was supplied by the hospital, and Dr. Medford frowned. Nobody had checked to see whether one of Charlie's suits had been missing, and yet they'd all assumed that he'd dressed and gone outside somewhere.

Judith drew in her breath sharply and suddenly. There was a finger missing from one of the hands.

Dr. Medford nodded. "We'll have to notify the police, and I intend to do it before I say anything to Dr. Smith. If we let him in on it first, he'll want to put poor old Charlie back to bed and pretend that he passed out in the usual way. But you couldn't fool the nurses, and, sooner or later, one of them would talk."

"I can't see why he'd object to the police," Judith said. "Accidents often happen in a hospital, and the police have to come in, but it's merely a matter of routine. You can't entirely control the patients, and every once in a while they do something to get themselves killed. Do you think the elevator killed Charlie? Only he doesn't seem to be crushed."

"No." Dr. Medford put his hand under the elevator, and she saw the bottom move up a little. "This is a safety device. If the bottom of the elevator touches anything at all, the cage stops at once."

Judith nodded, and drew a long breath. "We'd better not touch him, I suppose, until the police get here."

"I'll put the call through at once. You can go and tell Dr. Smith. It will be too late for him to interfere with me by the time he gets out here."

Judith went to the Smith quarters and knocked on the door, but there was no answer. She waited a little, and then went in. She could see into Dr. Smith's bedroom through the half-opened door. Vera was helping him to bed, and Judith moved forward and rapped sharply on the panel.

Vera swung around, and her face colored angrily. She said, "Yes?" with her eyebrows elevated.

"I knocked on the outer door," Judith explained, "but nobody answered, so I came in because it's important. We've found Charlie. He's dead, and Dr. Medford is calling the police."

Dr. Smith began a frantic effort to resume his clothes. He yelled wildly to Judith to go and stop Medford, and she backed away and went out into the front hall. She met Dr. Medford, retreating from the switchboard, and said dubiously, "He's coming. He's getting back into his clothes, but I've been sent out to stop you from calling in the police."

Dr. Medford nodded, and grinned faintly. "That's on schedule. The call has already been put through. I'm going to the back hall and see that Charlie stays where he is until the police get here."

Judith followed him with a little wrinkle between her brows. "Do you think he's going to sneak off while we're not looking?"

"He'll never sneak off again," Dr. Medford said impersonally, "but I want to make sure that no one takes him off. I believe someone brought him here. I can't seem to convince myself that he lay down in that pit to die, neatly tucked in, the way he is."

"Well"—Judith pulled at her lip—"I suppose he could have fallen there and been unable to get out again."

Dr. Smith appeared, his chair propelled by Vera for greater speed. He looked down at Charlie, and at the same time Vera snatched up the candle, which was standing at the edge of the pit. She said unsteadily, "Who brought this here?" and tried to keep her mind off the odor and the thought of Charlie, dead in this undignified way.

Dr. Smith was furious. "You know very well that I am still head of this place," he fumed. "You had no right to go yapping to the police without first consulting me."

"It's a police case," Dr. Medford said flatly. "I thought I'd save you the trouble of putting through the call."

Dr. Smith lowered his eyes and twisted his helpless hands together. He hated the damned police at any time, but just now it was worse than ever. That girl in the house, and Willie too. Where was Willie? He ought to be here. No, better not; he might be drunk.

It was all too much for him. Sick as he was, he ought to have help, and there was no one to help him. Charlie had always been a pest, and now that he was dead he was still making things difficult. He'd known there was something wrong with the elevator. It wouldn't go all the way down, and he'd intended to get someone in to fix it. Then for a while it had seemed all right, so he hadn't bothered. He'd like to fire Bob Medford, kick him right out. He'd put that officious call in for the police right away because he knew he'd be stopped if he waited. It would have been easy enough to do a little arranging and to have kept the whole thing quiet. But people like Medford had to parade their stuffy honesty for fear you might miss it. He had much better control over Willie. But of course Willie must go. That was definite. He shuddered. Willie would have to go. And there was Medford, honest Joe himself, proclaiming that the corpse was missing a finger, and that it had been cut off after death. A finger wasn't so much, but that was only the beginning. Just an easy way to start. Damn Angie, running off like that. Somehow, it wasn't her way of doing things.

He heard someone come into the front hall, and he composed his face and allowed it to fall into lines of gloom. He didn't have to put on any silly smile for them this time; his old friend, Charlie, was dead, and a decent grief would be in order. That police clown, Knotty, had a head only for the obvious; anything beyond that was apt to confuse him.

Knotty, chief of police and proud of it, was questioning Dr. Medford in the front hall and thinking, at the same time, that boy, was he ever glad he hadn't had that last drink. He said loudly, "I want to see the orderly," and refrained from hooking his thumbs into his vest because that was lowbrow. The orderly was probably the guy, anyway.

Dr. Medford asked, "Why?"

"Listen, mac, you ain't astin' the questions. I am."

Dr. Medford shrugged. "Lucius is at his home. He's always there in the evenings. His wife won't let him out at night."

"So?"

"Don't you want to see the body?" Dr. Medford asked. "We haven't touched it. It's still where we found it."

Knotty sighed, and allowed himself to be led into the back hall. He took only one quick glance into the pit, and then backed away hastily. "Get him out," he muttered, "and find out when he died, and what of."

He returned to the front lobby, and Dr. Smith followed in his chair. Betty was standing up at the switchboard, her eyes wild and frightened, and Dr. Smith said quickly, "Sit down, my dear, and relax. It's nothing. Just routine."

Betty perched nervously on the edge of her chair, and Knotty stopped suddenly, as a new idea slid into his mind. "Say, this guy Lucius is on days, ain't he? Where's your night orderly?"

"We don't have one," Dr. Smith said coldly. "If anything comes up that can't be handled by the nurses, they wake one of the doctors."

"If you want me to get Charlie to the morgue," Dr. Medford interposed, "you'll have to give me a hand. I can't get him out of there alone."

Knotty paled, and then strode to the door and peremptorily called in a young assistant, who was ordered to help Dr. Medford in the removal of the deceased. The assistant paled too, but went off with his quivering chin raised bravely.

Knotty began to question Judith, but Dr. Smith interrupted impatiently.

"I think you're on the wrong track, Chief. Poor Charlie died a natural death, but he fell into the elevator shaft, and we did not know that he was there. He was inclined to wander off. He'd done it several times."

Judith nodded. "But it's odd about that finger." She turned to Knotty and explained, "One of his fingers had been amputated after he died."

Dr. Smith compressed his lips and hoped that the fury he felt did not show on his face. Why did the officious, interfering girl have to mention that finger?

"Somebody musta had a grudge against him," Knotty suggested, without too much interest.

Dr. Smith agreed eagerly. "That's it. That must be the explanation. It had not occurred to me until you mentioned it."

Knotty smiled and carefully lit a small cigar which he had pulled from his vest pocket.

Dr. Smith sighed, and settled more comfortably into his chair. "We knew what had happened, of course, since he was apt to get out of bed and wander around. He had a stroke, some time ago. He was not paralyzed, but his mind was affected and he was not responsible. I suppose he had another stroke and tumbled into the shaft out there."

Knotty nodded wisely, and then fixed his eyes on the sheeted figure that was being wheeled through into the new wing.

"They have to go through to the other building," Dr. Smith explained. "The elevator in there goes to the basement, but this one doesn't."

Knotty squared his shoulders. "I think I'll go with them."

"Do," Dr. Smith said cordially. "And if there's any information or help that you want, please call on us."

"Sure, mac. I'm the police, ain't I?"

Knotty made off, and Dr. Smith sent a coldly malevolent look after him. It was too much. Angie ought to be here, helping him. She'd no right to run like a lousy rat. She must have known that he'd talk to her; they could have fixed it up between them. She was being dramatic, that was all. Only where had she gone? Nowhere. There was nowhere she could have gone, at least not without paying out some of her money, and she'd never do that. So where was she? But of course he knew; he should have known all along. She was hiding here in the house, somewhere.

Chapter 20

Down in the morgue Knotty was conscious of a feeling of exasperation. He eyed Dr. Medford,and said peevishly, "Why can't you tell me when he died? Don't they learn you guys anything in them fancy butcher schools? You got a pretty diploma which cost you plenty of dough, and you can't even tell me when this stiff croaked."

Dr. Medford, leaning against the wall with his hands in his pockets, smiled amiably. "They don't put things like that on the diploma–there isn't room. I told you that in my opinion he has been dead for some time, and yet, if that's true, I can't understand why we didn't find him sooner. Dammit, he *has* been dead for some time–and yet he seems well preserved, in a way—"

"The fact that you didn't find him sooner is my department," Knotty said austerely. "All I'm astin' you is how long he's been dead, and what killed him."

"I'd say he had another stroke."

Knotty looked disappointed. "If he did, why didn't onea you guys find him lyin' around?"

"That's your department," Dr. Medford said courteously.

"O.K., O.K. Only you gotta fix the time of death for me."

Judith stirred and said quietly, "You don't need me any longer. I'd like to get some sleep. I've a lot to do during the day."

Knotty frowned at her. "You'll have to wait till Doc gets here."

"What doc?"

Bob Medford grinned at her. "Go on up to bed. We'll call you if you're needed. The police doctor has to examine the corpse officially to determine whether I'm lying about my findings. I don't see why he'd need you. If he wants a nurse, we can get one of the girls from the floor."

Knotty was offended. He said, "Listen, mac, I'm givin' the orders around here, see? And I need this here nurse, see?"

Dr. Medford sent an impersonal gaze up to the ceiling, and murmured, "I see."

Judith flicked Knotty a cool glance and walked out of the room without another word. She went upstairs, and found Dr. Smith still in the front lobby, and Vera still with him. They had a few frantic questions for her, but she answered briefly and went determinedly on her way up. She met Willie coming down, attired in a robe of many colors and obviously excited.

"Vera woke me," he explained feverishly. "I understand Charlie's been found dead, poor fellow."

Judith nodded. "Your father and sister are downstairs. They'll tell you all about it."

She had one more interruption. Shirley was standing at the head of the stairs on the top floor, and she asked simply, "What's going on down there?"

Judith explained briefly, ordered her back to bed, and then went on to her own rooms. She looked under the bed before locking the door, and then derided herself for being a neurotic fool. But this place *was* queer—Charlie's finger cut off after he had died, and left on the floor of the morgue...

Judith lay down on the bed and closed her eyes. She had not expected to sleep, but she went off soundly, and when she awoke again, it was broad daylight. She looked at her clock in a mild panic, and flew out of bed at once. Apparently the policeman had decided that he could get on without her, which was just as well. She was tired, mentally tired, perhaps.

She found the bathroom empty and was hurrying back to her room when she ran into Shirley.

"You're late, pal," Shirley said cheerfully. "Better hurry."

Judith decided that she looked better, in fact, entirely recovered.

When she got down to the dining room, she found them all there, with the exception of Vera, which was routine. Shirley was holding the floor.

"You guys can sneer all you want to, but if I had this place I'd cheer it up some. Look at this room, for instance. All it needs is a coffin in the corner."

"People's tastes differ," Judith suggested as she seated herself.

"Oh, sure." Shirley was tolerant. "But when a person's taste stinks, they oughta have sense enough to change it."

"Would you be good enough to show me your contract?" Dr. Smith asked her carefully. "I want to satisfy myself that there are no loopholes by which I might get rid of you at once."

Shirley laughed heartily. "You sure are a scream, Doc. I don't mind showin' you my contract, but I warn you, if you tear it up, I'm stayin' anyway. I like it here, and you and no one else is gonna get me out before I want to go."

"No?"

"N.O.," Shirley said firmly.

Judith glanced at her curiously, and Willie cleared his throat.

"Well, did the police close the case? They seem to have left, but I haven't heard what they decided about Charlie."

"They agreed that he died of the second stroke, as I told them;" Dr. Medford replied, "but they want to know where he died and what happened to his finger."

"They enjoy occupying themselves with nonsense," Dr. Smith said impatiently. "You can see why I did not want to bring them in. They'll be annoying us for a month, probably."

Dr. Medford shrugged. "I'd prefer they nose around here than that they have me nosing around the four walls of a cell. Remember, I have a title here and I feel responsible. But you know that I intend to step out as soon as arrangements can be made and Willie can take over. He'll need an assistant, of course."

"Don't try to tell me my business," Dr. Smith said irritably. "It so happens that I expect you to remain until Willie gets back."

"Where am I supposed to be getting back from?" Willie demanded, staring.

Dr. Smith gave him a smile that was free from the usual malice. "I'm sending you to my old friend, Dr. Crockett, at Wildwood, for a while. It will be good experience for you, and when you come back you'll be ready to take over here."

Willie was not pleased, and desperation lent him courage. "You know that's nothing but a high-class nuthouse he runs there. What do I want with psychiatric experience? I'm a medical man."

"Well—" Dr. Smith allowed the malice to return. "That's one way of putting it. But nuts get sick too, and you might as well be prepared."

"It's a waste of time!" Willie said, in helpless fury. "I'll be sitting around there, yawning, painting a throat, or tying up a cut finger. It's utterly absurd. I—"

"Willie!" Dr. Smith interposed sharply. "You will do as I say. Psychiatric experience has its own value, and it won't be wasted. You'd better start packing. I want you to leave today."

"Today!" Willie stood up and flung his napkin onto the table. He faced his father for a moment, and then his figure sagged into defeat, and he left the room.

"Now, I wonder why you're booting him out right at this time," Shirley said thoughtfully.

"Shut your evil mouth." He glared at her, but the color had deepened in his face.

"Oh no." She looked him full in the eye. "I'll shut my mouth when it feels good that way, and I'll open it when it happens to suit me too."

Dr. Medford stood up abruptly. "Dr. Smith, you'll have to get someone in to take over while Willie's away. I shall be leaving within the week."

Dr. Smith gripped the arms of his chair, and said quietly, "I'm sure you won't make things so difficult for me, Bob. You know that I cannot replace you in so short a time."

"Then you'd better keep Willie here." Dr. Medford started for the door. "I repeat, I'll be leaving within the week."

There was blackmail going on, he thought, as he went out into the hall. The West woman was doing it, sponsored by Miss Ewell. Shirley seemed confident and unafraid. Perhaps she had decided to play it alone, and had chased Miss Ewell. That dressing up to look like Vera—trying to make out that she was a natural daughter of the old man, no doubt. But she seemed to be getting away with it, and if she'd had no proof, Dr. Smith would have disposed of her long ago. Well, high time to get out of the place. It seemed to be an unsavory mess, whatever it was.

Judith came up behind him, and he stopped her.

"I'm opening up my office in the village here. You can come and be my office nurse, if you like."

"Oh no." But she smiled at him. "In the first place, I don't want to be anybody's office nurse, and, anyway, with you going and Miss Ewell gone, I couldn't possibly leave here until they're more settled."

"I suppose not. Nurses seem to be harder to get than doctors. Still—" He looked down at her thoughtfully. "When the lid blows off Smith Hospital, and it may take the walls with it, you can always come to me. At least until you can get another job."

"That's nice of you, and I appreciate it," Judith said soberly. "But I really think you're making too much of it. It's probably a private family scandal of some sort that will blow over quietly."

He shook his head, but did not argue it. "I'm going out for about an hour," he said abruptly. "I don't think any of my patients is due to turn his toes up, but you can always call on Willie. You'll find him complaining to Vera, as usual, when he's upset. I'm going to buy a house."

"In an hour?"

"Why not? I merely need one in the village that's handy for people to come to."

"But there are other considerations," Judith protested. "I mean, when you go to buy a house—"

"The house can be fixed up later," he said carelessly. "What I need now is the location."

"Supposing the furnace doesn't work and the roof leaks? There are so many things. You shouldn't be too close to your neighbors, because they might have noisy children. Besides, there can't be much of a population around here. What sort of a practice—"

Dr. Smith wheeled himself into the hall, and Bob Medford went out in a bit of a hurry. Shirley sauntered in, and Mary Gore, who had been sitting at the switchboard, got up stiffly. "You're late, Mrs. West."

"So I'm late," Shirley agreed airily, "and the world's still goin' on."

Judith went up to her room for a cigarette. She felt out of patience with Shirley and all the rest of them. And she was uneasy, too, might as well admit it. She'd like to leave, but she simply couldn't abandon them just now.

She was in the small sitting room, and as she smoked, she found her eyes fastened on a folded blanket that lay on the divan. She hadn't noticed it before, but then how could she? It hadn't been there before. She was sure of it.

Someone had slept on that divan last night, and had forgotten to take the blanket away.

Chapter 21

Judith tried to remember whether the blanket had been on the divan that morning, but there was no picture of it in her mind. She had rushed out in a hurry, and would not have been apt to notice it in any case. But someone had slept here, and this time it was not Charlie.

The blanket was neatly folded, and she went over and lifted a corner of it. She couldn't identify it. It was like all the other blankets in the place, a rather ugly pinkish plaid. Probably some bargain lot. Well, anyway, she still had a lock on her door, and it was a comforting thought.

She crushed out her cigarette and went downstairs. Shirley was seated at the desk in the front hall, and she gave Judith a cheerful grin. "Hi there. Listen, are you running this shebang now? If so, you got to get another girl for the switchboard in the daytime."

Judith turned and looked at her. "Are you leaving?"

"Not right off, but I got to have the new girl right off, and I'll help around some until I go. Don't worry, I'll be here for a while."

"But we won't need you if we get a new girl."

Shirley winked at her. "Maybe some of the dusty old stiffs around here would like me to stay on and cheer 'em up."

"Well"—Judith shrugged—"it isn't exactly my department, but I'll speak to Dr. Smith and Miss Smith about it for you."

She expected a reaction, but got none. Shirley nodded, and said airily, "O.K. I didn't think of it until I got stuck here this morning."

"How's your head?"

"It's doin' pretty good, but I'm not gonna sit here all day. I might need my head for something, like pourin' a cocktail into it. So I got to take care of it."

Judith nodded. "You'd better go to Dr. Willie when you get off. He might want to see it."

"Him!" Shirley snorted. "I'm not gonna trust my skull and brains to a guy like that. Old Stinky Stuffshirt can look at my head, even if he has to do it through a monocle."

"Now, just a minute," Judith said quietly. "Dr. Willie is a dependable doctor, and extremely thorough. I've worked with him, and I know what I'm talking about. He treated that wound on your head, and if you have any sense you'll let him finish the job."

"Yeah?" Shirley looked impressed. "That's good to know, I guess. I thought he just had an in because he's the boss's son."

"Certainly not," Judith said firmly. "He's in because he's a doctor with a degree, and experience. He's a medical man, not a surgeon. Dr. Medford does the surgery, and they work well together."

"I'll bet that Medford wears kid gloves when he butches around," Shirley said, laughing, "instead of them common rubber ones. So Willie's all right, huh? I thought he was a menace, the way they kick him around. And now they're sendin' him away. Why? Can you answer me that?"

"I've no idea, and it's none of my business. But one thing is sure: they can't send him off until they get another doctor in."

A voice from the door said, "Maybe you're talking about me," and they turned to see a young man standing there, with his hat in one hand and a suitcase in the other. He added, "I'm Dr. Burrell. Dr. Smith sent for me yesterday."

Shirley stared frankly, and as Judith started forward, Dr. Smith wheeled himself into the hall. He greeted Dr. Burrell, thanked him for having been so prompt, and introduced him to Judith. They acknowledged each other, and Dr. Smith swung his chair around. "Now, where's Medford?"

"He went out to buy a house," Judith said absently.

"A *house*?"

Judith recovered herself. "He'll be back soon. He went out for a while," she said hastily.

Shirley leaned over the switchboard and tapped Dr. Burrell on the arm. "He forgot to interdooce me. I'm Mrs. West, temporary switchboard."

Dr. Burrell bowed, and Dr. Smith interposed testily, "I'm sorry that your room is not yet prepared, but I shall have it attended to at once. In the meantime, you can leave your bag here, and Miss Onslow will show you over the place."

Dr. Burrell bowed again and lowered his suitcase to the floor, and Dr. Smith nodded at Judith and then abruptly wheeled himself off.

He made grimly for his own quarters, and stopped outside the door. He could hear the murmur of voices, but although he strained his ears, he was unable to make out what they were saying. It didn't matter–let them talk. He pushed through the door, and Vera and Willie fell silent at once, and looked at him. Accusingly.

Dr. Smith spoke first, and firmly. "Dr. Burrell has just arrived, Willie. I want him to have your room, so you'd better get your stuff out of it. Dr. Crockett expects you tomorrow, so you'll have to leave today."

Dr. Willie raised his chin. He had wanted to sound firm and definite, and was horrified when he realized that his voice was weak and timid.

"I'm not going."

Vera was more defiant, although the shrill quality in her voice betrayed her nervousness.

"He's not going, and you can't make him go. It's time and to spare that you stopped kicking him around."

Dr. Smith wished fiercely that he had a workable leg with which he might kick Willie around. But he had only his tongue, and he used it. "You'll go where I say, for as long as I say, or you'll get out of here at once and set up on your own."

Willie raised his chin again. "You forget that I now have a few patients of my own here. I can't just go off and leave them."

"Why not?" Dr. Smith asked, with the most insulting inflection.

"He is not going," Vera said quickly. "He is staying here where he belongs. You can't throw him out just for some whim of yours. He is not going to pack a thing, because he isn't leaving. He's needed here. I have an interest in this place, too, you know."

"That's merely an assumption," Dr. Smith said nastily. "This place belongs to me, and I believe I'll phone my lawyer today."

Vera muttered, "You wouldn't dare!" and her face went gray.

"Dare?" Dr. Smith laughed, and swung his chair around. "You will leave today, Willie."

Willie's face and back slumped together, but Vera bravely followed the wheelchair out into the front hall. Dr. Burrell had returned there, and she allowed herself to be introduced to him. Her father told her, tersely, to find a room for him and have it fixed up.

There were no rooms left, she thought agitatedly. She'd have to put him in one of the patients' rooms. Charlie. She could give him Charlie's room for the time being, and they'd move him later. She quite warmed to this personable-looking young man, and undertook to show him over the hospital, and the house as well. She remained with him through lunch, and well into the afternoon. Dr. Burrell was tired, and Willie was infuriated. He felt that Vera had gone over to the opposition, and that he was abandoned and alone.

He was surprised and decidedly cheered when Shirley told him that Dr. Medford was leaving.

"But no one told me. I haven't heard anything about it," he said wonderingly.

"You will." Shirley nodded her head. "Me, I think it's good riddance."

Knotty came in during the afternoon. He was unhappy about Charlie's finger, and said so. He liked to do a thorough job at all times, and could have closed the case with a clear conscience, except for that finger. He spent some two hours roaming the hospital, and getting in everyone's way.

Dr. Smith eventually caught up with Bob Medford, and relieved a good deal of pent-up irritation. He ended his tirade by shouting, "If you had to interfere in my business by calling in the damned police, why couldn't you have sewed the blasted finger back on before they saw it?"

Medford was laughing, and Dr. Smith wheeled away from him with his temper still hot, but with an uncomfortable feeling that the thing was laughable, after all. He was losing Bob. It was inevitable, and he knew it. So he had Willie and this young Burrell.

He passed Mary Gore with his face averted, but she followed him until he had to say hello. She helped him into the elevator, and he was glad to see the door close her face away from him. He went down, all the way down to the basement. He'd go to the morgue. Nobody would be there now, and he liked it. He often went there. It was quiet, and he could remember the days when he was a practicing surgeon himself and he could be away from all that rabble upstairs.

How could he get Willie out? He couldn't, actually. He could turn him out of the house, but that was all. Well, he *would* phone his lawyer, just so that Vera could hear him. Do her good.

Someone was coming. He tensed himself, and muttered that he'd spit at the person, whoever it was. If he couldn't have peace and quiet in the morgue, then where could he have it? Of course, if it were Lucius, he wouldn't mind. Lucius was all right. Only it wasn't; this was a different step. Lucius sounded, and looked, too, more like an ape than anything else. Funny. All he had to laugh at, these days, were his own corny jokes. Nothing amusing about Vera and Willi. They were merely dull. That other one was different, though.

He heard a click, and twisted around in his chair. What was it? The door. Closed now. He wheeled over and pushed, but it would not open. Locked. His own fault too. He'd had the lock put on it.

He listened for a while, and decided that Lucius had closed the door by mistake. But it hadn't been Lucius. Those steps belonged to someone else. A little flash of fear went through him, and he tried to brush it away. Silly. Lucius wouldn't have shut the door without looking in. So it was some officious, interfering pest, and the hospital was infested with them.

Well, he'd have to get out; he'd better start shouting. Would they hear him? Lucius might, but he was probably busy upstairs, and it was possible that he'd be busy until he left to go home.

Dr. Smith shook his head, and gripped the arms of his chair with his crippled hands. He could pound on the door. Someone would surely hear him eventually. He might be heard from the cellar of the main house, even. In fact, there was someone there, now, moving quietly.

He was conscious of cold moisture on his forehead. Of course someone was in the cellar; they knew he couldn't escape that way, and so they had locked the new wing door and circled around to this one. Why had he been so careless, so stupid? That girl had been hit over the head, and he hadn't paid any heed.

The cellar door rattled, and his thoughts began to race like a squirrel in a cage. He wouldn't have cared so much, but that new treatment— he might have had a chance—

The door moved slowly inward, and belatedly it occurred to him to scream, but the first hoarse cry was choked off by firm, unrelenting pressure on his throat.

Chapter 22

Judith had been very busy all the afternoon. Knotty had wasted time for her on several occasions by stopping her to ask questions which she either could not answer or had answered before. She kept her patience, but when she glanced out a front window at five o'clock and saw his car disappearing down the driveway, she heaved a sigh of relief that seemed to come up from her shoes.

At seven she wearily climbed the stairs and changed from her uniform into a dress. She would have preferred to drop straight into bed, but she realized that a cocktail and some hot food would make her feel better.

She met Shirley in the hall, and with a glance at her bandaged head asked if she felt well enough to come down to dinner.

Shirley gave her a pert grin. "Sure do. I hadda swell nap the last couple hours. That dopey drip Mary came and told me she'd handle things for a while."

Judith nodded, and consciously turned her eyes away. Shirley was made up like Vera again; a different dress, this time a plain, dull blue. Her hair was pulled back tightly into a prim little knot.

They went down together to the Smith quarters, and as they entered the living room, Judith was unable to suppress a little giggle.

Vera had gone glamorous, as far as it was in her power to do so. Her mouth was bright with lipstick, and her hair had been curled and loosened around her face. She wore a dress of beige-colored lace, and a red rose from the garden bobbed on her shoulder.

Shirley stiffened, and muttered, "Why, the damned, double-crossing bitch!" After which she made straight for Dr. Burrell, who was standing alone, with a cocktail glass in his hand.

Willie was standing by the window, looking both sulky and determined, and Les was seated on the couch. He watched Shirley float up to Dr. Burrell, and heaved a sigh that could be heard all over the room.

"Give the new one a play, girls," he lamented, "and leave all us familiars to pine." He turned to Willie. "Get out the drinks, boy. We've been deserted, and we might as well drown our melancholy."

Dr. Burrell blushed, and Shirley yelled something at Les, who turned his attention to Vera. "Darling," he said plaintively, "aren't you ever going to look at me again?"

Vera gave a laugh which had a note of excitement in it. She said, "Don't be silly," and he followed her as she carried a drink to Judith.

"Judy," he mourned, "you are my last chance. Will you give me a little attention, even though it may bore you?"

Judith took her drink, and murmured, "Why not?"

Les sat down beside her, and Vera, after one quick look at Shirley, who was telling Dr. Burrell a series of off-color jokes, sat down with them.

Les leaned toward Judith a little, and his voice became intimate. "You know, I hate to think of you getting stuck in this town. I saw your intended looking at houses. He's serious."

Judith sipped her cocktail, and Vera asked, "What do you mean, Les?"

"I mean that he was looking at houses, a place to live, a hearthstone. It's the first step. Following that you acquire a wife and, eventually, the patter of little feet. It makes me feel lonely. I have no house, no girl, and the patter of little feet is very far away. All I have is my drink."

Vera's face became very serious. "Why, you know that isn't so, Les. You could get any girl you wanted to, practically."

Les leaned back and raised his eyes to the ceiling. "How? The church social, perhaps? Or take up charity work—"

"Or grow a mustache," Judith said, and took another sip.

Vera laughed, and then became serious again. "You shouldn't drink so much, Les."

Dr. Medford came in, and Les jumped up.

"Sorry, I was only sitting beside her to keep her warm. I was not trying to make myself fascinating."

Vera looked up. "Bob, Les says you were looking for a house."

Dr. Medford looked at Les, who pulled up the collar of his coat, and muttered, "I'm just the forgotten man. Nobody loves me."

"Stop clowning," Medford said, helping himself to a cocktail. "Yes, I've been looking at houses. I'm leaving here, as I told Dr. Smith."

"You told Father?" Vera asked.

He nodded. "I understand he got another man in, so that relieves me."

Vera's face burned with sudden color. "I must tell you, Bob, what Father's trying to do to Willie. Only we're not standing for it, Willie and I—"

Nora came in and announced without enthusiasm, "Dinner's ready."

"But Father isn't here yet," Vera protested.

"So." Nora swept the room with a look of cold dislike. "I guess the dinner didn't know that; it kept right on roasting itself until it was ready."

Vera's face froze, but she dared not say anything, and Nora turned to leave.

"It's going on the table right now," she said indifferently, "and it'll go off in twenty minutes, so's I kin git washed up."

Vera relaxed her face because she realized that Nora was no longer looking at it. She went over to Willie and sent him off to find Dr. Smith, and then herded the rest of them into the dining room.

They had barely started the meal when Willie appeared at the door with a set, white face. He said quietly, "Bob, will you come with me, please?" And something in his voice produced a dead silence as Bob Medford got up and went out.

He asked in an undertone, "What is it?" but Willie shook his head and seemed incapable of further speech.

Down in the morgue they looked together at Dr. Smith's dead face and still figure in the wheelchair. Medford drew a difficult breath, and broke a heavy silence by saying flatly, "Bruise marks on his throat. Strangled. Easy job for whoever did it. Knew just where to hold."

Willie was shuddering throughout his body at regular intervals, and Medford presently glanced at him and told him to go upstairs and get a drink. When he had gone, Medford picked up the phone and called Knotty.

Knotty excitedly warned him not to touch anything and to let no one near the body until he arrived. Medford dropped the phone back into its cradle and looked around the room. He did not touch anything, but he noticed that the door into the cellar was locked, as it should be, and he wondered who had the keys. The other door was fitted with a lock, but the catch was kept on so that it would stay open, and the catch was on now as usual.

Knotty appeared in a space of time that made it seem probable he had ignored all speed laws. He was very serious, and determined to be very thorough. Several times he said darkly, "I knew that cut-off finger meant something."

The hospital routine went on, but with difficulty, since Knotty insisted that police routine came first. Vera retired to her room and would see no one, and Willie started to drink in earnest. Les put his car, and himself as driver, at the disposal of the police, and was told that they were well equipped with both, but that he'd better stick around if he knew what was good for him. Dr. Medford answered most of the questions, and Judith, knowing that she would not be allowed to go to bed, wandered around and helped the nurses when Knotty's activities caused them to fall behind with their work. Knotty, scorning all respect for people's rooms and possessions, went everywhere like a whirlwind.

Shirley had been quiet, but her eyes were watchful. When she had a chance, she went quickly and silently up to her room, where she faced Miss Ewell. She told her breathlessly that the police were going in and out of all rooms at will, and when Miss Ewell agitatedly demanded to know why, explained bluntly that the "old man" had been murdered.

Miss Ewell quietly fainted dead away.

Shirley looked at her, lying across the bed, and chewed worriedly on her thumbnail. What should she do now? Go and get someone? But if the old bag woke up and found someone else there, she'd go off into another fit. Oh well, rub her hands, or her wrists, or something, or maybe stick a pillow under her feet.

Miss Ewell revived without any real help from Shirley, and after gazing wildly at the ceiling for a while, moaned, "Oh, my God! I must get up and go."

"Go where?"

"It doesn't matter. I must go. The sooner, the better."

"How you gonna get out without being seen?"

Miss Ewell's lip quivered, and her terrified eyes closed for a moment. "I must try. I'll have to try."

Shirley felt a slow shiver sneak through her body. The old man had been strangled; she'd heard that much from Willie, who was beginning to talk in his cups. And this skinny old hag, once so sure of herself, was now a blubbering little coward. Maybe she ought to get out with her. But she had a stake here, and she did not want to abandon it. Miss Ewell had finally told her, the first time she'd turned up in her room. But she had consistently refused to reveal why she was hiding out. Shirley chewed on her thumbnail again and wondered whether she could still bull the thing through, now that the old man was dead. She narrowed her eyes at Miss Ewell and asked, "Listen, what about me?"

Miss Ewell was putting her few things into her suitcase with shaking hands. She closed it, put on her hat, and picked it up while Shirley watched her, and then she put it down again and whispered desperately, "But where will I go?"

"You sure are yellow," Shirley observed impersonally. "Why go? Why not come back?"

"How can I come back? I can't. I dare not stay here now."

"If you know what's going on, all you got to do is to come back and tell the cops. How about tellin' me, by the way?"

"Oh no. No, not you. I'll tell the police. I'll have to. Oh, God—"

"Come on, you can trust me," Shirley said, with her eyes on the gray little face. "I got a right to know so I can watch out. I got hit on the head, didn't I? I mighta been killed."

Miss Ewell picked up the suitcase again. "I'll go, and I'll come back right away. I—the afternoon train— It would be in half an hour ago, but—"

Shirley nodded. "That's O.K. You walked from the station, and you didn't see anybody on the way. I'll go down to the front door with you, and you can ease out and then walk in again. I'll get that dame at the switchboard talkin' about something, so she don't see you."

Shirley went ahead down the stairs, and walked to the switchboard where Betty Robinson sat with her eyes snapping excitedly. Shirley started a long ramble of gossip about people in the hospital. It was entirely imaginary, but lurid enough to be interesting, and Betty listened with her mouth hanging open. Shirley had to stop eventually for breath and to think up further material, and Betty, not to be outdone, offered an item of her own.

"Did you know," she whispered, "that that new Dr. Burrell says he has a hunch that poor Dr. Smith was killed by someone real close to him—someone who doesn't remember anything about it now, because of some sort of insanity trouble?"

Chapter 23

Miss Ewell had not gone out. She opened the front door quietly, then shut it firmly and walked over to Betty at the switchboard. Betty gave a little scream, and Shirley tried to look properly surprised.

"Hi, Miss Ewell. You back?"

Miss Ewell was able to do a better job of acting. She said severely, "Yes, young woman, I am back. Please tell Miss Smith that I wish to see her at once."

Shirley loped off, feeling well satisfied. Now she could have her room to herself again, and maybe this business could be fixed up in a hurry so that she could get what was coming to her. That dullard, Vera, would have to give.

Vera was still shut away in her room, but she had neglected to lock the door, so Shirley simply walked straight in.

"How dare you intrude on me at a time like this?" Vera demanded furiously. "Even you should know enough to have a decent respect for my grief. Get out of my room! At once!"

Shirley looked at the untidy hair and the thin red nose, and shook her head. "Look, pal, what good you think you're doin' anyone by lyin' here and leaking tears? Snap out of it, for Pete's sake. Anyways, I got news for you. Our dear Miss Ewell is back."

Vera was interested in spite of herself. Her sodden face firmed, and became hard. From now on things were going to be different. Miss Ewell would find that Miss Smith was in complete charge of the house-keeping. In fact, she was very glad that Angie had come back. There were several things that she wanted to point out to her without delay. The first, and the most important, was that Vera Smith and Dr. Willie Smith were the heads of Smith Hospital.

She swung her feet off the bed and raised her hands to her disordered hair. "Lead me to Miss Ewell, please," she said haughtily.

Shirley grinned at her. "Find your own way. She was out in the front hall, last I saw of her."

Vera stalked out, and Shirley lingered, eying the room with half-scornful curiosity. Not bad. It had class but was kinda gloomy. Let Vera wait and see what Shirley could do in the way of decoration. She'd show Vera how a room oughta look!

She left, walking slowly. Her head was hurting again. But then, she hadn't had any dinner. Nobody had. She made for the dining room and found that the food was still on the table, and that Les was sitting there alone, eating heartily.

Shirley greeted him warmly and thought again that he was really her dish. She sat down and began to eat, and at the same time started what she hoped was an interesting conversation. Les was receptive in a slightly abstracted way, but the time came when they both fell into an uneasy silence, their thoughts winging to the all-important consideration of what was going on in this place.

Judith came in and sat down, and they passed food to her and informed her that she wouldn't like it much, because it was cold.

She sighed. "Oh well, just so long as it's something to eat."

Dr. Medford and Knotty came in after a while. Dr. Medford applied himself to the cooling meal, but Knotty said, "No, thank you, I don't care to eat," and then proceeded to pick up bits and pieces of the food and stuff them into his mouth.

When Miss Ewell and Vera appeared, there was not much left. Les sprang to his feet with his mouth full, and greeted Miss Ewell with enthusiasm, but the others had taken note of her return, and were apathetic.

Les swallowed, choked, and extended a welcoming hand. "So glad to see you back, darling. Where have you been all this time?"

Miss Ewell murmured, "Just a little visit," and sat down heavily at Dr. Smith's place. She could not have eaten, even had the food been fresh and hot.

Vera called Nora, and when there was no response, went purposefully out to the kitchen. She found Nora, eyes red, sitting at the kitchen table.

"Why didn't you take the food back to the kitchen and keep it in the oven? They're all in the dining room now, and everything is cold."

Nora drew a long, uneven breath and muttered, "I should worry."

"That's no way to answer me."

"No kidding?"

Vera was defeated, and she knew it. She considered several reprimands, abandoned them in view of possible retorts, and flounced out of the kitchen with her thin nose twitching.

Judith watched her return, and took a shrewd guess as to what had happened. But she felt badly in need of some hot coffee, and she got to her feet and said to Vera in a mild voice, "Do you mind if I go out and make some coffee?"

Vera shrugged and turned her attention to Miss Ewell, who was telling everybody where she had been. Knotty was prodding her with questions, and Miss Ewell was being very careful.

"I went to town and registered at a large hotel in the name of 'Mrs. Smith.' I didn't want anyone to find me, because I wanted to think things out."

"You used our name?" Vera said coldly.

"Yours, and a million others," Miss Ewell snapped. "I merely wished to be nobody for a few days."

Vera colored angrily, but before she could speak, Knotty asked smoothly, "What did you have to think out, Miss Ewell?"

"Personal problems."

Knotty chewed on a cigar he had picked up from Willie, and Judith came back from the kitchen with hot coffee.

Dr. Medford extended his cup gratefully and asked Miss Ewell, "Did you know that Charlie has been found?"

All the color faded out of her face, and her hands tensed into fists. She said quietly, "Yes, I know. He was found in the elevator shaft. But how did he get there?"

Knotty flicked ash from his cigar. "You know he had a finger missing?"

"Yes."

"How do you know? You just came in, didn't you?"

Miss Ewell floundered a little, but recovered herself very quickly. "Mrs. West told me after I arrived here tonight."

"Who's Mrs. West?"

"That's me, bud," Shirley informed him composedly.

"Somebody told me your name was Miss Shirley."

Les stirred, and announced, "I think I'll get going. I've a lot of calls to make tomorrow."

Knotty swung around on him. "You stay where you are, guy. Where were you all day, anyways?"

Les groaned and sank back into his chair. He named the places where he had called during the day, and added that he had then returned to his hotel, showered and changed his clothes, and come over to Smith Hospital.

"You spend a lot of time hanging around this joint?" Knotty asked.

"Certainly. I find it interesting and amusing here."

"He wanted to be a doctor," Miss Ewell interposed, "but his parents could not afford it."

Knotty sighed and left the dining room rather abruptly. He went out into the hall, and up to the switchboard.

"Betty."

"Yes, Uncle Jacob?"

"Have they come yet? Doc, I mean, and that lousy photographer."

"No." Betty shook her head. "You know, I don't know what Dr. Burrell means by 'split personality.' I told Shirley about it."

"Yeah? What she say?"

"She said, 'For Chrissake!' "

Knotty frowned. "You don't have to soil your lips with language of that sort, a nice girl like you. Did the West dame seem to be upset, or scared, or anything?"

"No," Betty replied, a little regretfully. "She just swore, like I told you. Gee, Uncle Jacob, I don't want to stay here. I want to go home. I feel cold all over."

Knotty was stern. "You can't rat out on a sinking ship because you got cold feet. It ain't done. The patients can't leave, or the nurses. You behave yourself."

Doc and the so-called lousy photographer came in at that point, and Knotty led them down to the morgue. They were both happy and eager. Nothing like this had happened in their small town since they could remember, and they found it stimulating. They were conscientious and thorough, and Knotty lounged against the wall, chewing on a tooth-pick and wishing that he'd eaten enough to make a toothpick worth while. These two would take ages to do the job, and then they'd write it all down. Knotty yawned, and made for the door. The young police-man who stood there guarding the corpse asked if he could go, and Knotty said, "No" and went on upstairs.

As a matter of fact, he'd had a wonderful idea, and he wanted to do something about it as soon as possible. Mary Gore. She was quite nutty enough to spill any beans she might be holding, and surely she ought to know something about the bunch of dopes in this joint.

He was lucky. She had not yet gone home, although he found her in the hall, attired in her hat and coat. She had been talking to Betty, but she turned to him as soon as he appeared.

"You're just the man I want to see. That young fellow down in the morgue wouldn't let me in. Said he had orders from you. Now, I'm sure Dr. Smith is not dead, and if you'd only let me—"

"Maybe." Knotty eyed her speculatively. "Look at this note I found in his coat pocket. From Miss Ewell. Know what it means?"

Mary took the note, read it carefully, and turned it over and back again.

"Well, she wants a decent funeral. She knows she won't need a fu-neral at all—" She stopped suddenly and put her hand to her mouth.

"Oh, dear. I suppose she was afraid they wouldn't respect her dead body."

Chapter 24

Betty Robinson gave a little gasp that had something of macabre enjoyment in it, and Knotty gave her a stern glance.

"Why would she think that?" he asked.

But Mary twisted her head to look over her shoulder in an uneasy fashion, and murmured, "I have to go now. I'll be late getting to bed as it is."

She made determinedly for the door, and although Knotty tried to stop her, she pushed him aside and went out. He scowled after her for a while, and then shrugged and went down to the morgue, where Doc and the lousy photographer were still busy.

Dr. Willie had been waiting halfway up the stairs, and when he saw Knotty leave, he came down and made for the dining room. They were all in there. He could hear them. He was still shaking a bit, but he was going to join them. He'd have something to eat, and some black coffee.

As he walked in, Miss Ewell suggested that Dr. Smith had, perhaps, committed suicide. Dr. Medford snorted and declared that it was absolutely impossible, and Vera observed that she really didn't think Father would do a thing like that. Les, who had not yet left, told them that, after all, you never knew.

Miss Ewell drew a long breath and told of a man she had known who had done just that, strangled himself with his own hands.

Willie nodded at her, battling desperately with the liquor to keep his face and body firm. "You're quite right. I've heard of that too, although you wouldn't think it was possible—"

Dr. Medford muttered, "For God's sake, Willie, you know better than that."

Willie sank back into silence, and Shirley said animatedly, "I hear he was missing a finger, like that Charlie."

Miss Ewell screamed, in a faint and ladylike manner, and Willie started to shake again. He'd have to have a drink now, he'd simply have to. He stood up and lurched out of the room.

"Where did you hear that?" Dr. Medford asked.

Shirley shrugged. Actually, she hadn't heard it anywhere.

Dr. Medford ran a cool eye over her. "Nonsense. I can assure you that it is not true."

Miss Ewell opened her mouth to speak, and then closed it again.

She looked blindly down at the table and told herself that she ought to eat something. She'd had very little food in the last two days. She got to her feet and went to the kitchen, and Shirley, after watching her go out, turned to Les and started a gay conversation.

Judith was longing for her bed. She wanted to go to her own room and lock the door, lock everyone out.

Dr. Medford said, "Now that Miss Ewell is back, you should have a little more time for yourself. Will you come with me and look over a couple of houses? I can't make up my mind which would be better, and I'd like another opinion on it."

Judith swallowed a yawn. "Why ask me?"

"Who else could I ask in this damned madhouse?" Dr. Medford demanded irritably.

"Well—" Judith thought it over and decided that, actually, there was no one who could advise him as well as herself.

"Besides," Dr. Medford added, "who else would be willing? They'd want to know why you weren't in on it."

"When do you want me to go?"

"Tonight. I have no other time, and I want the thing settled."

"*Tonight*? But surely we ought to stay here—"

"Oh, stop making difficulties."

He went off and announced to Miss Ewell that Judith would be absent for a while, and then hunted up Willie to arrange for his own departure. He had to extract a drink from Willie's hand and then steer him to the kitchen and feed him black coffee before he felt reasonably safe in leaving him.

He eventually emerged from the kitchen muttering profanities under his breath. Shirley and Les were still in the dining room where they were conversing gaily to the accompaniment of a couple of highballs. Vera sat staring at them, and Miss Ewell and Judith had disappeared.

He went on to the front hall, where he met Dr. Burrell, who had many questions to ask, and who wound up by observing that he wished he'd never come to this place. Dr. Medford advised him not to worry, assured him that he was badly needed, and declared that there was a good future for him in Smith Hospital. Immediately, he felt a bit guilty for having said such a thing. Willie was head of the place now, and if he continued to drink too much, he would almost certainly run it to ruin. Dr. Smith had been out of active practice for some years, of course. But at least he had been there, with a watchful eye on things.

Dr. Medford had to go all the way up to the third floor to get Judith. She had retired to her room, but she had not undressed, and when she opened the door for him he said impatiently, "Come on, a bit of fresh air will be good for you in any case. You've been closed up in this damned place too much."

Judith put on a hat and a light coat, and they went down the stairs together in silence. In the front hall they met Knotty, who asked rather coldly, "Where you going, you two?"

Dr. Medford frowned at him. "We have an errand in the village. We'll be back shortly."

"What kind of an errand?"

Vera appeared quietly behind them, and stood there listening while Dr. Medford explained irritably, "I'm buying a house, and I want Miss Onslow's opinion. And she needs to get away from this infernal place for a while, anyhow."

"I understand," said Knotty carefully, "that you two are engaged."

Judith looked him straight in the eye. "We are not."

"They are too," Vera interposed shrilly. "She keeps on trying to deny it, but I happen to know that they've been engaged for a long time."

Knotty shifted his eyes from one to the other and decided with satisfaction that there was something decidedly suspicious here.

Dr. Medford took Judith's arm and urged her toward the front door. Knotty followed, silent and observant, and watched them get into Dr. Medford's car. As it rolled down the drive, he went over to his own car and instructed the policeman who sat behind the wheel to follow them.

"See what they do and where they go, and write it down so you won't forget it."

"I ain't got nothing to write it down on, boss."

"Well, get something, you dimwit," Knotty thundered. "Use your cuff, or the seat of your underpants–if there's any seat left after all the sittin' around you do on the taxpayers' money."

He returned to the front hall of the hospital, muttering darkly to himself, and came upon Vera and Miss Ewell in agitated discussion.

"It's Nora," Miss Ewell was saying, fluttering her small hands. "She simply refused to do the dishes, and she's gone up to bed. She said she was too upset for any more work tonight."

"*She's* upset!" Vera cried. "What about me? I am only his daughter, of course."

"My dear, I know, but suppose we do the dishes anyway? There's no one else, you see, and Nora simply will not be forced."

"No." Vera turned away with two crimson spots on her cheekbones. "It's not to be expected of me at a time like this. You'll have to get someone else."

"*I'll* have to get someone else?" Miss Ewell straightened her small body. "Indeed, it's no concern of mine. You have just informed me that you are running this place now." She turned toward the back of the hall, apparently headed for her own room.

Knotty clicked his tongue. "See what you done now? She was all set to help you with them dishes, but you got her tail up, and you also got all the dishes to handle by yourself."

Vera's eyes blazed, and she shrieked, "You mind your own business."

Shirley and Les wandered in arm in arm, and Shirley asked vaguely, "Wassa matter? Wass goin' on?"

Vera turned on her. "As for you, you miserable creature, you can pack up and leave."

She ran off without waiting for an answer, and shut herself into her room. She stood behind the closed door waiting for someone to come after her, but nobody did.

Miss Ewell had locked her door firmly, and was already attired in her long-sleeved, high-necked nightgown. She shivered a little as she slipped into bed, although it was nice to get back to her own bed again and her own things. It had been bad, sleeping on the couch in the little outer room of her old quarters. Not that she'd been able to sleep much, expecting every moment to be discovered. In the beginning, when Charlie had her bed, it hadn't been so bad; but later, when she was supposed to have left the place— Well, she needed sleep, and now she'd be able to get some. The door was locked, and nobody could get in. But nothing had worked, nothing at all, and now he was dead. She'd tried to tell him, and if she hadn't pretended to run away, he wouldn't have believed her. She'd had to do it that way, only it hadn't worked. And now where was she?

She turned over and went to sleep.

Shirley and Willie were washing the dishes. Knotty had informed them of Nora's defection, and Shirley had tried to get Les in on the job. But Les had remembered that he ought to get home. Willie had wandered by, and Shirley, philosophical by nature, had marched him firmly off to the kitchen. Knotty was lounging against the wall and annoying them with questions.

It had been apparent to him for some time, however, that their answers were not reliable, since they had both had too much to drink. Knotty had his code, and he was privately a little shocked at the way Willie was laughing and joking with his father lying dead.

"Can you tell me," he asked sternly, "why Miss Ewell ran away and then came back?"

Shirley dropped a cup on the floor, and, ignoring the pieces, said reasonably, "Whyn't you ask her?"

Knotty frowned. "I did. She told me to mind my own business."

"Well, whyn't you mind your own business then?"

"Dr. Smith," Knotty said peremptorily, "can you answer me on this subject?"

Willie, who was unaccustomed to being addressed as Dr. Smith, went on washing dishes in silence.

Knotty pulled at his sleeve and repeated the question.

Willie turned around from the sink and looked up out of eyes that were a bit glazed. He laughed for some time, and then said carelessly, "Yeah, I know. Old Ewell was afraid that I'd cut her up into little tiny pieces."

Chapter 25

Shirley screamed and dropped another cup. "Willie! Shut up! Are you nuts or something?"

Willie flipped soapsuds from his hands and said mildly, "'Struth."

Knotty pulled him away from the sink. "Explain what you're talkin' about, guy."

Willie wrenched himself free and returned to the sink in one loping stagger. "Ahh, how do I know what goes on in her head?" he muttered. "She's bats."

"O.K., so she's bats. But why was she afraid?"

Willie ignored the question, and Knotty found his mind circling around Charlie, from whose dead body a finger had been severed.

"Did you do that?" he asked in sudden excitement.

"Did I do what?"

"That finger that was cut off the old guy under the elevator. I guess you musta done that. I'll have to take you into custody."

"Watta you mean, you ape?" Shirley demanded indignantly. "You can't take him in. You got nothing on him. Why would he cut off a dead guy's finger, anyways?"

Willie was already regretting having said anything. He was beginning to sober up a little, and he knew that he should have kept his mouth shut. He bent lower over the sink, hunching his shoulders together.

Knotty pulled insistently at his arm. "You gotta answer me, Dr. Smith. This is important."

"Why don't you leave us alone while we get these damn dishes done?" Shirley demanded peevishly. "We're almost through here, and then we'll sit down and have a drink all around and answer all the dumb questions you can think of."

Knotty was furious. "That'll be swell!" he shouted. "I can hardly wait. Suppose I had to help my wife with the dishes first, every time I got an emergency call? Where'd this town be?"

"Where's it now?" Shirley asked.

Willie raised his head from the sink. "Your comparison is faulty. Mrs. West is not my wife, and I am not helping her. She is helping me. This is my hospital."

Knotty, still in a blind fury, picked up a towel and dishcloth and went through the kitchen like an avenging spirit. The place was neat and immaculate in a matter of minutes, and he led the two of them to the dining room and sat them down.

"Now," said Knotty through his teeth, "I want some truthful answers to my questions. You, Dr. Smith. Why did you cut a finger off that poor old guy?"

Willie had always been one to give up easily, and he felt that Knotty had found him out at this point, and he'd better tell the truth.

"They wouldn't ever let me try," he said in a tired voice. "I wanted to be a surgeon too, but they wouldn't give me a chance; they wouldn't let me do anything."

Knotty was a little puzzled, but he kept a stern frown on his face and asked, "Who do you mean by 'they'? Who wouldn't give you a chance?"

Willie sighed. "My father and Bob Medford. They were solidly together, and they kept me out. They said I was not capable, but they were wrong. They should have let me try."

Knotty, in his own vernacular, felt that he was now cooking with gas. He said tensely, "So you tried your skill on old Charlie?"

Willie sighed again. "Only after he had died. It could not hurt him then—so why not? They never allowed me to do any autopsies, even. It was not fair, but they sided together and told me that my hand was not firm enough."

"Where did you cut the finger off?"

"Well, at the joint, of course. I wanted to try—"

"No, no, no." Knotty wiped moisture from his forehead. "I mean, where was he? Under the elevator?"

"Oh." Willie sank back into his chair and studied the ceiling.

Knotty moved restlessly. "Come on, surely you know where you did it."

"Yes, of course. I found him under the elevator. He was lying there, and I picked him up and carried him down to the morgue. He'd been missing for a while, and I knew that he'd have to go to the morgue anyway. I took him through the house. I went down the cellar stairs with him. He was so light, you know—"

"And you didn't want anybody to see you," Knotty supplied.

"Well, it seemed more diplomatic not to arouse anyone. I could see that he had been dead for some time, and certainly it could no longer matter to him. I wanted the practice. I needed it so badly. I knew I was capable—"

"What happened?" Knotty asked quietly.

Shirley moved uneasily in her chair. "Yeah, what happened next, Willie boy?"

Knotty gave her an evil look, but Willie still had his eyes on the ceiling.

"Well, I got him onto the table and I thought I'd start with the finger. Such a small thing—"

"Sure, sure," Knotty murmured. "What next?"

Willie's voice had a defeated quality in it now. "The finger jumped. I tell you, it jumped at me, and I couldn't find it. It might be that I'd had too much to drink. That was my trouble, and I realized it. I shouldn't have attempted the thing without authority. I knew that. And when I couldn't find the finger, I was frightened. I thought I'd put him in the freezer, but then it seemed better to come back when I hadn't had so much to drink and try again. Only, I couldn't hide him anywhere; there was already an odor. It was then that I thought of the old freezer, outside in the cellar under the old house. My father had intended to sell it, but could not get what he thought it was worth, so it was still there. I switched it on and found that it was working all right. It's an old thing, and noisy, and I began to be afraid that it would wake everyone up, but nobody came, and I realized that you would not be able to hear it so clearly upstairs. I went back to the morgue and picked up Charlie and put him in. The freezer was still pounding away, and it got on my nerves, so I ran upstairs to my room. But it wasn't much better up there. I was in a bad way. I lay down, but I must have had a nightmare, something of that sort. I believe I screamed, let out a yell, something—"

Willie stopped and looked at them, and was a little taken aback at their absorbed faces. He wished now that he hadn't said anything. He was always talking too much. He should have kept quiet and let Knotty find things out for himself.

"Go on, Willie hon, tell the rest," Shirley whispered.

Willie looked down at his hands and shuddered. He said slowly, "I was worried about that finger, and I went down to the cellar again with my flashlight. I thought it might somehow have dropped in the cellar. I searched. I was sweating and frantic, but I searched thoroughly. It wasn't there, though. I couldn't find it. I went back upstairs and decided I'd have a nap, and then try my skill on him again. After all, it couldn't hurt him. He was dead, and I intended to sew him up again. I never meant him to be buried without his finger, but I couldn't find it. When I read that note that Angie left, I knew she must have seen Charlie. She was always terrified of being buried without her body being intact. She had some crazy idea that she wouldn't be able to rest unless she was all there, and she'd often told us that no one was ever to touch her body to find out why she'd died. So I knew she'd seen him with his finger gone, and I thought I'd better get him back to where I'd found him. I thought she'd tell Father, sooner or later, and I didn't want to get mixed up in it. It took a bit of maneuvering, but I managed it in the end."

Shirley let out a long breath and muttered, "Gee-zus!"

Knotty rumpled his hair. "I can see why you didn't tell you'd found the old guy, though I ain't sayin' it was right—and don't let me hear of you doin' a thing like that again—but if Miss Ewell found him, finger or no finger, why in hell didn't she squawk right away? Instead of which, she pulls up her little pants and runs away."

Shirley opened her mouth to say, "No, she didn't," and then closed her lips on the words, and remained silent.

Willie shrugged. "She was always odd—secretive."

"What did she mean when she wrote, 'Like father, like son'?"

Willie stared at him blankly, and Knotty said impatiently, "You know, that note she left for your old man. She sez 'Like father, like son.'"

"I was not like my father in any way," Willie said remotely.

"You musta been like him in some way. A guy hasta get something handed down to him from his old man."

Willie had lost interest and was looking around for another drink. Knotty said desperately, "Did your father like cutting people up?"

"Father was a very good surgeon in his day. If that's what you mean."

Knotty sighed in exasperation and sent a glare at Shirley, who had found a toothpick and was idly picking her teeth. She knew that Knotty was looking at her, but she pretended to be far away and deep in thought. She didn't want him starting on her. Not that she'd tell him anything anyway; not until she'd had a few more words with the old bag, to see what was what. She had an ax to grind, and she wanted to grind it right.

Knotty suddenly walked out on them. At least he knew a few things now–he was getting along. But he wanted to talk to that Miss Ewell. She'd been skinning out on him long enough.

He walked into the front hall and slowed down as he saw Betty talking to a stranger. The woman was tall and well dressed, and appeared to have plenty of assurance. A suitcase stood on the floor beside her, and Knotty thought, until she spoke, that she was a patient.

"I shall wait for Dr. Medford," she said in a clear voice. "I am his sister, and I have come to live with him."

Chapter 26

Shirley, who had followed Knotty out to the hall, spoke up in a loud but earnest voice.

"Don't you do it, sister. You go and find a dump of your own to hang your hat in. No place is big enough for two families, especially when that stuff-shirt brother of yours is one of them."

The woman straightened her back and divided a chilly look among them. "My name is Mrs. Barstow, Mrs. Medford Barstow. My brother is not married, and now that his engagement is broken, I'm beginning to think that he never will marry. Therefore, I am accepting his invitation to come and live with him."

Shirley gave a loud and uninhibited laugh. "Oh, sister, are you ever on a bum steer. He's out with his girlfriend right this minute, buying a house. That engagement is on, babe, but good."

Mrs. Medford Barstow paled, and spoke directly to Shirley for the first time. "What do you mean? What on earth are you talking about?"

"I shall bring you abreast of the facts," Knotty said, and was surprised to hear himself using a cultured accent that he had not known he possessed. "The girl came out here to find out why the son of a—why your brother was delaying the marriage, and it looks like everything is hotsy again now. He announced it himself, only the girl is trying to keep it secret for some reason."

Mrs. Barstow had regained her color, and she said firmly, "Oh no, you are making a mistake. The girl to whom he was engaged married someone else last week."

Shirley stared, her eyes wide and interested. Some slick worker, she thought, and admired Judith without malice. Shirley herself would have been willing to swear that he was not ready to be picked up. But perhaps this old bag of a sister was mixed up about his girlfriends. She opened her mouth to speak, and closed it again as Judith and Bob Medford came in through the front door.

Dr. Medford was laughing, but his face sobered at once as he caught sight of his sister. He said, "Elizabeth!" and seemed unable to find further words.

Mrs. Barstow and Judith were looking at each other, and their expressions seemed to indicate a mutual dislike. Mrs. Barstow eventually turned to face her brother and demanded, "Do you mean to tell me you were out with this slut?"

Dr. Medford colored violently and snapped, "Elizabeth! For God's sake, watch your language! Miss Onslow has been a victim of circumstantial evidence, but she has every right to expect courtesy and respect from you."

"That's tellin' her," Shirley muttered approvingly.

Mrs. Barstow was furious. "How can you be so gullible as to be taken in by a woman like that? With Bill it was different. But you! Can't you see that she's just trying to pay you back for the evidence you gave against her?"

Dr. Medford said, "Be quiet, Elizabeth. Come into my office where we can talk privately."

She huffed away from the hand he put on her arm, and Knotty stirred and moved in. "You never told me anything about this, Medford. Come on, now. I want to know how you came to be giving evidence against her."

"It was a divorce action," Judith said flatly. "I was corespondent. But I believe that the divorce was never completed. They were reconciled, so that I couldn't have done too much harm. And now I'm going to bed."

Judith walked upstairs, and Shirley looked after her admiringly. "She sure has class, don't she? It's these quiet ones who always end up in the middle. Why didn't the dirty rat get rid of his wife and marry her, anyways?"

"Please!" Mrs. Barstow moaned, and turned to her brother. "Bob, I had come to live with you in response to your own invitation, but I see that I shall do no more than stay here overnight. I can only hope and pray that you come to your senses before she gets you. But I can do no more than that."

"Oh, shut up, Elizabeth," Dr. Medford said tiredly, "and mind your own business." He asked Shirley, "Do you know of any room where she could stay tonight? I realize that we're pretty well filled up—"

"They don't confide in me about the housekeeping, Doc," Shirley said amiably, "but I'll go ask Miss Ewell. She's in her room, and she's the one knows all about that sort of stuff."

She went off in the direction of Miss Ewell's room, and Knotty moved over to the switchboard and closed Betty's sagging mouth. He pretended to engage her in a low-voiced conversation, but his ears were alert for anything that might pass between brother and sister.

Mrs. Barstow dropped her voice, but it had a carrying quality that allowed Knotty to hear every word.

"You can't be serious, Bob! I realize that men cannot resist playing around with a creature like that, but marriage! Why, the woman might be the mother of your children!"

"Be quiet!" Medford said impatiently. "I reserve the right to run my own life, as you've run yours. Matter of fact, I think you're far more in need of advice than I am."

Mrs. Barstow gave him a stricken look. "How could you say such a thing to me? The unhappy life that I have had!" She extracted a delicate handkerchief from her bag and carefully touched each eye with it.

"If you start to cry, I'm going to bed," he said agitatedly. "Where are the children?"

"I put them in boarding school last fall. I told you that. I did not want them to hear the constant bickering. But now I have left him, and this is really the end. There is another woman, and I know who she is."

"All right," Dr. Medford said grimly, "this time you're going to Reno. I'll pay for it, and you can leave tomorrow. You'll have a lovely time. I hear there's a lot of fun to be picked up. As for the woman, we're not going to put her through the wringer the way we did that one upstairs."

"Oh, my God!" Mrs. Barstow murmured tragically. "You *are* going to marry her!"

Dr. Medford ground his teeth. "I shouldn't be surprised," he said savagely. "Everyone has been pushing me toward it, and now you're giving the final shove."

Shirley returned with Miss Ewell, and said brightly, "We woulda bin here before, but nothing would do but Miss Ewell gotta put on all her clothes, girdle and everything. She's got a swell-lookin' robe, but I guess she keeps it to hide herself from herself when she looks in the mirror."

"That will do, Mrs. West," Miss Ewell said repressively. "Now, Bob, I understand that you're in a little difficulty."

"My sister, Mrs. Barstow—Miss Ewell," Bob said, striving for suavity. "Is there a room anywhere in the place in which she could stay tonight? Rather than go to a hotel?"

Miss Ewell nodded. "But of course. We would not allow your sister to go to a hotel. Mrs. Barstow, we shall be happy to have you visit with us. It is only unfortunate that your arrival should have coincided with our tragedy."

"Tragedy?" Mrs. Barstow repeated hollowly.

"We got a murder on our hands," Shirley explained obligingly. "It was the boss who got chilled off, and they got me on the dome too, only not bad enough. Nobody knows who done it yet, including the police."

"Oh, my God!"

Knotty stepped forward and said reassuringly, "Now, don't worry, ma'am. We'll pick this guy up pretty soon. Miss Ewell, will you take this lady to a room somewheres, and then I got to talk to you."

Miss Ewell nodded, and her tired eyes were reflective. She'd have to talk to him, of course, sometime. And now she'd have to find a room for this woman at a time like this. It would be discourteous to refuse, only there were no rooms left. Dr. Smith's bedroom—But she could hardly put her in there. Where, then? The small outer room that adjoined Miss Onslow's bedroom. Surely she wouldn't mind, or she shouldn't. Shirley had told some garbled story of trouble between them. Dreadful if it was true, but Shirley was so unreliable. They were all waiting for her to speak, and she took a long breath.

"I'm really sorry that we're so crowded just now, Mrs. Barstow. You see, Mrs. West is occupying one of our guest rooms. But there is a small room available, if you'll come upstairs with me. Have you a suitcase?"

Dr. Medford picked up the suitcase and gave his sister a slight push. Knotty followed them, and Shirley brought up the rear. She said in a loud whisper, "Nosy Knotty, they call this guy."

"This is my job," Knotty replied in a furious undertone. "But I'd like to know what you think you're doin', snoopin' around here."

"It so happens that I live up here, mac. And I'll be glad to show you my bedroom so long as you don't set foot inside the door."

But they all stopped and stood in a group outside Judith's suite while Miss Ewell walked through and knocked on the bedroom door.

Dr. Medford had not realized her intention, and he said excitedly, "Angie, wait! You can't do this! Elizabeth can't stay here. Come back, will you?"

Judith opened her door as he finished speaking. She had not, like Miss Ewell, waited to dress, and she looked sleepy and exquisite in a dark green satin robe that was beautifully embroidered with gold dragons. Actually, it was not a thing that could have been in her budget. It had been given to her by a rich aunt.

There was a slightly awed silence, and Judith asked impatiently, "Well, what is it?"

"Some swell burlap you got there," Shirley sighed, her voice quite free from venom.

Miss Ewell murmured in astonishment, "What *is* that you're wearing?"

"You mean, who is she waiting for?" Mrs. Barstow said clearly.

Shirley turned to look at her. "You got a mean tongue, sister."

"Would you be good enough," Judith asked coldly, "to tell me what you want, all of you?"

"Well—" Miss Ewell showed confusion, which was unusual with her. "I was trying to find a room for Mrs. Barstow for the night, and I thought perhaps your sitting room here— But I see it wouldn't do."

"It would do very well," Mrs. Barstow said unexpectedly. "If Miss Onslow doesn't mind, of course."

Judith looked her over. "Not at all. I hope you'll be comfortable." She went back into her room and closed the door firmly behind her.

Shirley, regretful that an expected fight had not taken place, shook her head sadly. "She's too refined, that one. It ain't good for the psyche, or whatever you call it. Now, if you'd made a crack like that to me, lady, I'da booted your tail outa my room in a hurry."

"Bob!" Mrs. Barstow cried hysterically.

But Bob Medford had retired to the hall and was smoking a cigarette in a resigned sort of way. He was astounded when he saw Miss Ewell go for sheets to put on the couch and realized that the thing had been arranged.

Knotty waited quietly until Miss Ewell had finished making up the couch, and when he saw her start down the stairs he followed determinedly. She paid no attention to him until she had reached the ground floor, and then she looked back with a little sigh.

"You had better come into my office. It is still more or less mine, although of course Miss Onslow uses it now."

Knotty shut the door after them, and when they were seated, he wasted no words.

"Look, Miss Ewell. You left a note for Dr. Smith. Now in this note you say, 'Like father, like son.' You mean those two Smiths? It don't seem to me they was like each other, not in any way. But since they was father and son they musta had something in common. What was it?"

Miss Ewell sighed and closed her eyes for a moment. "No," she said, and pressed her small hand against her forehead. "No, they were not alike in any way. You see, they were not father and son."

Chapter 27

Knotty didn't believe her. This whole place was nuts, and this dame was a nut too. He said impatiently, "Oh, come off it, Miss Ewell. I'm a busy man."

She rose to her feet, looking offended. "If you do not believe what I tell you, I shall go to bed and save time for both of us."

Knotty eased her back into her chair with a muttered apology. "I want to listen to you, and I'm trying to take it serious, but what can I think when you tell me a thing like that? I even remember when he was born. I was a boy, and people were saying the doctor had twins, a boy and a girl, and that the mother died."

"Yes." Miss Ewell sighed. "Do you remember the orderly we had at that time? Jake?"

"Sure, I remember Jake."

"Jake's wife came in as an emergency. She had waited too long, as those people so often do. She was in the same room. We have only one delivery room, and, in any case, there was a flu epidemic and we were very short of nurses. Dr. Smith had just opened the hospital. He was desperately sure that he'd have a son—he wanted a son so badly—and two girls were born to his wife, while Jake's wife had a boy. You must understand that it was a very bitter disappointment, and that he had been working too hard and was not himself. He was in a livid fury, and I remember him saying, 'I'm not going to put up with this.'

"I was very busy at the time, and so was he. Mrs. Smith was dying. We could not save her, and I was upset and confused. I was astounded after a while to hear that the twins were a boy and a girl, and that Jake's wife had had a daughter. I spoke right out. I couldn't help it. I said, 'You've mixed them.'

"He turned on me savagely and demanded to know what I was talking about.

"I said, 'You had twin girls. Jake's wife had the boy.'

"He yelled at me. He battered me with words until I fell silent for the sake of peace. But I knew, and he knew that I knew. Every now and then after that he'd ask me if I'd got over my crazy idea, and I'd say 'No' and leave the room. It bothered him, of course, and he began to throw out hints as they grew up that he wanted to settle down and marry someday, marry a girl like me. Oh, he was smart."

Miss Ewell paused and glanced down at her handkerchief, which she had twisted into a rag. Knotty held himself still in his chair, and did not breathe until she went on.

"This kept me quiet, of course, even though I knew that he was going around with a series of women. I was stupid enough to think that he really loved me. I gave up chances. Then his arthritis began to get bad, and he depended on me so much. After he became really crippled with it I told him I thought he ought to marry me, so that I'd have some security. He put me off, said I must wait until he was better, because he would look foolish getting married in a wheelchair. I told him that I'd looked pretty foolish waiting around for him all these years–and then he made a mistake. He told me that I would look the same as I had always looked, and the way I'd look to my death. Foolish.

"He was right, of course. I was a fool. I realized it, and no one knows what I suffered inside. In the end, I decided to do something about it, and I told him that I'd kept in touch with Jake's family."

"Where was Jake by this time?" Knotty asked carefully.

"He'd been sent away. He was queer, and he was doing peculiar things, so Dr. Smith had sent him away. He'd got another job, and I think he did well enough, but I'd kept in touch with his wife. I'd heard plenty about Shirley, and I decided to bring her here, without telling her, of course. But Dr. Smith laughed at me. Only I had him. I knew they were identical twins. And no matter how many times he said that he had lost that other placenta, I knew it hadn't been around any-where—"

"What do you mean?" Knotty asked intensely.

Miss Ewell straightened her slender back. "Well, I need not be so technical. You see, I *knew* they were identical twins, no matter how different they might look, owing to a disparate upbringing. Still, I realized that they could be made to look alike.

"I worked for a year before I could get Shirley here for a sound reason. The switchboard girl was leaving.

"He was upset. I could see that he recognized her at once. He said, 'Your word against mine.' He wasn't looking at me, but he was talking to me."

Miss Ewell looked down at her mangled handkerchief again, and laughed a little.

"I had him, and he knew it but wouldn't admit it. He just kept smiling at me. He'd have had to give in to me finally. Only somebody got him first."

"Who got him, Miss Ewell?" Knotty asked quietly.

She shook her head. "I don't know. I wish I could tell you, but I don't know."

"Maybe you can tell me what 'Like father, like son' means?"

"Oh yes." Miss Ewell nodded. "And then I must go to bed."

She coughed, blew her nose, and sighed while Knotty waited patiently.

"We had discovered, as time went on, that Jake was taking bodies out of the freezer and cutting them up. He'd always been fascinated with the autopsies, and loved to watch. He was a good orderly, and Dr. Smith talked to him, but it did no good, and the undertakers were furious. Then, in the end, he took someone down who was not yet dead.

I'm sure Jake thought the man was already dead, but he wasn't. He was moribund, and I'm quite positive that he felt nothing when Jake cut him open, but of course it was a mess. He bled, and Jake was terrified. He ran and got me, and I had to get Dr. Smith. Jake had to go after that, but Dr. Smith got him a job in a mental institution, where the patients didn't die so often.

"But I kept in touch with the family. I thought the whole thing was dreadful. Dr. Smith made no attempt to keep track of his daughter. He seemed to want to forget it as completely as possible, and he always told me to shut up when I so much as mentioned it."

"Does the girl know?" Knotty asked. "The Shirley one, I mean."

Miss Ewell nodded. "I told her just lately. It seemed only right."

"Well"—Knotty shifted his cramped body—"when did you see old Charlie with his finger off? Because that's why you ran away, wasn't it? You thought Willie was doin' like his father done, especially after they was dead. And you didn't want that to happen to you."

Miss Ewell shuddered, looked blindly down at her little hands, and nodded.

"So when did you see Charlie minus his finger?"

"I happened to be in the cellar," she said through stiff lips, "and I heard the old freezer working. So I went and looked inside, and it was Charlie."

"Did you notice the finger was gone then?"

"Yes." Miss Ewell stared at the wall. "I left early the next morning."

"How early?"

But Miss Ewell stood up abruptly. "I could not say. I'm tired. I'm going to bed."

Knotty scowled, but he realized that he could hardly tie her into her chair. He said quickly, "Tell me, did Charlie know anything about the switch that was pulled on the kids?"

Miss Ewell paused and looked back at him. "Yes. Yes, he did. He came in shortly after the birth, and when he saw one placenta for boy and girl twins, he started prodding me. I wouldn't say anything at first, but how could I explain it? I had to admit it in the end. And now I'm going to bed. I cannot answer any more of your questions."

She went determinedly to her room, but she could not go to bed. She was too upset, and she had gone beyond ordinary fatigue to the point where she could no longer relax and rest. What was going on here? Who had hit Shirley over the head? And who had killed Dr. Smith?

She wept a little, and then squeezed her damp handkerchief between her fingers and tried to think the thing out clearly. Willie must have noticed how much Shirley looked like Vera, and probably he knew all about it. Charlie could have told him. So first he had tried to scare Shirley away by hitting her on the head. Only he had found out that she didn't scare easily. Then Dr. Smith decided to send him away, so he had killed Dr. Smith. The old doctor was dead, and Charlie was dead, and perhaps it was her turn next.

She found that she was shaking and could not stop it, and she went over and tried the door. Well, it was locked, firmly, but she could not stay behind a locked door forever. There was tomorrow, and he could get her then. But she'd be careful, very careful. The whole thing was ridiculous, anyway. Just imagine Willie killing anyone! Impossible, surely. She could do it more easily herself. Dr. Smith could have done it, except that it had been done to him. He could have killed himself just the way it was done if he'd felt like it. She didn't think, though, that he had felt like it. Crippled and all, he'd still wanted to live.

She was frightened again, but she undressed and got into bed. Well, she'd told the story after all these years, first to Shirley, and then to Knotty. It had been too big a burden, and it was better off her mind. Only her mind was still heavy. She didn't really feel any better.

She pulled herself up from the bed and went to the bureau to get a clean handkerchief. She opened one of the top drawers, and then stood very still, looking down at a black leather wallet that lay on top of the neat pile of handkerchiefs. She extended a cold, shaking hand, picked it up, and recognized it at once. It had belonged to him, to Dr. Smith.

Chapter 28

Miss Ewell dropped the wallet back into the drawer as though it had stung her, and sent a frightened look around the quiet little room. He had never allowed anyone to touch that wallet, so who had dared to take it even from his dead body? He had kept no money in it, just some personal papers. But he had always had it in his pocket by day and under his pillow by night. How had it come to be here in her room? Somebody must have put it in her drawer. And she never allowed anyone to come into her room; she had always made that clear to the entire household.

She went to the door and tried it again. Still locked, of course. She always locked it now. It was automatic. She backed away and looked under the bed and in the closet. Nothing, nobody. She was alone. Well, she'd look through the wallet. Why shouldn't she? It couldn't hurt him now.

She had an uneasy feeling that his spirit was standing at her shoulder as she drew the wallet from the drawer again, and she compressed her lips into a thin line. After all, he was dead. These things could not hurt him.

Curiosity and interest swallowed up her fear and uneasiness as she began to look through the papers. Several I.O.U.s from people she knew, people whom she would never suspect of being short of cash. And a mortgage! Really! People with a big house and several cars. It all went to show that you never knew. Several patients were listed, those who had paid about half their bill and no more. Miss Ewell knew them, all of them. The kind who said that that was all they could pay, and added that they thought it was quite enough, anyway. Dr. Smith had never liked that type, and Miss Ewell knew that there were ways of getting even with them. When they had come into the hospital, Dr. Smith had always given her a hint, and she had taken it out on them. She'd known how; she was good at that sort of thing. They'd never been able to put their fingers on anything, but they'd been uncomfortable. Not right, perhaps, but she'd felt that she'd been under orders, and it had been amusing. She'd almost laughed at times. And now everything was over and done with, and her prestige was gone. She was at the mercy of Vera. She had told about Shirley, but they would only tell her that she was a little soft in the head. Dr. Smith and Charlie had known, but they were both dead.

She pulled some more papers out of the wallet, and her mouth twisted with disgust. Love letters from women. She knew some of them, and one or two had husbands, nice husbands. And all that time he had led her to suppose that he was going to marry her. But she was not like these loose women. She had never let down the barriers of respectability. She found that she was crying, and that tears were dripping onto these disgusting letters. Why had he kept them, anyway? Some of these women were grandmothers now. But he was mean. He'd always been mean.

She folded the letters and decided that she would destroy them, now, at once. Only she couldn't leave the room. She wasn't going out there again–she was too frightened. It *must* be Willie–he was insane. And, God knows, he had had enough provocation. Dr. Smith had always treated him badly. But how *could* it be Willie? It couldn't. He was too soft.

She began to tear up the letters, patiently, into very small pieces. She kept the other things because it seemed to her that these people should be made to pay. It was only right. She kept the list of patients who had paid only half their bills too. Willie had a right to that list. If he could get the money, he'd need it.

She went back to bed and stared into the darkness with wide eyes. That sister of Bob Medford's. How would she and the Onslow woman hit it off, sleeping almost together like that? She'd had to do it. There'd been no other spare bed. Serve them right, anyway. If they were ladies, they'd put up with it gracefully. She drifted off into a sleep that was lurid with nightmare dreams.

Mrs. Medford Barstow, who would have resisted indignantly any doubt that she was a lady to her fingertips, was knocking softly and insistently on the door of Miss Onslow's room. It was some time before there was any response, but when at last Judith opened the door she spoke before Mrs. Barstow could so much as utter a word, and her voice was vibrant with quiet fury.

"If you cannot sleep, will you be good enough to find quarters somewhere else? I work hard, and I'm badly in need of rest."

Mrs. Barstow backed up a step and raised her chin. "Please! I realize that you need your rest, and of course I apologize for rousing you. But I cannot sleep, and I wish to talk to you. Won't you at least have one cigarette with me?"

"I can't have a cigarette with you," Judith said coldly. "I need sleep, and I intend to get it. If you have anything to say, say it, and let me get back to bed."

"As you wish." Mrs. Barstow touched a plain, clean handkerchief to the tip of her cold nose. "I merely wanted to warn you that my brother changes his girlfriends every few months with amazing regularity. I'm quite convinced by this time that he will never marry, and if you will heed my words, you will save yourself a lot of worry and pain."

Judith removed a foot from one of her slippers, wriggled the toes impatiently, and replaced it. "Thanks so much," she said indifferently. "Remind me to terminate the engagement the first thing in the morning, without fail. Good night, and kindly don't wake me up again."

She closed the door firmly, locked it, and went back to bed, but it was some time before she could get to sleep. She kept thinking of things she could have said to Mrs. Barstow that would surely have ruined her aplomb.

Mrs. Barstow had a cigarette by herself. She decided that she had failed in what she had set out to do, and she was miserable. If Bob married that woman, it would make her look so silly. And he'd look silly too. She must tell him that. Men always hated to look absurd in any way.

She crushed out her cigarette and began to pace the room. Why hadn't she gone through with the divorce that time? She'd have to do it now, anyway. And, by this time, Bob was getting soft and sentimental

about brazen girls being named as corespondents. The whole thing was
stupid and annoying. It would be nice to go to Reno, though. That
would be fun. Maybe she'd come back married to someone else. Well,
it was something to look forward to. But it would all be so much
pleasanter if first she could stop Bob from marrying that girl. She lay
down on the bed and began to think of what clothes she ought to take to
Reno. She'd have to have some new things.

Toward morning Knotty was awakened violently by a cramp in his
leg. He'd been sleeping in a chair, not much, of course, just a nap.
Because this was murder, and it had to be solved before the day was
out. All the others had simply stretched out on their fat backs and gone
to bed when they felt like it. He ought really to have made them stay
up. He'd been working, hadn't he? But every time he wanted to ask
someone a question, they'd gone to bed. Served them right if he'd gone
in and yanked them off their lousy, soft pillows.

He got up and stretched. He'd have something to say to his wife
when he got home about how hard he worked. Let her try sleeping on a
chair sometime. He would have demanded a bed here, except that he
didn't want them to know that he'd be sleeping at all.

Well, he must trap that Mary Gore dame when she came in. She
ought to know a few things. His face burned a little as he remembered
Willie's reception to the news that he was not Dr. Smith's son. Willie
had opened up his mouth and really distinguished himself. In fact, he
had used some impressive words that Knotty had never heard before.
All in all, he was beginning to behave like the head of the place, and
who would have thought that he had it in him? Of course, he'd have to
put on an act like that even if he knew the story, and knew it to be true.
But there was no proof, or anything, only Miss Ewell's word. And that
wasn't enough by itself. That Vera dame, the daughter, had opened up
her yap and howled that such a story was preposterous. And after bawl-
ing him out for even mentioning it, she had the crust to end up by
wondering out loud whether there *could* be anything to it. Willie wasn't
much like any of the family, really, and so on. But she sure did raise a
stink about the idea that the West woman might be her twin sister.
Absolutely impossible stupid nonsense. Mrs. West was a coarse, vulgar woman, and born that way. After which she said she had to go to
bed and get her sleep. The hospital had to go on, he should know that.
Well, he did know it. The lousy hospital had to go on, and they all had
to get a good night's sleep. Sure. All but Knotty. It didn't matter whether
he ever slept again or not.

He walked out to the hall and sourly regarded Betty, who was sleeping peacefully in her straight chair. He wondered enviously how she did it, and then yawned prodigiously and went out to the kitchen to get some coffee and something to eat.

He ate a large breakfast and left the mess lying around the kitchen, because, after all, he wasn't at home, and it was only at home that anybody expected a man to clean up after himself.

He looked at his watch and saw that it was only half-past six; the Gore woman wasn't due until about seven. Betty had said that she turned up at different times and went off at different times, but she could be more or less expected around seven.

He returned to the front hall and caught a glimpse of Miss Ewell going up the stairs, attired once more in her nurse's uniform. Betty was awake, and he asked, with a jerk of his head toward Miss Ewell, "Where's she going so early in the morning?"

"Oh"—Betty yawned—"she always runs upstairs, first thing, to snoop at everybody and see they get up on time. I guess she gets up about five o'clock, or something. She cleans her room and takes a bath first, and still she gets out here at the crack of dawn."

Mary Gore walked into the hall, and Knotty approached her and laid a firm hand on her arm. He led her to Miss Ewell's office, seated her, and then asked directly, "Did you know that Dr. Willie was not Dr. Smith's son?"

Mary unbuttoned the collar of her coat and leaned back. "Oh, sure," she said easily, "old Dr. Charlie told me. I said I didn't believe him, but he insisted it was so."

Chapter 29

Mary got up to go, but Knotty urged her back into her chair. "Wait a minute, Mrs. Gore. Who else knows about all this?"

"Nobody but me, I guess, and I wouldn't tell. He told me not to."

"When did he tell you the story?" Knotty asked.

"W-e-ll, now let's see." Mary frowned thoughtfully at the wallpaper. "When exactly was it? Two weeks ago, maybe, on a Tuesday, or was it Wednesday? Yes, I guess Wednesday. Only, it might have been three weeks ago—Yes, I think it was three weeks ago. But, on the other hand—"

"It was just lately, anyway," Knotty said impatiently.

"Oh yes. Tuesday or Wednesday, two or three weeks ago. Was I ever surprised! But, see, Charlie had got sort of queer in the head, so I didn't really believe him."

"Did you tell him that?"

"Sure, and he got mad as blazes. He said it wasn't right, and people ought to know about it, and that's why he told me. I told him I believed it then. Just to keep him quiet, see?"

"Do you believe it now?" Knotty demanded.

"Well, maybe I do. See, everybody is talking about this Mrs. West, and how she was trying to dress up to look like Vera. Nora was talking about it. Nora says she was trying to look like her twin sister, and that she does look like her too. So I thought about what Charlie said, and it seemed like maybe he was right. I remember Mrs. Smith when she was pregnant. And was she ever a size! She sure did look like twins, or even more. I was just married then—my son is younger—and now he's married already, with two children. It don't seem possible, somehow. Well, of course, he married young. Some wedding too! Everybody was there. Did you get to his wedding, Mr. Knotty? You sure missed something if you didn't."

"I missed something," Knotty said through his teeth. "Don't you think Charlie told someone besides you that Dr. Willie was not Dr. Smith's son?"

Mary shook her head. "I don't think so. See, people always tell me their troubles, and all sorts of things. That's why Charlie came to me when he wanted to open up. He might have told Miss Ewell, maybe, but nobody else. At least, I don't think so. Poor Charlie, he wouldn't be dead now if only they'd let me get to him. I raised him up from the dead once, you know."

"No kidding?" Knotty said, and began to chew on a toothpick.

"Certainly, I did."

"How'd you do that?"

"Well, we found him lying down in the morgue, Miss Ewell and me. She took a look at him and said he probably had a shock. She was all upset. She didn't want him to die, so I told her he didn't have to. Only she'd have to do what I said. She was agreeable, and I lifted him up. It was early in the morning, like now, and nobody was around except Betty, and she was asleep. Anyways, we brought him up in the elevator, and when we got to the main floor she said not to take him to his room where the nurses could interfere with him, but to bring him to her room where we could look after him without anyone bothering us. So that's what we did. We had to sort of sneak around Betty so that she wouldn't wake up and see us, because Dr. Smith never would let me try to work out my system on anybody. But we had Charlie all day in Miss Ewell's room, and the next day she came and told me that he had just got up off the bed and walked away."

"Chrissake!" Knotty said absently.

"Yes. He walked away, and then he must have fallen in that elevator shaft and died again. But I could have—"

"You mean he was really dead when you brought him back to life?"

"Certainly he was dead. Look, I'm needed at the switchboard. I got to go."

Knotty suffered her to depart, and Mary went off in a bit of a hurry. She wasn't really due to relieve Betty just yet, but that Knotty was entirely too nosy, and he made her uneasy. She walked past Betty and immediately met up with Miss Ewell, to whom she aired her grievance.

"That man Knotty, Miss Ewell, he's been asking me all kinds of questions, and it kind of scares me. I don't like it."

But Miss Ewell merely gave her a vague look and went her way without a word of consolation. She no longer cared who upset Mary Gore, or anyone else, for that matter. It was unimportant what happened now. She went on to her room and took Dr. Smith's wallet from her drawer. She had torn up the love letters, and Knotty might as well have what remained. It was his right.

She met him in the hall, and extended the wallet in her small, claw-like hand.

"I found this in the drawer of my bureau. I don't know how it came to be there."

Knotty took the wallet eagerly, and she told him what was in it, but she did not mention the love letters. He'd be furious if he knew that she'd removed anything, but it didn't matter anyway. Nothing mattered very much. He was still studying the various papers intently when she moved away quietly. He did not need her, really, and she had things to do.

Knotty put the wallet in his pocket as Willie came down the stairs. Willie's chin was up, and he had a defiant look on his face. He greeted Knotty with a faint sneer.

"Have you found out whose son I am?"

"Sure thing," Knotty agreed complacently. "I've found another witness too. This here Mrs. Gore knows all about it. She got it from old Dr. Charlie."

Willie stopped; his hand tightened on the banister, and his face went gray. Knotty, however, had raised his eyes to Dr. Medford and Mrs. Barstow, who were descending the stairs behind Willie's frozen figure. They were talking and laughing together, and Knotty was conscious of a feeling of offended decency. This wasn't old home week, it was a murder case.

Les came in the front door at the same time and immediately made himself charming to Mrs. Barstow. He took her into breakfast on his arm, and Judith, who had appeared in time to see it, curled her lip slightly and raised an eyebrow.

Dr. Medford was looking at Willie and wondering what was the matter with him now. His thoughts were interrupted by Judith, who said coolly, "Your sister woke me in the middle of the night to tell me that you are entirely worthless, so you may consider our engagement at an end. I want to get caught up on my work today, and I'll make out better if I'm free of all entanglements."

Dr. Medford laughed without venom. "You make the announcement then. I do dislike wasting my breath."

Willie said quietly, "Have you heard that they say I'm not really a Smith?"

"You're a Smith," Knotty corrected him amiably, "but not the Smith you thought you were."

"Where's Mary?" Betty asked from the switchboard. "I want to get home early."

Knotty turned on her. "You're not to repeat anything you heard around here, my girl. Hear me?"

"Yes, Uncle Jacob."

Knotty snapped his fingers. "That was it. Jake. Jake Smith was your father, Dr. Willie."

"What's all this?" Dr. Medford asked in a bewildered voice.

Dr. Willie stammered, with his sick eyes on the floor, and Knotty came to the rescue with a flourishing explanation.

"Who told you this nonsense?" Dr. Medford demanded.

Knotty smiled happily. "Miss Ewell. And that Mrs. Gore backs her up. Seems old Dr. Charlie knew it, too, and told her."

Shirley came down the stairs and gave Knotty a little nod. "So somebody gave you the right dope at last, brother. I've known it a long time. I'm Vera's twin sister, Gawd help me, and Willie really belongs to my pa and ma. They're nice folks, Willie boy, even if the old man gets drunk week ends and holidays. Anyways, they're not mean, like old Doc Smith was. And you can stop worrying, kid, because I'm gonna put you at the head of this hospital."

Willie threw up his hands as though in utter despair, and disappeared promptly. Knotty made off after him. Shirley grinned, and said to no one in particular, "The poor nut. Geez, I'm starved. Let's go and put on the feed bag."

She went into the dining room, followed more sedately by Judith and Dr. Medford. When she saw Les, she let out a yell.

"Why, you old s.o.b.—always rushin' the newest dame!"

Mrs. Barstow colored delicately, and Les muttered, "Try not to be yourself for a while."

Judith sat down at the table and said directly to Mrs. Barstow, "I'm sure you'll be glad to hear that the engagement between your brother and myself has been terminated by mutual consent."

Shirley let out another yell. "You mean old Stuffy is free again?"

Les gave Judith a slow smile. "So here we are, back where we started."

Mrs. Barstow patted her bosom. "I'm very glad to hear it, I'm sure. I feel convinced that neither of you will regret it."

"Shut up, Elizabeth," Dr. Medford said mildly. "How can you, or anyone, predict what will be regretted, or what won't? We're all groping blindly."

Miss Ewell came into the dining room in the ensuing silence. She sat down quietly, pushed food away from her but drank coffee feverishly. She had just come from her room, where she had gone to get a package of cough drops. Her throat was scratchy, but she hadn't been able to find the cough drops. She had found, instead, Dr. Smith's gold watch, right in her dresser drawer.

Chapter 30

First the wallet, and now his gold watch. She'd have to search the room and see if there were other things, and she'd have to put the watch somewhere. They'd miss it, because he had always worn it. She couldn't give it to Knotty, though. How could she? He'd think it was queer and suspicious. No. She'd watch for an opportunity, and put it in his room.

"Where's Dr. Burrell?" Dr. Medford asked.

Miss Ewell brought her thoughts back to the table with a painful little wrench and replied quietly, "He should be down. I woke him."

Dr. Burrell was down, but he was pacing the floor in the front hall. Betty had made several attempts to start a conversation with him, but he gave her only abstracted but polite grunts. He was a polite young man.

Knotty appeared and gave him a sour look, but he ignored it, and approached eagerly.

"Look, I understand that those two women are supposed to be twins, identical twins, and that Dr. Willie really belongs to the family from which Mrs. West comes."

"Where in *hell*," Knotty demanded, "did *you* hear all this?"

Dr. Burrell brushed it aside impatiently. "You can't keep a thing like that from the nurses. They're full of it."

"Gossiping dames!" Knotty said disgustedly. "This thing ain't proved yet. Sure, they're supposed to be what they call identical twins, but if them two dames is identical in any way, I'd like to know what it is."

"But you must allow for the difference in environment," Dr. Burrell said intensely. "One was allowed to develop, but the other, probably the weaker twin, was repressed by her father. I understand that Dr. Smith was somewhat of a martinet. If you will give me a little time, I shall observe the two of them, and I can tell you whether the thing is possible or not. Are there any other developments?"

"No." Knotty turned on his heel and made off. If there was one thing he couldn't stand, it was one of these officious kids who thought he knew it all. So cocky and sure of himself! He should have a job like Knotty's.

He waited until Dr. Burrell had gone into breakfast, and then he came into the front hall again and headed for the door. He had plenty to do today.

Betty called to him to wait for her. She'd be off in a minute or so, and he could give her a lift into town.

Knotty was infuriated. He said, "Listen, girl, d'ya think a murder case can wait while a young snip picks up a ride to town? What's the matter with you, anyways?"

Betty dropped her eyes with proper humility, while Knotty left in a hurry. She raised them only when Dr. Willie descended the stairs and approached the desk.

"Where's Knotty?"

"He just left, Dr. Willie, but I don't know where. He was in kind of a temper."

Willie turned away and went on to the dining room. His stomach seemed to be moving around in his interior, and he felt that some food might be able to anchor it.

He discovered that they were discussing him, and the possibility that he was the wrong Smith. Vera was not there, so that Shirley was able to express her ideas without interruption.

"Can you imagine dear old Vera and me bein' twins? She sure got whatever was missin', the poor kid."

"Identical twins," Les murmured.

"Sure." Shirley nodded at him. "Whatever that means."

"How can they be twins, Bob?" Les asked curiously. "I thought that twins, identical twins, anyway, had to be very much alike."

Dr. Medford nodded, and Dr. Burrell said eagerly, "Wait a moment. May I say something?"

Everyone looked at him silently, and he swallowed a piece of egg and mopped his mouth. "Identical twins *can* be different. I mean, it can be a matter of environment and parental influence. Parents always have a favorite in their children, you see. And so we have to look for characteristics—"

"They are both very determined," Miss Ewell observed to no one in particular. She hid her face behind her coffee cup, while Dr. Medford and Les agreed that they were both very determined.

Mrs. Barstow said, "Absurd! They are completely different in every way."

Nora, who had come in with fresh coffee, banged the pot on the table and declared, "They got the same color hair and eyes."

Mrs. Barstow did not answer her directly, but informed the table, "Many people have brown eyes and hair. It is very common." She touched her own reddish hair with a long white hand.

"It's our own natural shade, see?" Shirley explained. "We got no gray yet, so we don't have to cover up with henna. When you're young, you don't need to rinse, unless you want to be a vulgar blonde. But you've forgotten all that, maybe."

"My hair has always had a reddish cast," Mrs. Barstow said frigidly. "*Must* you be so abominably rude?"

"Relax, sister," Shirley said comfortably. "They done a good job on your hair, anyways, although I guess they charged you plenty for it."

Judith said, "One of them is left-handed, and the other right-handed."

Dr. Burrell sprang up from his chair, looking excited, and ran around to examine the top of Shirley's head.

She squirmed, and muttered, "I feel like a moth with a pin through my middle. Listen, why don't you ast me what you want to know, instead of pickin' around on my dome like a monkey lookin' for fleas?"

"Why should you complain?" Dr. Willie asked bitterly. "They are trying to prove that you belong here, which means that I am out and that you will inherit."

Dr. Medford put a match to a cigarette, and squinted through the smoke. "I presume the old man left a will. Chances are he provided for you, Willie."

Miss Ewell straightened her small body and said severely, "How can you be so callous, all of you, with the poor man not yet cold in his grave?"

"What difference does it make, in God's name," Willie demanded harshly, "how long it takes him to cool? He never liked me, and didn't mind showing it. And I never liked him either. Do you expect me to grieve because he's dead?"

His voice began to rise, and Dr. Medford said quickly, "All right, Willie, but suppose we let peace be with the dead. At the worst, Shirley has said that you are to be head of this hospital. So you won't be out of a job."

Les laughed, and Mrs. Barstow contributed a cultured giggle, but when they found that their amusement was isolated, they subsided.

Judith murmured an excuse and departed, and Miss Ewell followed close on her heels and went straight to her own room.

The gold watch was still in her drawer, and she lifted it out with shaking fingers. She must get rid of it, the sooner the better, and surely no one would be around just now. She went quietly to the Smith suite, and to Dr. Smith's room, and had a moment of panic when she discovered that the door was securely locked.

"May I ask what it is you think you want in my dead father's room?" Vera's voice asked from behind her.

Miss Ewell swung around with her chin up. She said gamely, "Be good enough to keep a civil tongue in your head, miss."

Vera was surprised into silence. She had supposed that Miss Ewell would cringe, now that Father was no longer around to back her up. Yet here she was, being as obnoxious as ever. It was all wrong, and Miss Ewell would have to learn that things were going to be different. She braced herself to express this view and saw the small, straight back disappearing out of the door before she could utter a word.

Miss Ewell returned to her room and put the watch away again. She searched the room carefully, but could find nothing else that belonged to Dr. Smith.

How could these things have come into her room? Well, before she started locking the door. Only she'd been locking it before he had died. Not all the time, perhaps. For instance, it wasn't locked right after he was strangled. It was open then.

She gave a little shudder. She'd have to go out. She hurried through the door, locked it after her, and dropped the key into her pocket.

In the front hall she found Judith talking to Betty Robinson, who was attired in hat and coat and apparently ready to leave. Shirley was at the switchboard.

Judith turned to Miss Ewell. "I'll have to get hold of that policeman. Several of the patients on this floor are complaining that someone came into their rooms last night."

Miss Ewell frowned, and muttered, "Nonsense."

"It seems," Judith added, "that the intruder was wearing a long cape, the sort of thing under which sinister characters hide daggers."

Chapter 31

Miss Ewell felt her lower lip trembling, and caught it between her teeth. It could not have been Charlie. Charlie was dead. He had roamed around a lot, she knew, and people had complained, but that was all over now. Only someone else was roaming around. Who could it be?

Betty turned to go, and Shirley called after her, "Don't forget about that girl for the day switchboard, pal. Send her up right away, huh?"

Betty nodded. "I'll phone her as soon as I get home. I'm pretty sure she'll come."

Miss Ewell released her lower lip, and gave Shirley a severe look. "Young woman, don't you think you're being a bit officious?"

"Nah." Shirley gave the base of the switchboard an idle kick. "How you think it would look around here, one of the owners of the joint wearin' out her pants sittin' at a switchboard all day?"

"It will be quite comparable," Miss Ewell said primly, "to the sound of this same owner's voice. You must surely be aware that your grammar and diction are appalling, and that your manners leave a good deal to be desired, as well." She touched a spotless handkerchief to her little nose, and walked briskly away.

Judith looked after her, laughing, and Shirley said ruefully, "The old bag ain't all wrong, at that. I guess I gotta learn to talk refined. It would make better business for the hospital. Say! You help me, huh? When I talk wrong you jump on my neck, every time."

"Well—" Judith shrugged. "All right, I'll help. But you must remember that it's a very irritating thing to be corrected all the time. And if you start snapping back at me, I'm going to stop, then and there."

"O.K.," Shirley said cheerfully. "I'll be good."

Mary Gore summoned Judith, and led her down the hall. "It's that Mr. Lister, Miss Onslow. He's carrying on like crazy. He wants to see you. Maybe you can shut him up. I can't do a thing with him."

Eva was in Mr. Lister's room, and Judith thought that she should never have put Eva and Mary on the same floor. She ought to have one of the younger and more cheerful girls around. But it had worked so well to have those other two upstairs. Down here they were chronic cases, some incurables.

Mr. Lister greeted her with enthusiasm and yelled, "Send those two old washerwomen out of the room. I want to speak to you alone. It's serious. Now get 'em out."

Judith got them out, but not before Mary explained, with great dignity, that she had never taken in washing in her life. She was a professional woman, a nurse. She had always been a nurse.

Judith winked at her, smiled, and shut them both outside, and Mr. Lister gave a loud sigh of relief. "Damned old biddies," he muttered. "Next thing they'll be coming in here with talcum powder and a three-cornered garment for me. You'd think I was in my dotage."

"What's your trouble?" Judith asked, grinning at him.

"It's about that thief who came into my room last night. I was awake, so that he didn't get off with anything. But I wanted to tell you about him. He was a short fellow. I didn't tell you how short he was. In fact, he was *very* short."

"That's a big help," Judith said seriously. "Knowing that he's unusually short should make it a lot easier to catch him. In any case, we're going to have people all over the place tonight, so I'm sure that you won't be bothered again."

Mr. Lister nodded and relaxed back onto his pillows. "You're a girl with a bit of sense to you," he murmured drowsily. "Can't understand why some bright young fellow hasn't snapped you up. No enterprise in the boys these days."

Judith went out quietly and sought Eva at the desk. She asked, "Are you having any trouble with the others?"

"We had plenty of trouble with them, Miss Onslow, but by now they're mostly asleep. I don't know how they found out that Dr. Smith was murdered, but most of them seem to know it. And then to have this intruder with the cape creeping into their rooms— Well, it's no wonder they're excited and upset."

Dr. Burrell came down the hall, and Judith went to him and told him about the disturbance. She ended up by explaining, "Most of them are catching up on their sleep now, and I think it would be better not to disturb them."

"How many of them saw this intruder?" Dr. Burrell asked.

"I expect that three of them actually did see him," Judith replied. "There's a fourth who thinks she did, but I believe it's only her imagination."

Dr. Burrell took a small notebook from an inside pocket and carefully wrote something down.

Judith left him to it, and went out to the switchboard to ask Shirley whether Knotty had returned.

Shirley shook her head. "Nah, he's probably in a poker game."

"No."

"No, what?"

"Just no," said Judith. "Not nah."

"Oh," said Shirley. "No, no, no, tiddy, no."

Dr. Medford approached, and asked Judith to accompany him to his office. He ushered her in, seated her, and offered her a cigarette.

Judith took a puff, and murmured, "I hope your sister didn't see me coming in here; she'd be very upset."

"Oh, cut it out, will you?" Dr. Medford said impatiently. "I want to talk business. Matter of fact, it's about Miss Ewell. Dr. Burrell thinks she's gone a bit off."

"You mean in the head?"

"If you want to put it that way, yes. I haven't noticed anything in particular myself. She's always been busy running around in under-cover doings, and I can't see any change. But just in case he's right, keep an eye out for her."

"Do you want me to follow her around?" Judith asked.

"No, I realize that you haven't the time. But keep your eyes peeled when you do see her."

"All right. Lynx-eye Onslow. Have you bought that house yet?"

"I'm going to phone him this morning."

She nodded. "Good. I think you'll find that it will work out very well."

"Perhaps. I don't know why I listen to you. I still think it's too much like a house, not enough of an office—"

Judith tapped ash from her cigarette, and said, "It's near the bus stop, it looks affluent, and it's a bargain. You can settle down there without any idea of moving again. And you can have your office right in the house, which will save you a lot of trouble."

"It's hard on the family though."

"What family?"

Dr. Medford's gaze strayed to the ceiling, and he said, "My future family. I don't intend to remain an old maid all my life."

"Really?" Judith smiled, and then brushed it off her face. "Your sister told me most positively that you would never marry. She said you were a philanderer and would continue to philander. She's your sister, and she ought to know."

"Yes, of course. I've been so busy looking after her escapades that I've had no time for my own life. But things are going to be different."

Judith nodded. "So you see, I was right about that house. It will be nice with your sister, her children, and your own wife and children—quite a merry household."

"Ah, shut up," said Dr. Medford, "and get out. And keep your eye on Angie."

Judith sauntered out to the hall, where Shirley still sat at the switchboard. She was filing her nails, and she looked up and yelled, "C'mere."

"Come here," Judith said clearly.

"No, you c'mere. You know I can't leave this gadget. I'll beat that Betty's brains out if she don't get a dame up here soon."

Judith approached the desk and asked, "What is it?"

"You'll love this. I just had a scrap with that dusty old skeleton, Vera. She come out here—"

"Came."

"Huh? Oh, came. Sure. Anyways, she opens up and wants to know what I think I am, see?"

"I do see, but you don't need to check on it every few minutes."

"I gotta leave out 'see'?"

"Every one of them."

"O.K. Well, she ast how I thought I'd get away with all this, so I ast her what's her worry. Willie's the guy who ought to be chewin' his nails. She has a fit, and swears she's goin' off to see her lawyer, when I sez, 'Lookit—'"

"There's no such word."

"Lemme tell ya the story," Shirley moaned.

Judith sighed. "All right. Go on."

"I sez, 'What's eatin' you, sister? Now you know Willie's no relation you can have him for a husband. You can get him, all right, anybody could. And it so happens I don't want him myself.' Well, gee-zus! Did she ever tell me what I am, and they don't come no lower. I should be ashamed to mention such a thought, and I was a low bum for havin' such a thought in the first place. But, anyways, she didn't rush out to get her lawyer yet. She changed her mind because I did a little mentioning."

Judith laughed. "Don't be silly. She probably has him on the phone right now."

"Hold it," Shirley murmured. "We got company."

Vera had come into the hall, and she walked straight to the switchboard with a set face.

"I have been talking to my lawyer on the phone, and he has confirmed the whole frightful story. Father left him a letter to be opened after his death, and it's all in there. You are my sister, Mrs. West, and Willie is not related to us. But Father left everything, the hospital, in equal shares to the three of us."

Chapter 32

Vera turned and walked stiffly away, and Shirley let out a yell.

"Hear that? I'm rich! Geez, I'm *rich!*"

"Hush!" Judith said quickly. "In the first place, you must stop saying 'Geez', and in the second place, you're not as rich as you think. Remember, you have to share with the other two, and even a private place like this doesn't make too much. Sometimes it's hard to keep it out of the red."

"Never you mind, hon. There'll be enough." Shirley stretched her arms above her head and grinned happily at the ceiling.

Knotty walked into the hall and glared at her. He asked Judith, "What's she clowning about?"

Judith explained, and went on to tell him about the caped intruder of the night before.

He stopped her with an impatient gesture. "Wait a minute, wait a minute. One thing at a time. If Dr. Willie gets his share of the gravy, why did he hit her over the head?"

Shirley dropped her arms and stared at him, and Judith asked, "Do you mean that you think Dr. Willie killed his father?"

Knotty gave her a rather abstracted eye. "I've just come from that lawyer, and I got all the dope about the letter. It's been there for years. I guess Doc felt bad about his kid, which he should of, and he figgered to fix her up after he died. Dr. Willie must of known. That's it, he found out. And he figgered this girl would get him pushed out, so he tried to scare her away. Where is he?"

Dr. Burrell had quietly added himself to the group, and he said, "Beg pardon, Mr. Knotty. Dr. Willie is in the morgue with Dr. Medford. But the point I wish to make is this: If you are under the mistaken impression that Dr. Willie has committed murder, I should like to correct you."

Knotty put a cigar into his mouth and chewed savagely. "Go ahead," he muttered, "correct me."

Dr. Burrell cleared his throat. "You must realize that I have made a study of these matters, and I can assure you, positively, that Dr. Willie is constitutionally incapable of committing murder."

Knotty said, "Do tell," without bothering to remove his cigar.

"Yes. I shall avoid the technical terms, since you couldn't be expected to understand them, but Dr. Willie's activities are almost entirely mental. The physical act of strangling his father would be quite impossible to him. In fact, Dr. Willie is out."

"Sure is," Knotty agreed. "Out to the courthouse."

He headed for the morgue without a second glance at Dr. Burrell, but he was uneasy. The trouble was, he thought unhappily, that he had no real proof; nothing that would stand up in court. Maybe, if he was smart, he could get a confession out of Willie. How could it be anyone else? Willie was the one who had been kicked around, and he sure had had a reason to smack that dame on the head.

In the morgue he found Dr. Medford and Dr. Willie sitting talking to each other. Doctors had it easy. They should have his job, once.

"Dr. Smith, would you mind coming down to the courthouse with me?"

"Why should he?" Dr. Medford demanded.

Knotty bristled. "I want him there for questioning, that's why. And you can kindly go about your own business, Medford."

"Keep your shirt on," Willie said, standing up. "I'll go. Why not?"

They went upstairs, followed by Dr. Medford, and in the front hall Shirley greeted Willie with loud cries of joy.

"Have you heard the dirt, Willie boy? We divvy this joint three—"

"Quiet!" Knotty roared.

Willie stopped short. "What? You mean we three—Where did you hear this?"

"Vera, the poor old skinny hen. she's my sister and none of your own, Willie boy. Look, we'll run the dump with a view to makin' a lot of money. That suit you, hon?"

But Willie had been forced out through the front door by an outraged Knotty.

Dr. Medford stood looking after them uneasily for a while. They were not taking Willie to the courthouse for nothing, that was certain. He turned back into the hall and asked Shirley, "What was that you were talking about?"

Shirley told him in brief and colorful language, and he said in a bothered fashion, "How can the lawyer give information like that over the phone at this time? Where's Judith?"

"She was tryin' to tell Knotty about this character who's been runnin' around with a cape, scarin' the pants offa the patients, but she had to go. Some dopey patient wouldn't use his potty, or something."

Dr. Medford departed, feeling somewhat annoyed. Caped intruders were probably imagination on the part of the patients. They knew about Dr. Smith, of course. You couldn't keep a thing like that quiet, and it was inevitable that they would build nightmares on top of it.

He found Judith and asked her irritably, "Why couldn't you have stopped this thing before it got out of control?"

"Are you trying to tell me my business? These people actually saw someone in their rooms. I've had separate descriptions from them, and they tally. I've told them that the intruder has been apprehended by the police, and I'm getting extra help on tonight so that the floor will be watched."

Dr. Medford swore quietly. "Damn this place! I can't wait until I get out of here."

"Well—"

But he put his hand firmly over her mouth. "Don't say it. I'm getting to be a bit afraid of your tongue. They've taken Willie off to the court-house, to question him, so they say."

Judith was held silent by a strong feeling of sympathy for Willie. Somehow, he was always the goat.

Dr. Medford looked down at his shoes and rattled the change in his pocket. "I don't suppose he'll get to Charlie's funeral. It's today, and there won't be many there."

"What about you?"

"I'll get there if I can. I suppose Vera will go, perhaps Les, and certainly Miss Ewell and Mrs. Gore."

"All right, I'll have to arrange to do without Mary."

As it turned out, there were more people at Charlie's funeral than Dr. Medford had anticipated. There was a fairly large group from the town, and some older people from the rural districts. Les appeared, wearing a black tie and escorting Mrs. Barstow upon his arm, which infuriated Dr. Medford. He got close enough to her to mutter out of the corner of his mouth, "I hope you're enjoying your date, and the obsequies."

She colored faintly and ignored him.

Lunch was delayed an hour, on Vera's instructions, until they all got back. Shirley was annoyed and kept telling anyone who passed that if she could only leave the switchboard, she'd go and make a better arrangement. But until Mary came back, there was no one to relieve her.

When Mary did at last return, she was immediately pinned down into Shirley's seat and told to stay there. Over her protests, Shirley announced, "I'm one of the owners here, see? I'm tellin' you to look after the switchboard. You can feed your face when I'm through feedin' mine."

"One of the owners?" Mary asked, her eyes alive with interest.

"Sure. I'm Vera's twin sister. They made her outa the scraps that was left over when they got through makin' me."

Shirley went off to the dining room, where she was a bit annoyed to find Les and Mrs. Barstow talking and laughing most intimately together. Vera was sitting at the end of the table as usual, but her face was so forbidding that Shirley made for the head of the table where Miss Ewell usually sat.

"You are taking Miss Ewell's place," Vera said sharply.

"Yeah, but I thought I'd save her the trouble of servin' the grub like she always does. She's gettin' old and needs a rest. And anyways, this place oughta be mine."

Miss Ewell and Dr. Medford came in, and Miss Ewell displaced Shirley without so much as raising her voice.

"You have my chair, young woman. Kindly return to your own place at once. You have a few things to learn before you can possibly take over the duties of the head of the table."

Shirley retired to her old place with only a murmured, "Gee-*zus!*"

Vera asked, with a shrill note of hysteria in her voice, "What are they doing to Willie?"

"Questioning him," Dr. Medford said flatly.

"Poor Charlie!" Vera sighed.

Shirley glanced at her. "Poor Willie, you mean."

"I meant poor Charlie," Vera snapped, "and I was not talking to you, in any case."

Shirley spread the five fingers of her right hand, but refrained from touching the thumb to her nose. She said cheerfully, "Hey! Where's Judy?"

Dr. Burrell came in and went over to speak in low tones to Dr. Medford, but since everybody ceased operations to listen, they all heard his words quite clearly.

"I should like you to come with me for a few moments, Doctor. I have something to show you."

Dr. Medford frowned, swallowed, and said civilly enough, "Very well, directly after lunch."

"I, er, think it had better be now."

"Sit down and have your lunch," Dr. Medford said crossly. "Surely whatever it is can wait until we've finished here."

Dr. Burrell sat down in Judith's place and received a plate of food which obviously did not interest him.

Miss Ewell was eating her lunch with her little finger stuck out as usual, but she realized that her appetite was not the same. Nothing was the same. What did the Burrell man want to show Bob, anyway? Had he somehow got into her room? But how could he, when it was locked?

Les stood up and said, "Well, off to business. I'll drop in on poor old Lister first though. I saw him this morning, and he's all upset. I'll give him a cigar. All right, Bob?"

Dr. Medford shrugged. "It'll do him good as long as he thinks he's smoking it against orders."

"You didn't kiss us girls good-by," Shirley yelled.

Les laughed at her, and said, "Later. Look, Bob, I'll run Judith in to lunch. I know you can't eat until she gets here."

Mrs. Barstow frowned. "Really, Bob—"

"You'll get your ticket to Reno this afternoon," Dr. Medford told her, "and you can take off immediately."

"But, my dear, I've only just arrived. I've hardly seen you. After all, I came only to see you. One would think—"

"You'd have seen more of me if you hadn't been so involved with Les and a completely strange funeral," Dr. Medford retorted.

"I must admit that I was a little surprised to see you there," Vera contributed acidly.

"Don't let 'em get your goat, sister," Shirley observed. "If I'd known you was goin', I'da gone too."

Miss Ewell had her eyes on Dr. Burrell, who seemed to be studying them all intently. He made her uneasy, and she presently slipped away from the table and hurried to her room. But it was all right. The door was still locked. Only she'd have to get that watch back to his rooms now. She could leave it on a table in the sitting room. That part was all right, but what should she do about the other!

She went to her closet to look at it again. There it was, her old blue nurse's cape with the red lining. The girls didn't seem to wear them these days. But someone had worn this, and recently. It was soiled with fresh mud.

Chapter 33

A voice, directly at her elbow, said, "Ah!" and Miss Ewell gave a little scream and would have fallen except for a firm arm around her waist. She looked up and saw that it was Dr. Burrell.

He steered her to a chair and then went to the closet for another look at the cape. He said "Ah!" again, with a pleased inflection.

Miss Ewell collected herself, and drew a long breath. "It must be sent to the cleaner," she declared, and added severely, "What are you doing here, young man?"

"Nothing in particular," Dr. Burrell told her pleasantly. "As a matter of fact, I'm merely trying to help."

"Then you had better go and help somewhere else. The patients, for instance."

"Oh, they're all right." Dr. Burrell dismissed the patients with a wave of his hand. "Do you ever have dizzy spells?"

Miss Ewell snapped, "When I want your professional advice I shall ask for it."

He reached into the closet and held up a fold of the soiled cape. "How did you get it so muddy?"

"I did not get it muddy. I am never careless with my clothes."

He turned around and looked at her. "You can't remember getting it muddy?"

"I did not get it muddy," Miss Ewell said quickly. "There is no question of remembering. I did not soil that cape."

"Well, who did you lend the cape to?"

Miss Ewell got a bit catty. She said, "I presume you mean, 'To whom did you lend the cape?' I am really surprised, and you a college man. I loaned the cape to no one. Someone has borrowed it, someone who is trying to frighten the patients, perhaps trying to ruin the hospital."

Dr. Burrell shook his head, and Miss Ewell was infuriated. "Why do you shake your head? What other explanation could there possibly be?"

"I was shaking my head at the idea of someone trying to ruin the hospital by scaring the patients," he explained, and made for the door.

Miss Ewell called after him, "You would do better to expend your energy on the job for which you were hired."

Dr. Burrell saw that she was tearing agitatedly at her handkerchief as he closed the door. He went through to the front hall. Mary Gore, who was sitting at the switchboard, called to him, "Doctor, doctor, please find Mrs. West for me. She must be through with her lunch by now, and I'm needed on the floor. We're shorthanded."

Dr. Burrell barely glanced at her, and he had no idea of what she was saying. Now, he thought, he had everything straight. That clod-hopper Knotty would have to be told. How could he get hold of him?

Knotty walked through the front door before the thought had left his mind. Mary saw him first, and she called, "Oh, Mr. Knotty, do please see if you can get someone to relieve me here."

Knotty glared at her. "That's something, isn't it? With all I got on my mind, I should get someone to relieve you at the switchboard. This dump is sure fallin' apart at the seams."

"Mr. Knotty—" Dr. Burrell said eagerly.

Dr. Medford walked into the hall, and observed, "Oh, there you are. What about Dr. Willie? Is there any news? His sister would like to know."

"He hasn't got a sister," Knotty said coldly. "That lawyer guy has it in a letter. One of these dusty old stupes who put their fingers together and look at you over their glasses. He didn't want to give with anything until the reading of the will. He never heard of murder. He just wasted my time. And that Dr. Willie Smith wasted more of it."

Dr. Medford shrugged. "You mean you couldn't break him down? That's simple enough, he isn't guilty."

"Who told you?" Knotty snarled. "And if he isn't guilty, who is?"

"How would I know?" Dr. Medford said carelessly. "That's your job. All I know is whether your tonsils ought to come out or not, and so on."

"Mr. Knotty," Dr. Burrell said intensely, "I have a theory. If you could spare me a little time, I should be glad to explain it to you."

"Sure." Knotty gave him an evil eye. "I suppose you know whether my tonsils ought to come out or not, and then some. I got no time to waste on theories."

"What have you got to lose?" Dr. Medford asked. "You might as well listen. You don't seem to have anything else to do."

"O.K., shoot," Knotty muttered. "I'm waiting. Give with your theory."

He stood still, staring at the wall in front of him, and Dr. Medford had a distinct impression that he had closed up his ears.

"Can't we be private?" Dr. Burrell suggested timidly.

"Nah!" Knotty transferred his gaze to the ceiling. "There's no one around. Mary here don't count. She's nuts."

"I'll thank you to be a bit more careful of your language, Mr. Knotty," Mary said spiritedly. "I have all my buttons, but you—" The switchboard buzzed angrily, and she was obliged to suspend her remarks while she attended to it.

"You see," Dr. Burrell murmured in a low voice, "Mr. Lister insisted that the intruder was short, very short. Now I should explain that insanity takes many forms, and there are people who appear to be perfectly normal. They have no idea themselves that there is anything wrong. They know that they get dizzy spells occasionally, nothing more. Now—"

"I take it all back," Knotty moaned. "Mary ain't nuts. He is."

"Thanks for nothing," Mary said tartly.

"Wait a minute." Dr. Medford made an impatient gesture. "Perhaps you haven't heard that several of the patients complained of an intruder in their rooms last night, someone wearing a cape."

"Miss Onslow was shootin' off her mouth," Knotty admitted, "but with everyone talkin' at once, or not talkin' at all, how can I get things straight? As for him"—he jerked a thumb at Dr. Burrell—"I don't understand a word he says, so what's the use wastin' time?" He walked off abruptly, looking furiously active.

Miss Ewell, who had been trying to listen down at the end of the hall, went quietly to the elevator, and dropped her soiled cape and the gold watch down into the shaft. She waited for a moment, and then returned to her room.

"Dizzy," she whispered. "But I'm not— I don't, not ever."

She began to cry quietly, the tears sliding over her cheeks. Her room had been locked all the time since yesterday. How could anyone have come in and taken her cape? And why was it encrusted with all that mud? Well, of course it had rained during the night, so someone must have worn it outside. It would be simple enough to get into the patients' rooms. Those on the first floor opened onto a terrace where the patients were seated in the sun, when they were well enough. But how had this person managed to get her cape?

Anyway, she wasn't dizzy. She never had spells like that. Sick, perhaps, with all this trouble. That Knotty would be coming to see her. He'd find the cape and the watch, and then he'd come and ask her questions.

It wasn't Knotty who came at last, but Dr. Burrell. He had the cape and the watch, and he said, "Look here, Miss Ewell."

She dried the tears on her cheeks. "Your manners are abominable, young man. You didn't even knock."

"There is no sense," he said earnestly, "in a gesture of this sort. After all, I saw the cape here. Don't be so foolish, and don't be frightened. Now, this watch. Do you know anything about it?"

"Certainly." She straightened her narrow shoulders. "I know a lot about it."

"It belonged to Dr. Smith, of course."

She did not reply, and he asked, "Do you know how it came to be in your room?"

"No."

Dr. Burrell seemed pleased. "That's what I thought." He turned abruptly and left the room, and she was alone again.

Well, it wasn't good to be alone when you had the blues. She'd go out and do something. She could hear that Mary Gore was still at the switchboard, and she turned back and went through to the kitchen.

Nora was sitting at the kitchen table reading a newspaper, and Miss

Ewell slid into a chair beside her. She asked mildly, "What does it say?"

"Never mind what it says," Nora replied discontentedly, "it's what it don't say. Never so much as a word about him bein' murdered in cold blood. They make out like it was an accident. That was some accident the poor old gentleman had, indeed. Now how in the name of mercy do they keep all the dirt out of the paper, I'm askin' you?"

"I don't know, but I'm glad." Miss Ewell got up restlessly and went to the Smith quarters.

She heard Vera singing as she approached, but the song was cut off sharply as she went in. She made her way to the bedroom and assumed an appropriately mournful expression.

Vera was almost civil. She said that her thoughts had been with her poor father all day, and having disposed of this conventional remark, she went on to discuss Shirley.

"You see, I just don't believe she's the one. I think she's an impostor. She's trying to take the place of my dead sister."

"Dead?"

"Well, of course. Shirley must have known that she had died, so she decided to step into her place. If she were alive, she'd take her own place."

"Absurd," said Miss Ewell. "If Shirley were a little thinner, we would not be able to tell you apart."

An ugly red burned on Vera's cheekbones. "How can you say such a thing? That—that creature, that slut. And you pretend that she looks like me. Her face, everything about her, is coarse and common and nasty."

Miss Ewell usually left when Vera went into a temper, and she did so now. She returned to her room and discovered that the cape and watch, which Dr. Burrell had brought back, had disappeared. The police had them then, and they'd be after her with their relentless questions soon. First Willie, and now herself.

She was tired, very tired, and there was a little time before dinner. She'd have a nap. She knew she could sleep now, only she didn't want to dream. She must not dream. She locked the door, and after a moment's hesitation went to a drawer and took out a ball of twine. She tied a length around the bedpost, and tied the other end carefully around her ankle. She stretched out on the bed and muttered, "Now, we'll see."

Chapter 34

Knotty was tired. He had questioned everybody in the place, and he had even listened to Dr. Burrell and his fool theory. He had Miss Ewell's cape and the gold watch. So what?

He stood in the front hall and mopped his damp brow. He had just been out to send that dumb jerk of a kid off to round up the men; they'd have to be stationed around the place tonight. That nurse dame was the only one who knew about it, Miss Onslow. Her idea, matter of fact. Only he would have thought of it himself without her telling him, but some dames always thought they had to rush in and tell a guy what to do. Like his wife. Anyway, this Onslow knew the layout and she could help him put the men in the right places. He hoped that prowler in the cape would come back again tonight. He'd catch him, and this lousy case would be over.

He'd tried to talk to Miss Ewell. He'd gone and rapped on her door, but she'd called out sharply that she was resting and that he was to leave her alone. So what could you do, outside of taking the door off its hinges and batting her over the head with it, which was what he'd felt like doing. He wondered whether it would be all right for him to get a drink. He needed one. Bad.

Shirley was back on the switchboard, and she said, "Say, are you deaf or something? I've spoke to you twice."

"Make it three times for luck," Knotty snarled.

"I ast you, have you got Dr. Willie locked up?"

"He is as free as a mountain goat, which he looks something like," Knotty said furiously. "I merely wanted to question him where I could have some peace and quiet. If you try to question anyone around this crazy dump, some jerk always horns in."

Shirley had already acquired some pride of ownership, and she was offended. "Waddya mean? We got a couple offices right on this floor, belong to our head doctor and our head nurse. Nice rooms too."

"Sure are," Knotty agreed. "Everybody uses them except the head doctor and the head nurse. Mary Gore's sittin' in one of them now, playin' solitaire."

"What!" Shirley shrieked. "And me sittin' here, one of the owners, workin' my ears off! Go get her and tell her—"

"Do your own housework, sister," Knotty said coldly. "I'm busy." He walked off purposefully in the direction of the Smith quarters.

Shirley rang the office of the head nurse and the office of the head doctor in quick succession, but there was no answer from either place. She fumed, with a picture in her mind of Mary ignoring all telephones while she devoted herself to solitaire. It became too much for her at last, and she left the switchboard and ran down the hall, but both offices were empty, so she hurried back again.

Judith was there, and she said directly, "You shouldn't leave this alone, Shirley."

"Yeah, I know. I was only gone a minute. I was tryin' to find that old pickle, Mary. She was supposed to come back."

"Now, look," Judith said firmly, "she'll be here at seven to relieve you, and no matter what you may think, we do need her. You'll just have to sit it out until we can get someone to replace you."

"O.K., pal. So I'm a bum, huh?"

"You must face facts."

"I'll beat that Betty's brains out when she comes in," Shirley muttered.

"Now, look, Shirley," Judith said reasonably, "you'll have to learn this business. Don't think that you can know it all at once. Whatever you may think of Vera, she still knows a lot more about running this place than you do. You have a lot to learn."

Dr. Medford came into the hall and asked, "Any news? Has Knotty figured it out yet?"

"Nothing," Shirley said dispiritedly. "How you expect that guy to figure anything out when he has a turnip where his head ought to be?"

"I believe Dr. Willie was released," Judith told him. "But I don't know where he is."

"Well, I wish he'd show up," Dr. Medford said fretfully. "That Burrell has his head so full of theories that he doesn't know what he's doing."

He went off upstairs, and Shirley said in a loud whisper, "Now here's where I could teach you something. You just let the guy walk off, and you could have him. You don't even swing your hips around when he's lookin' at you."

Dr. Medford heard this and took the trouble to come downstairs again. He said, "You are entirely wrong, lady. Haven't you ever heard of 'hard to get'?"

"Yeah, sure. But—"

"But nothing. As far as getting me is concerned, it's been easy. She already has me, wrapped up in brown paper and tied securely with string. I believe her next move is to throw the package in the wastepaper basket."

Judith murmured, "I wouldn't say that."

"Me either." Shirley nodded. "You're doing pretty good with your practice, and she's only a nurse. Any girl oughta be glad—"

"Shirley," said Judith, "you shouldn't bring that part of it into the open. We women are supposed to marry only for love, not to further ourselves financially."

"You girls talk it over," Dr. Medford suggested, moving away. "You can let me know later what you have decided."

Shirley giggled as he went up the stairs. "I guess he ain't so bad at that."

"Don't say 'ain't.'"

"O.K., pal. I know that much myself."

There was an immediate disturbance at the front door. It sounded as though several people were in trouble, but it turned out to be Willie alone, with a load of imbibed liquor. He waved a cheery arm and said gaily, "Hi there, girls. What's new?"

"You wanna cup of strong corfee," Shirley told him austerely.

"Take your coffee slops and dump them down the drain," Willie said with dignity. "What I need, and what I intend to have, is another drink. Been a long time, much too long. Another drink, ladies, and at once."

"Come on upstairs," Judith suggested. "It's time to dress for dinner. You can have more drinks when you come downstairs again."

Willie thought it over and decided that it was reasonable. He followed Judith upstairs, and Shirley looked after them with a knowing grin.

Judith took Willie to his room, ignoring his zigzag progress, and said, "You'll have time for a sleep before dinner."

"Whatza time?"

"Don't worry." She urged him toward his bed. "I'll wake you when it's time to get up."

He considered it for a moment, and then staggered to his bed and fell heavily. Judith gave a little sigh of relief and went along to her own rooms.

Mrs. Barstow was in the outer sitting room. She was stretched out on the couch, draped in a negligee, smoking a cigarette. Judith hesitated, and could feel a chill creeping over her face.

"Come in, do," Mrs. Barstow said. "I've nowhere else to go, or I wouldn't annoy you this way."

"Quite all right." Judith headed for the inner door. "Make yourself comfortable."

"Wait, please!" Mrs. Barstow raised herself from the couch. "Have a cigarette with me. We might as well learn to be friends, since we are to be sisters-in-law."

"I'm glad you told me. I hadn't heard."

"Oh—" Mrs. Barstow ran a troubled hand through her hair. "You mustn't mind me. It's just that I've been so upset. Please sit down. I must talk to someone. Bob will give me the devil, I know. I was supposed to go today, you see, but I don't want to. I haven't had any fun for so long. I'm getting used to you, now. But surely you can realize that it was difficult at first. Quite honestly, I'd like to be friends. As I said, I haven't had any fun for so long. I'd like to stay here for a while, just for a few days, and then I'll go on to Reno. But it's so exciting here."

Judith sat down and lit a cigarette. She was conscious of an odd feeling of pity. The woman was not frightened by murder. She found it exciting and pleasurable. And of course she was having fun with Les. It was probable that she had been unhappy and bored for a long time, and why not? Bill always running around with other women, while she was stuck with a couple of children in a suburban home with not too much money. Bill always needed so much. He liked nothing but the best in women, drink, and cigars.

Judith smiled. "I think you're quite right. Stay here for a few days. There's no rush about Reno. Use this room, and have fun. Never mind what Bob says."

She saw a look that was faintly puzzled and a little humble in the woman's eyes, and she was glad that she hadn't been stuffy. It was better to have friends than enemies, anyway.

"They dress up a bit for dinner here," she explained. "Miss Smith always serves cocktails before the meal, makes a party out of it."

"Oh, good!" Mrs. Barstow glanced at herself in an opposite mirror and touched a hand to her hair.

"I'm not sure whether she'll go into the usual routine tonight, of course. But suppose we go down and see."

"Oh yes." Mrs. Barstow pulled herself off the couch. "I'll wear my black dress."

Vera had no intention of abandoning the cocktail gathering before dinner. She had been looking forward to it. She'd been alone in her room all day and she wanted to see people, and talk. Of course she was the chief mourner, she'd have to remember that, since Willie was out of the picture, but a cocktail and sympathy from her friends were what she needed.

She put on a black dress which she hadn't worn much, but it seemed to be right for tonight. She fluffed her hair and applied a little extra lipstick, and then her cultured pearls on the black dress. She was a little surprised at how well she looked. And her costume was appropriate for a time of mourning too.

She went out to the living room and stopped short at the sight of Knotty sprawled in an easy chair with a drink in his hand. How dared he!

Knotty saw the look on her face and stood up at once. "I've been waiting for you, Miss Smith. I didn't want to disturb you before, knowing how you must feel. But I ought to tell you that I think I'm getting to the bottom of this thing. I hope you don't mind me picking up this drink, but it's been hard work and I'm about bushed."

Vera was appeased, as he had intended her to be. She became quite gracious and urged him to have another drink, then went on to say that he'd find out in the end that her father's death had been some sort of an accident.

Knotty didn't argue. Why look an extra drink in the face? And besides, perhaps tonight would tell the tale.

Les came in and approached Vera with a solemn look on his face.

"My dear, what's all this about poor old Angie being some sort of a Dr. Jekyll and Mr. Hyde?"

Chapter 35

Knotty said nothing, but Vera gasped and put a hand on her thin bosom. "But what do you *mean*?"

"That Dr. Burrell," Les said. "He seems to think he has it all figured out—a split personality, or something like that. Says he has the evidence, but the police won't listen to him. He put an adjective in front of 'police.' "

Knotty refrained from asking what an adjective was, exactly, and said instead, "Where is he?"

"I don't know."

Knotty went off, and Les sank into a chair. He gave Vera a nice smile and said, "Do get me a drink, dear."

Vera mixed him a highball and then began to make the cocktails.

Everyone was quiet that night, and Mrs. Barstow was disappointed. Les seemed to be thinking about something and was a bit vague when she talked to him, and Miss Ewell and Willie did not appear at all. Shirley did her best to be gay, but she found it heavy going.

When Dr. Medford came in, he went directly to his sister and asked when she was leaving.

"I am staying on for a few days." She avoided his eyes, and looked at Judith for support.

Judith nodded. "Mrs. Barstow will stay for a while. She is using my little sitting room, so that she won't be in anyone's way. We have decided to become acquainted with one another."

Dr. Medford's lower jaw dropped slightly, and after a moment of silence he turned away and went to get himself a drink. He found Les busy at the same task, and muttered to him, "Women are nuts."

"Are you finding that out only now?" Les demanded. "God, you're slow, boy."

Knotty had been talking to Dr. Burrell, and now he was sitting on a chair in full view of the door to Miss Ewell's room. He was munching on a sandwich.

Mary Gore, at the switchboard, knew that he was there, and kept calling to him.

"Mr. Knotty, why don't you come out front here? We could talk a little."

He left his chair and walked to where he could see her. "You hush up!" he said fiercely. "Do you think I got time to sit around and gab with a dame? I'm workin' on a murder case, and I'm busy."

"Yes, but what are you doing back there?"

"What I'm doing is nothing you need to know. Stick to your own job, and keep quiet."

He returned to his chair, and had barely settled himself, when Miss Ewell emerged, neatly dressed and combed. She stopped and looked at him with raised eyebrows.

"May I ask what you are doing here?"

Knotty shifted his position on the chair, scowled, and said at last, "I'm eatin' a sandwich."

Miss Ewell nodded. "That's very obvious, but I should like to know why you choose this spot to refresh yourself."

Knotty assumed a faintly pathetic expression. "I'm so busy," he sighed. "I didn't get time to go home to eat, so Nora fixed me this sandwich. I don't want any of them to see me eatin', so I came back here."

"Nonsense," said Miss Ewell, and reminded him of his sixth-grade teacher, of whom he still dreamed occasionally. "There is no earthly reason why you could not come into the dining room and eat with the rest of us."

Knotty choked on a piece of crust, and said in a strangled voice, "No, no. I'm busy. I, er, hope you got a good nap."

"Very good, thank you." She went on with her chin up. She was glad he had been sitting there. That Burrell man must have talked to him, and she was sure that she hadn't even moved the foot on which she had tied the twine. Nor did she feel dizzy, not even slightly.

She went to the dining room and discovered that the rest of them had not yet come in. Well, she was not going in there to watch them all drinking. It was disgraceful, anyway.

She sat down at her place. Nora came in twice to complete the table arrangements, but they did not speak to each other. Miss Ewell was thinking, and her eyes had an absent expression. She was not going to be afraid any more. She felt quite confident now. Somebody had gone wild, and she ought to be able to guess who it was. She closed her eyes and tried to concentrate.

They all came into the dining room in a group, and she opened her eyes and looked them over coldly. No one paid any attention to her except Vera. And Vera gave her a very peculiar stare.

They were unusually quiet. Even Shirley was subdued. She had given up trying to make any fun, and was practically talking to herself.

"This place is a damned morgue, for sure. I got to get outa here. I can't stand it. I'll go to a movie. That's what I'll do."

She ate heartily, and began to eye Dr. Burrell. "You wanna take me to a movie, pal?"

Dr. Burrell said, "No, thank you," in an abstracted voice, and appeared to be concentrating on the wallpaper in front of him.

Shirley asked the table in general where Willie was, and Judith volunteered the information that he was sleeping.

Dr. Medford immediately wanted to know how she knew, and Shirley spoke up pertly. "Oh, she spends lotsa time in his room, drinking and flirting with him. So who oughta know better when he's sleeping, or not?"

No one laughed, and there was no comment of any sort; Shirley sighed. There was Les, too, sitting next to that Barstow dame. But anyways, he wasn't talking to her, or anything. He was just eating. She swallowed a mouthful of food and said brightly, "Les, how about *you* going to a movie with me?"

Les didn't even bother to look at her. He said shortly, "Sorry, can't make it tonight."

Shirley finished her meal and left them all sitting there. She went through to the front hall where Betty was now at the switchboard, and Betty spoke up hastily. "She couldn't make it today, my girlfriend, I mean, but she'll try and make it tomorrow."

"*Try* and make it!" Shirley yelled. "For Pete's sake! Does she think we're all gonna sit around here on our rear ends while she makes up her mind?"

Betty shrugged, and put a stick of gum in her mouth.

"I gotta go to the movies tonight, or I'll go nuts," Shirley muttered.

Knotty, appearing from the hospital wing, shook his head at her and said firmly, "Not tonight. You can't go tonight."

"Watcha mean, not tonight?"

"What I say. You stay home and get a rest. You're gettin' circles under your eyes."

Shirley gave him a suspicious look while he carefully inspected his fingernails. He had a line of men around the hospital, and he didn't want any interference. He wanted them all inside.

"What makes you think you can keep me in, brother?"

Knotty drew back his shoulders. "If you try to get out, you'll be sent back in."

Shirley looked at him doubtfully, and as she was trying to figure out just how far his authority extended, Willie appeared on the stairs.

He asked in a weak voice, "Dinner ready?"

"Over and done with," Shirley said shortly.

"But she promised she'd wake me."

"Who?"

"Judith. She told me—"

"Ahh, she thought you needed your sleep, which you did."

Willie went on to the dining room, taking slow, careful steps. Mrs. Barstow, Les, and Dr. Medford were still there, and they were talking about trains. Les was telling them just which train Mrs. Barstow should catch.

"Is there any food left?" Willie asked in a wavering voice.

Dr. Medford looked at him and then told him to sit down while he went to the kitchen to see what could be done. Miss Ewell was there, giving Nora instructions for the following day. Between them, they arranged a meal for Willie,and sent it back to the dining room by Dr. Medford.

Miss Ewell finished with Nora and then went straight to her room. Knotty saw her inside the door, unobtrusively, and immediately sent Shirley off to find Judith.

Judith had gone to her room and was reading in bed. She did not welcome the summons from Shirley, and relieved herself with a little quiet swearing.

Shirley said, "I'm surprised atcha, a nice girl like you!"

Judith belted herself into a wrapper, applied lipstick, and combed her hair. She went downstairs with Shirley trailing her.

Knotty bowed to her, and, after a brief look at the flapping ears of Betty and Shirley, drew her back to the little hall that led to Miss Ewell's room.

"I got the place surrounded outside," he explained in a low voice, "and extra men on the terrace. But I don't want them inside. I figure this is an inside job, and I don't want to scare the guy away. I'll be watching here, but I got to keep myself hidden."

"How can you watch and keep yourself hidden?" Judith asked.

"You learn such things in my business, young lady," Knotty said austerely. "Now, that Burrell butch has some idea about Miss Ewell, and I want you to sit here in this chair and see if she comes out of her room. If she does—"

"For heaven's sake!" Judith groaned. "When am I supposed to sleep? I work hard during the day."

Knotty assumed pathos again, and did it well. He looked like a man out of a job, with starving children at home.

"I shouldn't ask you, Miss Onslow, I know that. But I want someone who isn't a policeman and who has a bit of sense in her dome. Because if Miss Ewell does come out, I need to have you follow her around and see what she does, and where she goes. See, you could do it easy if you have your nurse's uniform on. She's used to uniforms around the place. I know I can trust you. You're not in with the rest of the gang. It would be swell if you'd go up now and get into your uniform."

Judith sighed deeply and turned toward the stairs. "Oh well, it's a dog's life, but I suppose I went into it with my eyes open."

Knotty followed her as far as the front hall and was relieved to see that Shirley was still there.

"Poor girl has to go on duty again," he said. "Seems they need her tonight."

"She oughta never been a nurse," Shirley said crossly. "Like I oughta never fooled around with a switchboard. If we'd had any sense, we'da married rich men and drunk ourselves to death in comfort. Which floor is she gonna work on?"

Knotty shrugged. "I don't know. She's just gone up to get into her uniform."

Willie had come into the hall, and he gave a little sigh. "I'm glad she's going to stand by. There will be blood shed when they find the Black Smith."

Chapter 36

Knotty asked sharply, "What do you mean?"

Willie shook his head, and pressed his fingers against his temples. He'd eaten something, but now he was dizzy, everything spinning around. He'd have to get up to bed.

Knotty took him by the arm and said sternly, "You got to explain what you said. Who do you mean by the Black Smith?"

"I don't know," Willie muttered. "I don't know. I was reading Father's notebook. Nothing in it, really. Don't know why he wrote it."

"What do you mean, there's nothing in it? Don't it tell about the Black Smith? Where is it, anyways?"

"Upstairs. I have it upstairs. I found it, it's mine."

Knotty didn't waste any more time. He steered Willie to the stairs, and ran him up so fast that they were both panting when they reached the top. Willie pushed into his own room, fell heavily onto the bed, and appeared to go to sleep at once.

Knotty looked at him in virtuous disgust. And him a doctor, too! The same guy who would sit in his office with a smug look on his puss and tell you to give up drinking because you had a sore toe.

He found the notebook in the first drawer he opened, and took it straight downstairs. Judith was waiting for him in the front hall, dressed in her uniform, and with a book under her arm. She was a bit sulky.

Knotty took her down the hall toward Miss Ewell's room, and said anxiously, "Do you think she came out of her room while I was upstairs?"

"How would I know?"

"Knock on her door and see if she's still there."

"What am I supposed to say?" Judith demanded. "'Are you there?' or something like that?"

Knotty was shocked. "Of course not! Ask her does she want something, like another blanket, maybe."

Judith sighed and rapped on the door, and Miss Ewell answered at once. "What is it?"

"It's Judith, Miss Ewell. I wondered whether you'd like a cup of coffee. I'm having one myself."

"No, thank you," Miss Ewell's voice said firmly. "I don't think you should be drinking coffee at this time of night either."

Judith made a little face at Knotty over her shoulder, and then said mildly, "Well, I seem to feel the need of it. Sure you won't have a cup?"

"Quite sure," Miss Ewell replied from behind her closed door. "Good night."

Judith murmured, "Good night," and turned to Knotty. "What am I supposed to do now?"

"Sit here all night and see if she leaves her room. If she does, you got to follow her, only she mustn't see you. Find out what she does."

Judith nodded resignedly and sat down in the chair. "I shall have to have strong black coffee at one o'clock."

"But—"

"And if someone doesn't bring it to me, I shall have to leave my post and go out to the kitchen to get it for myself."

"I'll see that you get it," Knotty promised, and walked off. He supposed that the dame would need coffee to keep her awake, but a police officer conducting a murder investigation shouldn't be tied down to domestic jobs of that sort.

Betty said something to him as he passed the switchboard, but he ignored her and went on to the office of the head nurse. He walked in, and then backed out in a hurry. Mrs. Barstow, Shirley, and Les were there, drinking, laughing, and talking.

He went to the doctor's office and found Dr. Medford talking to Dr. Burrell. He backed out again, although Dr. Burrell called to him and would have followed him out if Dr. Medford had not snapped, "For God's sake, come back here and listen to the rest of these cases. I can't handle the entire damned hospital alone."

Dr. Burrell said courteously, "Sorry, I'm sure," and returned to his chair, and Knotty left them and went to the dining room. It was dark, and he had to grope for the light switch. He had no sooner turned it on, than Nora came padding in from the kitchen.

"I turned this light out," she announced belligerently.

"And I turned it on again," Knotty snarled.

"Electricity costs money, Jacob Knotty."

He faced her and spoke through his teeth. "Get out of here, and get out fast, or I'll put you inside to keep company with your brothers."

"I wouldn't be seen dead with either one of those bums." But she backed away a step, and her voice dropped. "I was only tryin' to do my dooty."

"Go and do your dooty somewheres else," Knotty said shortly.

She left, and he sat down and carefully opened Dr. Smith's notebook.

He had been reading for some time before he was forced to admit to himself that he had never been so disappointed in his life. It was all so uninteresting. Things like "Much better this morning. Worse this afternoon. Will try using the stuff on Lister." It was all the same, and there was so much of it. When he was about halfway through, he put the book down and went to the kitchen to get himself some coffee.

He found Dr. Medford there, and was annoyed, because he had expected, and wanted, solitude. He slammed the pot onto the stove, measured coffee and water, and turned on the gas.

"Make enough for Judith," Dr. Medford said.

Knotty frowned at him. "So you've found her?"

"Well, I ran across her trying to keep awake on that blasted uncomfortable little chair. I said I'd get some coffee for her."

"How many thousand people heard you talking there?"

"I carefully made sure that no one heard us," Dr. Medford said with dignity.

"Oh?" Knotty's eyes were on the coffeepot. "How come you ran across her when she's sittin' in that dead-end hall leadin' to Miss Ewell's room?"

"It also leads to the elevator. But I found her because I was looking for her. I was told that they were so short-handed that she had decided to work all night, and I intended to send her to bed. However, I understood the situation when I found her sitting in that back hall, reading in a bad light. Now look. Do you mind telling me what's going on? Do you really think that poor Angie has a split personality?"

"I don't know," Knotty said crossly. "I'm having everything watched tonight, including Miss Ewell. Nothing will happen, I suppose, and then I'll have to do the whole thing over again tomorrow. Which reminds me. Kindly dig up some other nurse to take Miss Onslow's place in the morning, because maybe I'll need her again at night."

"How much are you paying her?"

Knotty ignored him coldly, and turned the gas low under the coffee.

"All right, but I'd like to say this: If your suspicion of Miss Ewell arises solely from the ideas burgeoning from Dr. Burrell's fancy brain, I think you're barking up the wrong tree."

Knotty was stung into indiscretion. "She had the wallet in her room. Didn't she give it to me and wonder how it got there? She had his gold watch, which he always wore. Her nurse's cape was out and about last night, when all the patients was scared into fits."

Dr. Medford was startled into thinking about the thing. He had not given it too much thought before. But the old man *had* been murdered, and somebody must have done it.

Knotty poured coffee for himself, and then filled another cup for

Judith and pushed it at Dr. Medford. Dr. Medford put it on the table for a moment, poured himself a cup, and carried them both into the hall.

Judith was standing at the switchboard, talking to Betty, and she looked up as he approached. She said, "Oh, thank you," and Betty chirped, "Why, you brought coffee for me, too, Dr. Medford. Aren't you nice!"

He handed the cup over silently, and was about to feel sorry for himself when it occurred to him to go to the kitchen and pour another cup. It did not take him long, and he presently returned and joined the sipping party at the switchboard.

Judith said, "Miss Ewell went to her office and found some people sitting around in there drinking. She was annoyed, to put it mildly."

Dr. Medford laughed. "Who was there? Outside of Les, of course."

"Your sister and Shirley."

He frowned, and Judith added easily, "She chased them out, and they went to your office."

He put his coffee cup down with a bang and headed toward his office, and Judith and Betty laughed.

Miss Ewell came back, and gave both a cold eye. She had passed them before she said distinctly, "When I was head, I was always able to arrange it so that I never had to work at night."

Judith sighed and wondered why it was that trouble seemed always to follow her wherever she went. It was tiresome, and she longed for peace. She finished her coffee and then returned to the chair in the back hall.

Dr. Medford appeared with Mrs. Barstow, Shirley, and Les trailing him. He was trying to keep them quiet, with little success. He sternly ordered his sister to bed, but she told him to be good enough to mind his own business, and linked arms with Les.

Shirley was feeling gay and happy because a weight had been lifted from her mind. She had it all figured out now: it was old Doc Smith who had conked her on the bean. He'd known she was drunk that night, and he didn't want his dirty work to come to light, so he'd decided to get rid of her. Now somebody had fixed him, so she was safe.

"All right if I stay with you tonight, Bob?" Les asked.

"Sure, only I don't know why you pay for that room of yours when you never use it."

"Oh well—" Les laughed. "It looks better. It might make talk if I simply sponged on at Smith Hospital. Anyway, I need a place to keep my clothes."

"I'll tell you one thing," Dr. Medford said firmly. "You can't stay with me tonight unless you break up this party as of now."

Les bowed. "It shall be done, immediately. I'm beginning to drink a bit too much anyway."

Shirley gave a sorrowful little wail. "Oh no, please. You guys wanna spoil the first fun I had in weeks?"

But Les winked at her, and she fell silent. They went up the stairs almost quietly, and when they reached the top, they filed into Shirley's room, closed the door, and continued the party. About three minutes later, Willie came in and joined them.

Knotty was still wending his way doggedly through Dr. Smith's notebook. He lit a fresh cigar, recrossed his legs, and muttered hopelessly, "What a goddamn waste of paper."

And then, unexpectedly, he found it.

"There'll be blood shed if the Black Smith ever steps off the ledge again."

Chapter 37

Knotty took an excited puff on his cigar, and squirmed in his seat. This here Black Smith, whoever it was, *had* stepped off the ledge again and started all this ruckus. "Step off the ledge"? What had the old buster meant by that? Someone going nuts, like maybe Miss Ewell had. She wasn't a Smith, though. There weren't so many Smiths. Vera, Shirley, Willie. Who else? Nobody.

No, that was wrong. They were all Smiths, all of them in this joint. Old Doc had always called them Smiths, like it was one big family. Even his niece, Betty, because she worked here. Sure had liked himself, that guy. Bossed them all around and wouldn't take any back chat from anybody.

Knotty stood up. This made it easier, anyways. Somebody had gone nuts and shed blood, as advertised by Doc Smith. Only the old boy probably hadn't expected that it would be his own blood that was shed. Well, serve him right. He should have put this Black Smith away in the loony bin. It was just like him, though. Always did things his own way, and thought he knew more than anybody else, and nuts to the police, who could never catch up with him. Him and his Smith Hospital and his Smith doctors and his Smith nurses, and even Smith patients! He was probably busy in the next world bossing Smith angels around.

Vera, in the kitchen, had been peering at him through the half-opened door. She saw him sit down again and resume his study of the notebook, and fury brought an ugly red into her face. Several times, as she watched him, she had had an impulse to go in and demand that he hand it over to her, but a defeatist sense of caution held her quiet. He wouldn't give it up, and what could she do? She stayed in the kitchen, fuming, and called herself a fool for having given the book to Willie. Now he had allowed Knotty to get hold of it.

How badly Willie was behaving, she thought drearily. She'd been up to his room to get the notebook back, and had found him in the midst of a vulgar party in Shirley's room. Shirley, her twin sister. Oh, it was impossible! She herself never entertained men in her bedroom. She wouldn't dream of such a thing. Well, she'd put a stop to that party, anyway. She'd stood there until they'd all gone back to their own rooms. She could see now that Willie was not a real Smith, not of her family, or how could he join a cheap drinking party like that, with their dear father hardly cold in death? After herself, Angie and Nora were the ones who felt the most grief, and it was not right. Father had been surly, perhaps, but he had been beloved by all, and his passing would be a deep sorrow to the whole community.

She peered in at Knotty again, and saw that he was still reading. Well, let him read. She walked restlessly out of the kitchen, and thought that perhaps she might go and talk to Angie for a few minutes. Better not, though. Angie would have to learn her place now. She sighed, and went reluctantly back to her own room to get a cigarette.

As it happened, Miss Ewell would not have welcomed her. She wanted to be alone so that she could think. She knew this hospital inside out, and yet she did not know who had killed him. She *must* know, she *had* to know. All these people who could have done it— And if none of them had? Then she had done it herself, and the police would prove it.

She almost screamed, but swallowed it down firmly. She must not let go; that would finish her. Well, she was finished anyway. He was dead, and Vera was going to push her into a small corner and keep her there. Only Vera would have to fight Shirley if she wanted to take control. And Shirley was not a weak sister.

Miss Ewell drew a long breath and began to feel a bit better. She could get on with Shirley, all right. She could still have an interest here, through Shirley. All right, but she had to think now. She'd have to put her finger on the one who had done it. Things kept popping into her head. Those people having a party. Shirley— Well, of course she'd had no training.

Someone knocked on the door, and Miss Ewell started violently. She got up slowly and pulled a dressing gown around her.

"May I see you for a moment?" Knotty asked politely.

"Well—" Miss Ewell pulled the neck of her gown more closely

around her throat. "I am not dressed, as you can see."

"That's O.K., Miss Ewell. I just want to ask you a couple questions. Can I step in?"

"Certainly not." Miss Ewell took a backward step. "I can't come out like this either, and I'm sure that I don't intend to get dressed again at this time of night." She tried to close the door and discovered that Knotty had put his foot in it.

"Just tell me," he said pleadingly, "who Doc Smith meant by 'the Black Smith.' "

"I don't know." Miss Ewell had taken breath to say something more when a bell seemed to ring in her head. She gasped, and pushed the door hard. Knotty's foot disappeared.

He stood for a moment looking at the blank panels before his face and swearing a little, and then he went out to the switchboard in the front hall. Judith was still there, and he motioned her back to her post with a curved thumb. She made a face at him and returned to the uncomfortable chair in the back hall.

Knotty leaned over and spoke to Betty in a low voice. "Find Dr. Medford for me. I got to talk to him."

"I don't know where he is, Uncle Jacob."

"I didn't ask you where he is," Knotty hissed. "I said, find him."

"If I can't get him, will Dr. Burrell do?"

"No!" Knotty shouted.

Betty rang Dr. Medford's bedroom first, and was not too surprised when Les answered. He said, "My dear girl, he is not here. He is never here. He says he's busy, and I expect he is, busy running after the girls. Would it sound too selfish if I ask that I may be permitted to sleep?"

Betty giggled and hung up and presently located Dr. Medford in his office.

Knotty, appraised of his whereabouts, went straight to the office, walked in and sat down. "You keep late hours, Doc," he said mildly.

"Not usually, but I thought that someone in charge should stick around tonight."

"All right." Knotty brushed it aside impatiently. "Look, you must know who this here Black Smith is. Doc Smith mentioned it in a notebook he had."

Dr. Medford wrinkled his forehead and said slowly, "Seems to me I did hear him refer to someone as the Black Smith, but I can't remember when."

"Did I ask you 'when'?" Knotty demanded, chewing on a cigar which he had forgotten to light. "I want to know 'who.' "

"Oh, I don't know 'who,' " Dr. Medford said indifferently. "Seems to me he mentioned it at the dinner table. Sounded a bit like a threat. He said, 'Someone around here whom I call the Black Smith had better behave, or else."

"Or else what?"

"Just or else."

"You don't know who he was talking to?" Knotty asked, looking exasperated.

"No." Dr. Medford shrugged. "Except that it was not I."

Miss Ewell, lying on her bed, was thinking of that remark that Dr. Smith had made at the dinner table. It had been a threat, and he had been serious. He never threatened idly, either. He had ways of doing harm to people. All those papers he had left in his wallet, they could make a great deal of trouble. The wallet had been planted in her room, perhaps to get rid of it quickly. But of course the piece of paper that could do harm to the Black Smith had been removed. It was one of themselves, no doubt about it. Then that young fool, Dr. Burrell, had started talking of split personalities, and immediately she had found the gold watch in her room. Next, her cape was stolen and used to frighten the patients, and the whole thing was set up to be pinned on her. Well, that had been a mistake, a big one.

She flung aside the bedclothes, got up, and dressed herself in her uniform. She was tense but she felt a good deal better. She knew what she had to do, and the sooner it was done, the better.

She left her room and walked straight up to Judith, who was drowsing in the little chair.

"Wake up, young lady."

"I am awake," Judith said hotly. "Why do you always assume that nurses are asleep on their jobs?"

"Because they always are," Miss Ewell replied equably. "Come with me. I have work for you."

Judith followed her, and they went out to the switchboard, where Miss Ewell spoke crisply to Betty.

"Where is your uncle Jacob?"

"He was talking to Dr. Medford in his office, Miss Ewell. Unless they left."

Miss Ewell nodded and went to Dr. Medford's office, with Judith still trailing her.

The two men were just emerging, but Miss Ewell pushed them back, pulled Judith in, and closed the door. She looked Knotty straight in the eye, and said, "It's really too bad that a woman in my position must do a policeman's work in order to protect herself from a most unjust suspicion. However, I have done what I had to do, and all I need now is a little help from you. It should not take long, and then perhaps I can sleep in peace again."

Knotty carefully repressed his peevish frustration, and listened in silence while Miss Ewell instructed Judith and Dr. Medford to go down to the morgue and take Dr. Smith's body from the freezer. They were to lay it on the table and then get out of sight behind the door and wait. They protested, but instinct urged Knotty to order them, shortly, to do as they were told.

Miss Ewell nodded. "Now, Knotty, take that cigar out of your face and put it out."

"Why?"

"It's necessary," Miss Ewell said firmly.

Knotty sacrificed the best part of a good cigar and wondered whether the wish that it was Miss Ewell's head he was crushing was an abnormal thought.

"Now, you must follow me and listen carefully. Don't allow yourself to be seen, but be ready to protect me should I need it."

"Let's go," Knotty said, trying not to sound as sulky as he felt.

Judith and Dr. Medford went off to the morgue, and Knotty followed Miss Ewell to the Smith quarters, where she knocked smartly on Vera's door. At Vera's summons, she went in, and said clearly, "I'm on my way to get Bob, but I wanted to give you the good news first. Mary, you know, was supposed to put the body of your father away in the freezer, but she did not do it. Instead, she worked on him, and has brought him back to life, as she always maintained that she could. I have seen him, but he is still very weak, so that if you want him to live you must not go down yet. He should not see anybody for a while, at least."

Vera began a sort of incoherent wailing, but Miss Ewell left without further words, and Knotty trotted after her. She went to the elevator and waited for him to step in beside her before closing the door and pressing the button for the top floor.

"You think she believed you?" Knotty asked uncertainly.

"Of course. I never lie."

"Oh."

Miss Ewell repeated her performance with Willie, who said in a blurred voice, "Never heard s'ch nonsense. S'perfectly ridiculous."

"I have just seen him," said Miss Ewell. "He is living."

She went to Shirley's room, and Shirley said, "Ah, get out! I seen him. He's dead as a herring, although he still smells better."

"Watch your tongue, young lady."

Miss Ewell went on to Dr. Medford's room, and woke Les to give him the news. He murmured sleepily, "Shut up, Angie, do. I love you, darlin', but you're as nutty as a fruitcake."

"I tell you I have just seen him, and he is as much alive as I am. But you must not go down yet. I'm getting Bob as soon as I can, although he's tied up with a patient just now."

She returned to the elevator, and Knotty stepped quietly in beside her. He said in a subdued voice, "What happens now?"

"One of those is the person Dr. Smith referred to as the Black Smith. At the time, I thought he meant Shirley, but we shall see. Whoever killed him will run down and try to do it again. They'll figure on having time enough, because I told Vera I was coming up here. And I told those up here that Dr. Medford was tied up with a patient and I'd have to wait for him. So we shall see."

They stopped at the switchboard to instruct Betty to pretend to be asleep, and then went on down to the morgue to join Judith and Dr. Medford in a corner behind the door.

They had not long to wait. They were hardly settled before someone came in through the door from the cellar and shot the corpse several times at close range.

Knotty did his job well at this point. He flashed out from behind the door, possessed himself of the gun, and handcuffed the culprit in a matter of seconds.

It was Les.

Chapter 38

Miss Ewell sipped coffee with her little finger stuck out daintily. "We should all go to bed," she said, glancing at the clock."

"What's the use?" Judith asked. "You know we couldn't sleep."

Dr. Medford crossed his legs and banged the kitchen table as he did so. He muttered, "Dammit!" and added, "I don't see how Les was so taken in by your story that he actually came down and shot a dead body without any further investigation."

"I never tell lies," Miss Ewell said primly. "He knows that, so of course he believed me. Even if he'd looked before he shot, he couldn't have been sure. He's not a doctor. In any case, do you remember what he said when they took him away?"

Dr. Medford nodded. "He said, 'I won't fry, anyway. I'm a nut, remember?' "

"But surely he hasn't a chance to work anything along that line?" Judith asked curiously.

"Oh yes." Miss Ewell sugared a fresh cup of coffee, and stirred it without spilling a drop over the rim. "I knew that Dr. Smith was giving shock treatments to someone two or three years ago, and I wondered at the time who it was. I now assume that it was Les."

"I never heard of that," Dr. Medford said in some surprise.

"No. Dr. Smith did things his own way, and was a law unto himself. But it will help Les to establish an insanity motive."

"Can he prove it?"

"Oh yes. Dr. Smith always kept records, although some of them were secret. He'd have sent Les a bill, too; and although Les never paid it, he no doubt still has it. You will probably find an I.O.U. from him among Dr. Smith's papers."

"Was he killed because he had the I.O.U.?"

"Oh, dear me, no." Miss Ewell touched her white hair, which was coiled in smooth order around her little head. "Dr. Smith was not pressing for payment. But he kept the I.O.U. in case he should ever need the money, supposing Les should ever have it, which is doubtful. No, no, it was for a very different reason. You see, Les had decided to marry Vera so that he could move in here and live a life of ease, perhaps study to be a doctor, which is what he had always wanted. Why do you think he came here so often? Vera wanted him, and he knew he could get along with Willie. Then Shirley turned up, and he did not know what her game was. He tried to frighten her away by injuring her when she was, er, inebriated, but she did not go."

Judith stirred restlessly in her chair. "But Les has been hanging around here for two years or better, hasn't he? Why didn't he marry Vera long ago? And what has it to do with his killing Dr. Smith?"

"My dear!" Miss Ewell showed elaborate patience for a dull mind. "It's very obvious. Dr. Smith would not allow it, of course. He knew Les was unbalanced, and Vera *was* his daughter, if he did find her boring and tiresome. He threatened Les fairly recently, you know. Spoke right out at the table, and said that the Black Smith would have to behave, or else. Only Les knew what he was talking about, and Les retreated a little from Vera and began to play up to the other women. Not too much, but just enough. He knew perfectly well that Dr. Smith could fix his will, with the help of a competent lawyer, so that any husband of Vera's would be left out in the cold."

Dr. Medford recrossed his legs carefully, but managed to bang the table again. "So Les up and killed the old man because he wouldn't let him marry Vera and live on the bounty of Smith Hospital, such as it is?"

"Exactly." Miss Ewell drew a long breath. "He figured, right from the start, that he could put it all onto me, because I was behaving foolishly. I pretended to go away and didn't, and he probably knew that. Also, I had Charlie in my bedroom, dead, with Mary Gore trying to bring him to life, and I think he knew that too. Then Willie began to act like an idiot, taking poor Charlie and trying to practice on him. Oh, you don't really know Les, always pottering around this hospital. It fascinated him. You know how he killed Dr. Smith; strangulation in the vital spot. He loved the medical profession; he'd always wanted to be a doctor, and the only thing standing in his way was Dr. Smith. Les always knew what everyone was doing around here. He spent far more time wandering through the hospital than any of you realized."

"I still don't see how he hoped to pin it on you," Judith said thoughtfully. "Before Dr. Burrell stepped in, that is."

Miss Ewell gave her an abstracted glance. "I know now that he had keys, and always kept them with him. He was able to enter anyone's room at will. He put Dr. Smith's wallet in my room, and later the gold watch and the soiled cape. He'd used the cape himself, of course, and he'd crouched down, or something of the sort, to make Mr. Lister think that he was very short. When that young idiot, Dr. Burrell, got his fool idea about me, Les made it pay off. He was a bit too quick and eager about it, though. I couldn't quite swallow it, so I sat down and thought it out."

"Why should he take such a terrible risk?" Dr. Medford asked. "He was making enough to live on—"

Miss Ewell stood up. "It's simple enough if you stop to think about it. Dr. Smith mentioned it in his notebook. 'There'll be blood shed if the Black Smith ever steps off the ledge again.' So he stepped off. Perhaps he needs more shock treatments."

"Perhaps he needs an assortment of iron bars around him," Dr. Medford said grimly.

"I shall leave you two now," Miss Ewell said, moving toward the door. "I've had a feeling about you for some time that you like being left alone together, at least at this stage of the proceedings."

"Wait! Wait a minute!" Judith called. "How do you know that all of this is true?"

"I know these people, young woman. I know them far better than you can ever hope to. Good night."

She departed on quick, light steps, and Dr. Medford grinned. "She's not boasting; she does know them. I think you can believe her without reservation."

Judith shrugged. "She certainly moved fast, once she found herself threatened."

"Yes, and she moved in the right direction. She knows people, and she can talk them into anything. Look at us, we're as good as married right now."

"I dare say." Judith lifted her shoulders again. "On the other hand, she might change her mind before we get to the altar."

Dr. Medford nodded. "I think you have a point there, so I suggest we fare forth tomorrow and get married before we find ourselves paired off with two other fellows."

Shirley's voice spoke up from the door.

"Oh no—gimme a cuppa corfee, willya?—no. You can get the license tomorra, but you guys are faithful employees of Smith Hospital, and we are gonna give you a wedding here that will knock your hats right off."

THE END

About the Rue Morgue Press

"Rue Morgue Press is the old-mystery lover's best friend, reprinting high quality books from the 1930s and '40s."
—*Ellery Queen's Mystery Magazine*

Since 1997, the Rue Morgue Press has reprinted scores of traditional mysteries, the kind of books that were the hallmark of the Golden Age of detective fiction. Authors reprinted or to be reprinted by the Rue Morgue include Dorothy Bowers, Joanna Cannan, Glyn Carr, Torrey Chanslor, Clyde B. Clason, Joan Coggin, Manning Coles, Lucy Cores, Frances Crane, Norbert Davis, Elizabeth Dean, Constance & Gwenyth Little, Marlys Millhiser, James Norman, Stuart Palmer, Craig Rice, Kelley Roos, Charlotte Murray Russell, Maureen Sarsfield, and Juanita Sheridan.

To suggest titles or to receive a catalog of Rue Morgue Press books write P.O. Box 4119, Boulder, CO 80306, telephone 800-699-6214, or check out our website, www.ruemorguepress.com, which lists complete descriptions of all of our titles, along with lengthy biographies of our writers.